THE WHITE SHIELD

By the same author, available from Valancourt Books

RENSHAW FANNING'S QUEST
THE WEIRD OF DEADLY HOLLOW
THE KING'S ASSEGAI
THE SIGN OF THE SPIDER
THE INDUNA'S WIFE *(forthcoming)*

Also Available in Valancourt Classics

NADA THE LILY
H. Rider Haggard
Edited by Gerald Monsman

THE ROSE AND THE KEY
J. Sheridan Le Fanu
Edited by Frances A. Chiu

THE MYSTERY OF THE SEA
Bram Stoker
Edited by Carol A. Senf

THOU ART THE MAN
Mary Elizabeth Braddon
Edited by Laurence Talairach-Vielmas

THE SORROWS OF SATAN
Marie Corelli
Edited by Julia Kuehn

ROUND THE RED LAMP AND OTHER WRITINGS
A. Conan Doyle
Edited by Robert Darby

VALANCOURT CLASSICS

THE WHITE SHIELD

BY

BERTRAM MITFORD

AUTHOR OF THE SIGN OF THE SPIDER, RENSHAW FANNING'S QUEST, THE WEIRD
OF DEADLY HOLLOW, THE KING'S ASSEGAI, THE INDUNA'S WIFE, ETC., ETC.

Edited with an introduction and notes by
Gerald Monsman

𝕶𝖆𝖓𝖘𝖆𝖘 𝕮𝖎𝖙𝖞:
VALANCOURT BOOKS
2008

The White Shield by Bertram Mitford
First published in 1895 by Cassell
First Valancourt Books edition 2008

Introduction and notes © 2008 by Gerald Monsman
This edition © 2008 by Valancourt Books

Library of Congress Cataloging-in-Publication Data

Mitford, Bertram, 1855-1914.
The white shield / by Bertram Mitford ; edited with an
introduction and notes by Gerald Monsman. – 1st Valancourt
Books ed.
p. cm. – (Valancourt classics)
ISBN 978-1-934555-63-7 (alk. paper)
1. Zulu (African people)–History–19th century–Fiction.
I. Monsman, Gerald Cornelius. II. Title.
PR5021.M8W48 2008
823'.6–dc22

2008047779

Composition by James D. Jenkins
Published by Valancourt Books
Kansas City, Missouri
http://www.valancourtbooks.com

CONTENTS

INTRODUCTION

The White Shield (1895) is the second episode in a quartet of all-native historical novels by Bertram Mitford on the nineteenth-century Ndebele-Zulu peoples. It began with *The King's Assegai* (1894), resumes in this novel, continues in *The Induna's Wife* (1898) and concludes with *The Word of the Sorceress* (1902). Perhaps, following H. Rider Haggard's lead in *Nada the Lily* (1892), Mitford borrowed the idea of an all-native story for his tetralogy; Haggard then subsequently appears to have borrowed Mitford's idea of consecutive historical novels on Zulu history. Not only had Mitford lived and worked in the Cape Colony in the 1870s, but later "at the close of the Zulu War, he trekked alone through Zululand, exploring the battlefields and interviewing the principal indunas. On his various visits to Africa he has travelled in Matabeleland, and visited Zanzibar, Mozambique and other East Coast ports."[1] All good writers adapt to their purposes, in addition to their own experiences, secondary source materials: thus earlier in his classic *Renshaw Fanning's Quest* (1894) Mitford's mythical Valley of the Eye may be more than a little redolent of A. Conan Doyle's first published story, "The Mystery of the Sasassa Valley" (1879), though what Mitford does with Doyle's motif makes it fully his own. Undoubtedly here in *The White Shield* Mitford drew on missionary accounts such as those of Robert Moffat and David Livingstone; and his friendship with the legendary frontiersman Johan Colenbrander, to whom he dedicated *John Ames* (1900), provided him with original oral accounts.

The White Shield is a closely felt story of strange events by an author with an eye for the telling specifics of an African-animistic world of magic. Details of psychology and anthropology, supplied by the novel's inner narrator, Untúswa, afford solidity to a past rooted in a natural or mythic time, shaped before the conquests of European imperialism. In Africa one encounters many

---

[1] "Mitford," *The Anglo-African Who's Who and Biographical Sketchbook*, edited by Walter Wills and R. J. Barrett (London: Routledge, 1907): 117.

uncanny events not scientifically explainable: visions, premonitions, and—notably—ambiguous meanings. Thus if black symbolized fears of night-time spirits and underworld ghosts, it contrastingly could represent fertility and resurrection—the dark soil of Africa in its mysteriously renewed life. Death in Zulu terms as described by Mitford or Haggard is a "going down into the darkness," into "the Dark Unknown." Although such phrases may seem nihilistic to the Western observer, it is possible that Mitford reserved judgment on the limits of native spirituality and that Haggard credited the Zulu darkness with being the "yet unknown." Mitford explores the cultural differences between Western and African perspectives with respect to spirituality, social organization, justice, women's roles, and civic duty. His Africa is one of physical forces tinctured with magic; but such mythic patterns and powers are hidden, almost beyond the scope of human manipulation, never obtrusive.

Mitford described Ndebele-Zulu history so that, even though seemingly constrained by the politics of colonial fiction, his presentations of native cultural practices surpassed cursory European stereotypes. The Ndebele-Zulu, at the time Mitford wrote the first two of his novels, had been overrun by the Europeans—the Zulus by British troops in the war of 1879 and the Ndebele by the British South African Company under Cecil Rhodes in 1893. The period covered by *The King's Assegai* and *The White Shield*, however, begins and ends much earlier in the century, opening in the early 1820s with the *Mfecane*, a Zulu word meaning "hammering" or "crushing." The *Mfecane* denotes those largely internecine conflicts—although recent conjecture includes external socio-political stimuli, even "dendro-climatological" changes—out of which emerged both the Zulu empire, controlled by its warrior-chief Shaka, and the Ndebele nation led by Shaka's quondam general Umzilikazi. The particular focus of these novels—the history of the Ndebele and Zulu kingdoms, symbols of African independence—is seen in the perspective of hindsight after their conquest by the Europeans, particularly in *The White Shield* and *The Induna's Wife*, in connection with the intensifying conflicts with the Boers. Each of these narratives might strike a casual reader as merely nostalgia for a vanished culture and its traditional lifeways; yet both show the past to be not a mere shadow but still a palpable and perilous presence. Indeed, before Mitford could write the third of his novels, the Ndebele had risen up in 1896-97 against their British overlords and attempted to wrest back control of their hereditary lands.

Underlying Mitford's role as empire writer is his early poetry and journalism—the latter notably beginning with a 14 December 1886 announcement of his proprietorship of the *East London Advertiser* (East London, SA) "offering this journal to the public under new auspices." No data hitherto has been published on this news medium of Mitford that preceded his empire romances, but it is apparent he and his editor saw the role of the *Advertiser* as gadfly, provocative and intensely antagonistic towards colonial short-sightedness and pretensions, whether of race, religion, politics, or bourgeois "getting and spending." When the *Advertiser* came into Mitford's hands he had pledged journalistic independence and kept his promise: "if getting into the numerous rows and setting the town generally by the ears be allowed to count for anything we certainly may claim to have kept our promise." Mitford rubbed criticism into his readers as if they were spiced beef: "The 'rubbing in' process has been impartially distributed to young and old, big and little; from the Premier in his chair of office to the newly emancipated schoolboy in his first masher collar. . . . If we have done any of you some little good and turned you from the error of your ways, you're welcome to the service and we ask for no thanks; if some of you feel sore and bear malice it can't be helped, we shan't say we're sorry, for probably it served you right."[1] Mitford himself did not stay in South Africa very long after taking control of the journal. He departed East London on 16 December 1886 on board the *Melrose* via the coastal ports of Port Elizabeth (or Algoa Bay as it was called) and possibly Mossel Bay for Cape Town, connecting there with the *Pembroke Castle* which left for London on the afternoon of 22 December 1886. He apparently was traveling alone, without his bride, Zima, whom he had married in London in 1886 but whose family resided at the Cape.[2] On 4 February

[1] "Hail and Farewell," *Advertiser* (21 February 1888). The local editor of the *Advertiser* was probably Colonel R.A. Bettington who came to the Colony in 1872 and joined Bowker's Rovers (a cavalry unit of irregulars under the command of Mitford's second cousin) during the Kafir Wars of 1877-1878.
[2] His name only is listed for December in the shipping news of the *Cape Times*. Zima Ebden's previous divorce at the suit of her husband for adultery with a medical officer had been reported by *The Times* in lurid detail (4 April 1884; issue

1887 the *Advertiser* reported: "We hope shortly to give our readers the promised English letters. By last mail we heard that Mr. Mitford had reached Madeira." Mitford's series of "English Letters" covered British parliamentary events, social events and the odd local "strange but true" story.[1] Such travel between continents and interchange of news between cultures was typical of Anglo-African writers—even those born in the colonies, such as Olive Schreiner.

In connection with South African high romance it may seem strange to mention a gathering of writers at monthly dinners in the Grand Hotel, Northumberland Avenue, London. But if there was a home for England's novels of Africa—an ideological center of journalistic opinions and literary narration—it may well have been here at the Anglo-African Writers' Club in Westminster. Bertram Mitford, so we are told in one of his scanty biographical notices, was "a prominent member." Another literary member was W. C. Scully, author of *Kafir Stories* (1895) and *Between Sun and Sand* (1898). For most of the Club's existence, H. Rider Haggard seems to have been its Chairman, active in its monthly dinners from its beginning in 1894 or 1895 to the earliest years of the following century. In his autobiography, *The Days of My Life* (1926), Haggard refers to this group of which he was elected chairman as "a pleasant and useful dining society."[2] Invited speakers included such luminaries as Rudyard Kipling (May 1898) as well as political leaders in, and journalistic commentators on, Africa. Kipling, so the newspaper reported, was introduced by Haggard as a visionary of empire: "There was more in the idea of empire than

---

31099; pg. 3; col E); either she stayed in England to avoid her family or remained in Africa to visit a bit longer.

[1] Shipping news of 14 January 1887 in the *Times* of London says: "The Pembroke Castle left the Downs [where ships gathered either to go up or down the English Channel] today for London"; and on 17 January advertises the fact that the *Pembroke Castle* will be returning to the Cape from London on 2 February and from Dartmouth on the 4th. Mitford thus arrived in England in time to write and mail the first English Letter which came out in the *Advertiser* on 25 February 1887 with the heading, "Our English Letter (from our own)." With a few exceptions here and there this feature appeared every Tuesday. Often they are lengthy, taking up two or two and a half columns. Probably *all* the English Letters were written by Mitford himself and posted, rather than telegraphed, as often the letter bears a date about a month prior to publishing.

2 *People of the Period*, edited by Alfred Pratt (London: Beeman, 1897); Haggard, *The Days of My Life* (London: Longmans, Green, 1928) II: 110.

that of trade, and the poet and idealist had a nobler conception of empire than the trader, and none was better qualified to give expression to that conception than their friend Mr. Kipling, who realized as few had realized the Divine right of a great civilizing race such as ours." Kipling praised the "strong men who were working for our Empire" and who "had to deal with an agricultural simplicity which objected to the very elements of civilization—to simple precautions against the spread of disease among their sheep, against rinderpest, objected to railways and to roads of all kinds. (Laughter.)"[1]

At one meeting in 1898 the group was addressed by James Bryce, one of Britain's most intelligent and liberal statesmen. Bryce's *Impressions of South Africa* (1897) had mixed sympathy for the natives with an unwitting downplaying of abuses or outright misinformation. Yet in his speech to the Club, on "the relation which literature and literary men ought to bear to the outlying parts of the Empire," Bryce paraphrased the Club's belief that the colonies were "a powerful stimulus and a fertile field for writers." The *Times* reporter summarized his address:

> It might be asked what literary men could do for the colonies, and what the colonies could do for literary men. . . . There still existed in England an ignorance of colonial society and of the conditions of colonial life, and he thought literature could remove that ignorance. Literature might make people in England understand the deep and peculiar charm that South Africa had for all who lived in it, and also make them understand its difficulties. (Hear, hear.) The chief difficulty which beset South Africa was the difficulty of race, but that was a difficulty which would ultimately give way under tact and judgment. (Hear, hear.) . . . . As to the question of what the colonies might do for literary men, he thought they might give them new fields, new topics, new subjects which were very welcome now that the old fields had been tilled and crops reaped from them over and over again. . . . When the soil of the old country had been exhausted, there were abundant fields in the outlying portions of the Empire. The works of Rudyard Kipling, Thomas Pringle, Olive Schreiner, Mr. Scully, and Mr. Bryden, and the brilliant romances of the chairman [Haggard], were instances of what the study of new

---

[1] *The Times*, "Anglo-African Writers' Club," May 17, 1898; issue 35518; pg. 11; col. F.

conditions might do in the way of stimulating and developing the
force of the writer's thought, and he did not think it was idle to
suppose that the time might come when the literary activity of
the colonies themselves might be far more abundant than it was
at present.[1]

Bryce clearly was equating "writers" with Englishmen, inasmuch as
when colonial expansion occupies the natives' territory, either the
native or his language is likely to be driven out.

If one applies Bryce's analysis of the British colonial writers' role
to Mitford—his name is not mentioned by Bryce, most likely because
he avoided the limelight of interviews (much loved by Haggard) and
book-signings (Scully's promotional forte)—his quartet of novels
goes in the direction of Bryce's "new fields, new topics, new subjects" by leading "the people at home" to see "the difficulty of race"
in imperial Africa. This was a time of cultural exchange as well as
intense conflict within a shifting balance of power among indigenous
African communities themselves and between them and European
adventurers, traders, and settlers. But after the Zulu and Matabele
Wars (in 1879 and 1893), this see-saw of negotiation between races
and disparate economic systems was supplanted in southern Africa
by a monolithic industrial economy. Mitford, recollecting the once-
mighty Ndebele empire that had collapsed, presents Umzilikazi
as a ruler standing by chance in the crossfire of past and present.
Eurocentric power and a world economy destroyed indigenous
social and cultural traditions and expunged African self-determination and a sense of historic identity and national consciousness.

At several meetings of the Club in 1900, attended by Mitford
and chaired by Haggard, the tensions of the Boer War and its
future settlement—e.g., should English be the official language in
the colonies?—were discussed by the members. These discussions
must have been a prime instance of how language could be used to
create a political reality—perhaps consciously so on the part of the
speakers since a Rhodesian visitor not only "advocated the official
use of the English tongue in all affairs in South Africa" but added
(ominously in hindsight) that an official language promoted the soli-

---

[1] *The Times*, "Anglo-African Writers' Club," December 22, 1898; issue 35706; pg.
8; col. E.

darity of "race feeling."[1] Every speaker's experiences and ideas of the world are delineated and conveyed by a communal language; and this linguistic construct is pliable and vulnerable to such biased and ideological interpretations as might frame its discursive meanings. The totalizing effect on settlers and indigenes alike of such an imperially controlled standard assists the geopolitical construction of a British myth—of white settler superiority, heroic military self-image, religious truth, or whatever—evolving as the needs arise to "explain" conquests, insurrections, and disasters. Clearly the definition of imperial English as a civilizing force over against the "many languages and dialects" (Bryce) of natives and Boers who embodied "an agricultural simplicity which objected to the very elements of civilization"(Kipling) casts light on a theoretical truism: generally the stronger social group has the power to impose its official interpretation on the groups it dominates, refusing to recognise the narrative authority of the dominated and, usually, being unable to envisage a point of view other than its own. Yet among those *initiating* an international or African English not subservient to empire is Mitford. While utilizing the language of colonial occupation to tell Untúswa's story, Mitford, like native African novelists Sol Plaatje or Chinua Achebe afterwards, melds English with indigenous African words, idiomatic turns of phrase, songs, proverbs, and even changes of the meanings of words to match localized African concepts—as for example Untúswa's "My father" idiom, a form of respectful address among natives or by blacks to whites, authentic for the precolonial and colonial eras.

Because Mitford had experienced both traditional Africa and its modern industrial restructuring, his object was to visualize the old kingdoms before their conquest and subjugation, particularly in contrast to the Eurocentric Africa that emerged in the wake of the Zulu War. If the cultural imperialism of pulpits and crass commercialism of newspapers often inhibited the emergence of authentic native

---

[1] *The London Times*, 19 June 1900; issue 36172; pg. 11; col. E; also 18 December 1900; issue 36328; pg. 10; col. C. See Bryce, *Impressions of South Africa* (1897), 3rd ed. (London: Macmillan, 1899): 366 and Olive Schreiner, *Thoughts on South Africa* [written in the 1890s] (New York: Stokes, 1923): 354-355 on English as a language to be widely used in the future outside the population of its native speakers.

voices, Mitford articulated the social, economic, and political under-tows within his African experience without jingoistic rhetoric. In short, he recognised (and we may also include fellow Anglo-African Club members Haggard and Scully) that when descriptions of spe-cific events by groups with opposed interests and visions conflict, these versions reflect a broader social struggle to enforce an official story. Mitford as contrarian links the settlers' struggles to the history of the natives themselves, humanizing Africans in an era of European chauvinism. Just as seeing eyes define objects from two intersect-ing angles, so Mitford leads his readers to visualize "the colonies" through the eyes of both the settler and the indigene. There, at that cultural intersection or zone of contact, Mitford's readers look past the public respectability of amoral imperialism or the bloodshed of the old Zulu kingdom to the terror and pity of humanity's quest for survival and love on both sides.

* * *

In *The King's Assegai* Mitford had told the story of how in about 1821 Shaka's headman, Umzilikazi (nowadays, Mzilikazi), member of a clan conquered by Shaka, fled with a band of follow-ers (much smaller than Mitford suggests) towards the Transvaal. Shaka's initial attempt to intercept him was dramatically fought off, leaving—according to historical accounts—a considerably reduced group. Umzilikazi, expecting another punitive attack after escaping over the Drakensberg mountains, laid waste the highveld country behind him, absorbing those of the Sotho-Tswana tribes and their cattle that he did not kill. Mitford's contemporary, A. T. Bryant, remarked that, "This method of destruction and wholesale pres-sure into his service became from now on his settled policy, so that when the Boer farmers trekked up in 1836, they found the greater part of Orangia and the Transvaal a miserable wilderness." This has been disputed, but Umzilikazi's kingdom did not become power-ful without the capture of cattle and local populations. The Sotho youths and others absorbed into Umzilikazi's expanding army were trained in Zulu tactics and were expected to take on Nguni customs. Owing to his gift of leadership, his disciplined regiments and deadly stabbing spears, and his shrewdness in tactical and strategic objec-tives, Umzilikazi's power began to assume near-mythic dimensions of invincibility. His name, it has been alleged, meant Path of Blood; however, this would suggest that his parents who named him—chief Mashobane and Nompetu, granddaughter of chief Zwide—were unusually prescient to foresee these later events! His multiplying nation became known as the Matabele or Ndebele peoples ("those who duck" under their shields). In late 1823 he built his first military kraal on the Olifants river, calling it ekuPumuleni, the "place of rest." There the Ndebele remained for several years engaged in incessant warfare with all the bordering clans. Not only was this an unusual form of "rest" but Bryant observed that the place also was "somewhat prematurely named" in the light of the subsequent drought:

> "For three months," says a Native account, "they had no rain and suffered keenly from want of water. The chief thereupon ordered all rain-doctors to be brought before him. All made up some medicine, but the heavens were unwilling, and the doctors failed to procure rain. The chief therefore ordered their execution. They were bound and thrown into the river" (or possibly where a river ought to have been). An exploring party having already previously reported a fine land "of much water and green grass even during the dry season" away north, Mzilikazi forthwith determined to remove to those parts.[1]

The White Shield continues the narrative of Umzilikazi's Ndebele when this decision was taken, historically about 1827, to move through the territory of the "Bakoni" and their chief, Tauane.[2] The kraal of ekuPumuleni, the "place of rest," is historical; but the new kraal of Kwa'zingwenya which Umzilikazi establishes in The White Shield is a fictitious name that conflates, for the sake of fictional streamlining, multiple military kraals occupied at various times in this stage of the migrating Ndebele community. Kwa means "place of" and Zingwenya is the Zulu word for "crocodile"—one of the rivers in the new Ndebele territory and an alternate name for its Bakwena people. Historically, this would have been near the present sites of Pretoria-Johannesburg in the Transvaal.

---

[1] Alfred T. Bryant, A Zulu-English Dictionary with Notes (Pinetown, Natal: Mariannhill Mission Press, 1905): 52.

[2] "Bakoni" is the Sotho term for the Nguni peoples of South Africa which include the Zulu, Xhosa, and Swazi but here used in a Zulu-Ndebele sense to mean everyone not Zulu.

As with *The King's Assegai*, so also the title of *The White Shield* highlights the essence of Zulu military power—shield and assegai, a power that at the time of these novels' composition ostensibly had been conquered and superseded by the British rifles. Many historical and ethnographic specifics underlie Untúswa's tale, owing to Mitford's venturesome placement of himself in a tribal mind in order to speak with the cultural authority of a native "voice"—in English. As in Haggard's Zulu epic, *Nada the Lily*, the relationship of the story-teller (in this instance Untúswa) to the hypothetical listener (Mitford-in-the-story) is considerably more problematic than in customary ethnographic reportage, since both the teller and the auditor are of the author's own creation. Even ethnographic documentation is subject to distortion by a transformation from the spoken native word to the printed English text with its colonized preoccupations. Owing to the historical baggage that words impose upon users, linguistic "equivalents" are inherently incommensurable. In his novels Mitford is the sole mediator between colonial and native cultures, inventing scenes, selecting data, placing isolated events in a chronological order, and giving local color and native voice to Untúswa and the paramount chiefs, Umzilikazi and Dingane—all of this encumbered by popular attitudes shaping his sense of audience and market. It is very easy to suspect that a political, even propagandistic, function might contaminate the blurred distinction between fictional and historical data. But the touchstone here is not primarily the socio-political party to which the author belongs; rather, it is the explicit or implied values projected through his *dramatis personae*. Can those voices be relied upon—not for some merely literal historical accuracy, but for a humanistic and elucidating shaping of the past landscape, for insights that outflank the mindless botanizing of "facts" and their stereotypical interpretations?

Mitford's chief accomplishment is not the twists and turns of "what next" in the narratives, though surprise and suspense are there, but the contextualizing details, those multiple levels of thematic connections wrought by the power of his personal, creative imagination. One example of Mitford's subtly comparative assessments must suffice here. Since all his readers knew how central to the nineteenth-century's self-image the ideal of ancient Greek civilization was, the implicit parallels drawn by the authorial consciousness between Greece and South Africa may be understood as validating pre-colonial native life and lamenting the loss of the heroic and mythical in England's drawing-room culture, its emerging mass consumerism of accumulated possessions. Thus the astonishing Zulu / Ndebele concept that the warrior's life belonged to the king could not be explained by modern values of private choice and control. That enlightened sense of individualistic selfhood—the idea that one's life is one's own and that one has a right to resist sacrificing it at the whim of another—remained foreign to native concepts of social identity. Self-determination was a product of Christian values—life, liberty, and the pursuit of happiness were not inalienable rights for Zulus. For the Zulu his deepest definition of identity is collective and expressed through the king's "word"; therefore, the warrior had no independent life to lose. In this Mitford saw a parallel to the classic Spartan ethos. Those three hundred Spartans who died to the last man at Thermopylæ set the Western standard of moral as well as physical courage by their sacrifice. Like the contemporary Zulu, the ancient warrior's body did not belong to himself, but to his *polis*, ancestors and kin; and he was trained to cultivate an unqualified contempt for a personal identification with his body or its pain or fear of death. His courageousness on the battlefield and unity with his battle-group was a product of *esoterike* and *exoterike harmonia*, self-composure or harmony within himself and the larger fortunes of war externally. Mitford seems to have nurtured a frank sympathy for the Lacedæmonian-like Matabeles, despite the countervailing gospel of Christian peace.

Mitford, who appears at the opening of his novel in all but *propriâ persona* as a battlefield antiquarian or archeologist, is seated with the storyteller Untúswa "high up on the ill-omened Hlobane Mountain" where in the Zulu War the British had been grievously bested— briefly. Mitford's first volume had been a non-fictional work on the battlefields of this war, *Through the Zulu Country* (1883). Untúswa's story is set prior to this war of 1879, in the pre-colonial era of the Transvaal. The national events and figures of power are played off against local and marginal lives, both given equal priority. The outer narrator's portentous locale contrasts the pre-colonial with his own colonial era. Situated between a powerful past and the present, Untúswa's narrative thus dramatizes the act of calling up historic deeds from the shifting terrain of memory to show how modern society can be infused with—or threatened by—the values of the old; and, one might add, the twenty-first century reader's angle of vision adds yet another coordinate to the retrospective vector of Untúswa's account. The symbolism of the narrative setting here points to the end of the heroic, mythical period of native independence, the *ancien régime*. As in *The King's Assegai*, here also in Mitford's second novel the story opens with a spear in the hands of a native that the author offers to buy. The native's declination emblematizes a refusal by the Zulus to betray Ndebele-Zulu cultural traditions to the emissaries of the European world: "it took some time to explain that the weapon was wanted, not for use, but for show—in short, as a curio." No slow evolution over time—no turning a somersault by gradual stages—is symbolized by this proffer of trade; rather, a sudden, irrevocable and unbridgeable change between an old world of native weapons employed in war amongst independent tribes on broadly equal terms and the new world of global British rule in which such are now merely "curios." This new world is industrial, commercial, and its love of money is love itself. The most appalling instance in Mitford's fiction of this mercenary materialism is the offer Laurence Stanninghame receives in *The Sign of the Spider* (1896) to sell his Ba-gcatya maiden to an Arab slave-trader—and though a slaver himself, Stanninghame's horror at this commercial prospect is his only hope of eventual redemption. Whatever their faults, the Zulus lived by a code of honor of which Jo'burg and its pursuit of gold knew nothing.

About 1829 Umzilikazi encountered European trader-hunters and missionaries in the far interior. Quite possibly Bertram Mitford's Jesuit missionary among Umzilikazi's people in *The White Shield* may have been an evocative parallel to Robert Moffat who from his station at Kuruman visited the king on several occasions. Their personal friendship lasted many years, despite the fact that Moffat felt duty-bound to expostulate on what he perceived to be the chief's harsh and pagan practices:

> His government, so far as I could discover, was the very essence of despotism. The persons of the people, as well as their possessions, were the property of their monarch. His word was law, and he had only to lift his finger or give a frown, and his great-

est nobles trembled in his presence. . . . Though but a follower
in the footsteps of Chaka, the career of Moselekatse, from the
period of his revolt till the time I saw him, and long after, formed
an interminable catalogue of crimes. Scarcely a mountain, over
extensive regions, but bore the marks of his deadly ire. His experience and native cunning enabled him to triumph over the minds
of his men, and made his trembling captives soon adore him as an
invincible sovereign. Those who resisted, and would not stoop to
be his dogs, he butchered.[1]

This about the chief who bestowed upon Moffat his very own family
patronymic and out of respect called a son after the mission station
at Kuruman! Clearly the issue of which traditional values must yield
to the historical process and which others might be retained in a
post-enlightenment colonizing culture remained unresolved and
papered over.

Although Moffat and his associates were Protestant, Mitford
uses literary license to alter the novel's Christian missionary to his
own personal persuasion of Catholicism. Before Mitford's "white
isanusi" dies at his post of a fever, he offers himself in substitu-
tion for several of Umzilikazi's subjects who were condemned to
be fed to crocodiles, a form of Ndebele execution Moffat also had
described. The heroic ministry of Mitford's Jesuit may have been
a literary precursor to H. Rider Haggard's Rev. Mr. Owen in *The
Wizard* (1896), since in both novels the new gospel of Christian
peace is pitted against the tribal culture of war. Catholic missionaries had been the first to go to the interior of southern Africa;
however, when Jesuits reappeared in Matabeleland in the time of
Umzilikazi's successor, Lobengula, the Ndebele had no interest in
their religious teachings although their practical skills in the repair
of ox wagons were welcomed. Such unresponsiveness was not
entirely owing to Ndebele disapproval of priestly celibacy since,
as it has been asserted, the Protestant missionary William Sykes, a
colleague of Moffat's son-in-law David Livingstone, preached and
taught among them for almost thirty years and could not point to a
single convert. Partly the natives struggled not only with theologi-
cal concepts such as the Trinity or bodily resurrection (hyænas and

---

[1] Moffat, *Missionary Labours and Scenes in South Africa* (London: John Snow,
1842): 542-545. Moffat's is the Sutú rendering of the king's name.

crocodiles ate many bodies and the rest putrefied—so what's left for resurrection?) but also with the Christian rejection of polygamy, of initiatory and marriage customs, of witch doctors and their "dark superstitions," and of internecine warfare. Mitford more than half suggests (also noticed by John Moffat, Robert's son) that Umzilikazi was convinced opening his country to white settlers in the wake of the missionaries would erode or overwhelm indigenous social and religious practices.

Mitford's second novel is organized around three battles of increasing intensity and ferocity in the 1827-1837 period, reflecting a murderous frenzy shocking for his readers. In each battle, Mitford conflates multiple historical engagements into a single encounter—one that always tips the balance in favor of Ndebele success. At the time he wrote, Mitford had little documentation for the dates and details of these conflicts—thus, in historical fact Umzilikazi's move from Ekupumuleni predated the earliest wave of Afrikaner Voortrekkers ("pioneers") to his territory. But Mitford's character Kalipe (or MKalipe/Kaliphi as many modern accounts spell the name of this historically renowned Matabele warrior) was indeed the *induna* in command of several attacks when the Boers first appeared. Umzilikazi astutely realized the threat the coming swarms of Trekkers posed. This first fight in *The White Shield* must have in fact occurred about June or July of 1836 with the earliest Trekkers who crossed the Vaal River with horses and wagons and shot game. Accounts do say Umzilikazi sent an *impi* under Kalipe to kill the men and bring back their women and girls. Not long after, the tension between Umzilikazi and the Trekkers climaxed in a pitched battle against the Boers in laager at Vegkop (or Vechtkop)—also fictionalized later in Peter Abrahams's *Wild Conquest* (1950) as the climactic encounter before Umzilikazi's flight north to Matabeleland. Though the Ndebele captured many cattle, hundreds of the attackers were killed. Mitford's incident of a girl-child captured from the Boers and sent to Umzilikazi was true enough though this occurred in the previous skirmishes, not at the climactic encounter—and some later accounts say two girls and a boy. If the Boer women are amusingly described by Mitford as "ugly," this blue-eyed girl-child is British and "has the look of a child of a race of kings!" Indeed, her "eyes were blue as the heavens"; and since the Amazulu are "the People of the

Heavens," she is a sort of nordic Zulu, much superior to the peasant Boers, of whom Mitford thought much less, brave and good shooters though they were.

The next Ndebele battle described by Mitford—a foray against a tribe of the Bechuana clan of whom Tauane (or Tauana, "lion's whelp") was chief—actually had occurred prior to the fights with the Trekkers, about 1830. This second battle may very well have been the attack on the Barolong later described independently in the opening chapters of Sol Plaatje's *Mhudi* (1930) since the episodes in both Mitford and Plaatje are initiated by a chief Tauane who "dared offer violence to the King's ambassadors." Seen as an attack against the person of the omnipotent sovereign himself, Ndebele punishment must "rewrite" the crime on the bodies of the offenders—a blood-for-blood logic that revolved around spectacle. Although British reformers and missionaries felt that such manifestations of "monarchical 'super-power'" (the phrase is Michel Foucault's) were unevenly distributed and thus capricious, within native social formations such punishments were not felt to be irrational or excessive atrocities. And although Umzilikazi may have ruthlessly attacked Bakoni tribes, he was not the blood-thirsty despot described by the Boers. He welcomed small groups of strangers if they entered his country from Kuruman (where the missionary Robert Moffat screened visitors) and if they acknowledged his rule by asking his permission to shoot game. Interestingly, both in Plaatje's and Abrahams's novels a Kalipe-figure named Gubuza warns Umzilikazi of the political and/or moral consequences of his vengeful massacre. Although Plaatje attempted to present Umzilikazi more favorably than in Boer South African accounts or in Barolong oral history, Mitford's 1895 novel had anticipated an even more sympathetic stance. Mitford's stance is not to see the king as a moral monster but to adopt the perspective of the chief's second-in-command, seeing him as did his loyal (and disloyal) followers—a more impartial ethnographical approach or, perhaps considering the emotions displayed, a diversity of dissonant and subversive voices for the time and place in which the novel was produced.

The third battle of the novel is a large-scale retaliatory attack on Umzilikazi by Dingane's Zulus, probably the one in 1837. Although in this "battle of the three rifts" the actual Ndebele did in fact rally at the point of total collapse and thus stave off national destruction, the fictional success was nowhere nearly as unqualified as Mitford suggests. Dingane himself actually rated this same encounter a significant Zulu victory. The novel concludes as Untúswa wins Lalusini for his wife after this final battle. Historically under continued pressure from Boers, Barolongs and Zulus, Umzilikazi not long afterwards was pushed north out of the Transvaal to settle for the final time in Matabeleland between the Limpopo and Zambezi. As understood by Mitford, Umzilikazi straddled the Ndebele's formative stage as a military state and its future prospects for peace—probably not, however, as a wholly autonomous state; rather, as a future jewel in the imperial crown. What this meant for Mitford is best encapsulated by John Buchan, private secretary to Lord Milner, High Commissioner for South Africa, and author of *Prester John* (1910), who recalled his belief "that we were laying the basis of a federation of the world" (Tennyson's phrase from "Locksley Hall").[1] Neither a moral monster nor a tragic hero, Umzilikazi stands as a force for choice of direction, a facilitator of the historical transition between a pre-colonial Ndebele and what European colonization at its best could do for south Africa's future.

In contrast to Mitford's sense of Umzilikazi's heroic capacity to build a nation and chart its destiny, Peter Abrahams has achieved a more modern level of sympathy for the king as a tragic hero. Abrahams goes so far in *Wild Conquest* as to have both Gubuza and Umzilikazi deplore the "bloodlust" of their nation, a "darkness" that Mkomozi, the proto-Christian witch doctor, observes has tainted all parties.[2] This may be a profound insight, but it is a post-colonial and twentieth-century perspective. Thus his native slaves in 1835 speak of freedom from Boer control in the binary style of proletariat and bourgeois: "The child says 'what is freedom, papa?' I say: when that valley belongs to us, and that house belongs to us, and when the things we build and the food we grow is ours, and when we and our children can eat and sleep in that house and there is no Baas Koos and no Baas Kasper to take what is ours, I say that is freedom."[3] In this version of freedom, the rule of the owner will be replaced by

[1] Buchan, *Memory Hold the Door* (London: J. M. Dent, 1940): 125.
[2] Abrahams, *Wild Conquest* (New York: Harper, 1950): 210-211.
[3] Abrahams, *Wild Conquest*: 12-13.

the enfranchised natives who currently themselves have no means of production but must give their labor to live. Mitford, unconversant with Abraham's desideratum of a Marxist-like land reform, envisioned instead a future spiritual tenure of the land as jointly held within an imperial utopia, as at the end of *Renshaw Fanning's Quest* (1894) where husband and wife, masters and servants are in consummate balance with each other and the land. Perhaps Mitford believed this oxymoron of harmonious but unequal ownership might contain the seeds of a less-flawed society once its internal logic of interwoven relationships was fully worked out—though, in sad historic reality, that did not arrive in his lifetime (has not yet arrived) nor, so far, peacefully. In hindsight, such an "assimilationist" goal of progress—attested to by a British *lingua franca* that cherished smaller cultural "others" in a dialogic way, standing alongside those African tongues—was illusory, crushed by the power and wealth of words rewarding lies.

Gerald Monsman
Tucson

April 30, 2008

GERALD MONSMAN is Professor of English and former head of the English Department at the University of Arizona, where he specializes in nineteenth-century British and Anglo-African literature. He has published books with Hopkins, Duke, Yale, and in the area of South African literature has written *Olive Schreiner's Fiction: Landscape and Power* (Rutgers, 1991), has edited H. Rider Haggard's *King Solomon's Mines* (Broadview, 2002), and most recently has authored *H. Rider Haggard on the Imperial Frontier: The Political and Literary Contexts of his African Romances* (ELT, 2006). He has also edited four other novels by Bertram Mitford, *The Sign of the Spider*, *The Weird of Deadly Hollow*, *The King's Assegai*, and *Renshaw Fanning's Quest*, for Valancourt Books.

The White Shield

CONTENTS

" . . . . A heathen horde,
Reddening the sun with smoke and earth with blood."

TENNYSON.

" . . . . The eager jackal,
As the lengthening shadows more drearily fall,
Shrieks forth his hymn to the hornèd moon!
And the lord of the desert will follow him soon:
And the tiger-wolf laughs in his bone-strewed brake,
As he calls on his mate and her cubs to awake:
And the panther and leopard come leaping along,
All hymning to Hecate a festival song:
For the tumult is over, the slaughter hath ceased,
And the vulture hath bidden them all to the feast."

THOMAS PRINGLE.

PROLOGUE.

WE were talking about Rorke's Drift and of Kambúla, in the battles fought at which places these two warriors had borne arms. They were fine, tall, martial-looking Zulus, and both head-ringed. They carried small shields, and a perfect arsenal of assegais—beautifully-made weapons for the most part. With none of these, however, could they be induced to part.

"What should you white people want with our poor weapons?" said one. "Have you not much better ones of your own? Where is your gun, *Umlúngu?*"

"Yonder," I answered, pointing to my waggon, which, far away on the plain beneath, drawn by its span of twelve black Zulu oxen, seemed at that distance to creep along like some great centipede. "But I seldom carry it about, for there is little game in these parts, and a useless gun is much heavier than a stick."

"And a Zulu spear is no heavier than a stick, but more useful," cut in the other, with a quizzical laugh.

Then it took some time to explain that the weapon was wanted, not for use, but for show—in short, as a curio—in process of which explanation a voice from behind sang out—

"*Au! Nkose*[1] is fond of assegais!"

I knew that voice. Turning, I beheld the tall, gaunt form and sinewy limbs, the white-bearded countenance and bright eyes of old Untúswa, some time *induna*[2] under the great Umzilikazi, Founder and first King of the Matabeli nation.

"Greeting, old friend!" I said, as he plunged eagerly forward to bestow upon me a hearty handgrip; which, by the way, left a sensation as of having shaken hands with a remarkably energetic skeleton. "Greeting to you, son of Ntelani, *induna* of the Elephant who of late trumpeted in the North! Greeting also to the King's Assegai!"

"You are my father, *Nkose!*" cried the old man, sinking down into a sitting posture in our midst. "Yes, the King's Assegai is still alive, like its old owner," he said, exhibiting the splendid spear, and bal-

---
[1] "The Chief." A title of courtesy.—Mitford's note.
[2] Noble adviser or military commander; *izinduna* is the plural.

ancing it lovingly in his hands. "When I saw yonder waggon and the black oxen which draw it, I said to myself—'There goes the white man to whom I told that tale.'"

"True, Untúswa, and a right stirring tale it was. But I seem to remember, that when we parted on the Entonjaneni heights, the word was that other matters, at least as strange, remained to be told, should we behold each other again. And here now we do behold each other again, and the day is yet young. Further, here is good store of tobacco, and if there is anything which constitutes a better accompaniment to a story, why, I never heard of it."

The eyes of old Untúswa brightened as he received the much-prized, *gwai*,[1] holding out both hands for it, as the courteous custom of this people is, even though the gift be no weightier than a three-penny-piece. For to receive anything with one hand only, would, to the minds of these "barbarians," imply a contempt alike for the gift and for the giver.

High up on the ill-omened Hlobane Mountain we were seated, whose savage fastnesses I had spent days in exploring. It was early morning, and the weather was grey and depressing, seeming to threaten rain. Beneath lay a great panorama of desolate rolling plain and craggy spurs—treeless, forbidding—with here and there a kraal, dotted at intervals, symmetrical in its circular ring-fences. But here, where we sat, poised high above the world, I had come upon another small kraal, and, turning my pony loose to graze, had, as usual, tarried to make friends with its people.

Now, the older of the two warriors with whom I had been in converse, called aloud, and presently there appeared a couple of stalwart, shapely-limbed damsels, bearing a very large earthen bowl brimming with *tywala*, or corn-beer, and a basket containing roasted mealies. A goodly portion of the liquor was poured into a smaller bowl and handed to me, after the preliminary sip required by Zulu etiquette, the others taking draughts in common from the large earthen pot.

Zulus, like most uncivilised races, are extremely fond of listening to stories, and hold a good narrator in high repute; therefore, these two sat with faces all animation and heads bent eagerly forward. Then, having taken several copious pinches of snuff, old Untúswa commenced the tale which follows.

---

[1] Tobacco, especially snuff.

THE WHITE SHIELD.

CHAPTER I.

THE CHIEF OF THE BLUE CATTLE.

You will remember, *Nkose*, how we of the Royal House of Dingiswayo, of the tribe of Umtetwa, with the Amandebeli, went out from the land of Zulu to found a new nation, and how we shut back the overwhelming number of the spears of Tshaka in the gates of the great Kwahlamba mountains. So, too, you will remember how, having hailed our leader Umzilikazi as king we swept ever onward, to the west and to the north, stamping flat the tribes within our path and laying waste the land, leaving behind us a desert that the cubs of the Lion of Zulu would find difficult of crossing. So, too, you will remember, how we built the great Kraal of Ekupumuleni, and subdued all the tribes round about, and sat in our fair resting-place, feared as a great and mighty people. For of the races around, all came in to *konza* to Umzilikazi, and to pay tribute, and such as did not—well, it was not long before the trumpeting of the Elephant sounded in their ears, dwelt they even two or three moons distant. But there was one tribe or nation which refused thus to *konza*, and of it I shall speak presently.[1]

As time went by, our new nation grew in numbers and strength—though the latter might be our weakness in the day of grave trial. For we had incorporated into our army the youth of such tribes as we had conquered and whom the king deemed capable of bearing arms.

---

[1] This description recapitulates the theme of the first novel in the quartet, *The King's Assegai*. Tshaka, Tjaka is currently spelled Shaka; *konza* means to pay tribute or to acknowledge suzerainty.

These Amaholi, or slaves, were really our dogs, and even of this they might have been proud, for in our veins ran the clear unmixed blood of the "People of the Heavens;"[1] but did the spears of Tshaka show upon the skyline there would not be one of these miserable jackals within a day's march of them by the time they drew near. Howbeit, although they were too cowardly to fight for us, we did not fear lest they should turn and fight against us, for the spears of Tshaka would devour them just as readily as they would ourselves; nay, more readily, for we Amandebeli were as lions, and dealt back blow for blow, were the enemy tenfold our own strength.

Time passed by, and as our *impis*[2] went farther and farther afield, reports came in of a wonderful land to the north: of a land whose streams were never dry, and where the grass was ever green, and rich, and sweet. Now, around the King's kraal, Ekupumuleni, it was not always so, and for many moons we had suffered greatly for want of rain; indeed, the King had sent out expressly to take all the rain-makers of every tribe and race and to bring them in. These tried their powers, each and all, and failed, wherefore they were put to death, for Umzilikazi declared that, as they were highly honoured and loaded with gifts when they could perform their office, it was only fair that they should pay forfeit when they could not; and this fate befell most of our own rain-makers, who were tied with their heels round the backs of their necks, and flung into a water-hole. Indeed, the only one who escaped was Masuka, the old Mosutu, whom we took, and whose life I had saved at the burning of certain Bapedi kraals, and who, while declaring himself an *isanusi*[3] but no rain-maker, yet managed to bring rain, and thus not only escaped death but was advanced to still further honour. He was now of a great age, this old man, and was little else than a human skin loosely covering a skeleton; yet his eyes were as bright and marvellous as ever.

That Masuka stood so high in the king's favor and in such honour among the people delighted me greatly, for I knew that as long as this was so I was safe from any plots my enemies might lay against

---

[1] Such is the literal meaning of the word "Amazulu."—Mitford's note. "Ama" people of + "Zulu" the heavens above.

[2] Armies.

[3] *Is-* + *anusi*: diviner, wizard, witch-doctor; usually, a rain-maker.

me. I was now second fighting *induna* of the whole army, and a *kehla*, or ringed man.[1] I had won a place of great power, young as I was, and those whose bitter jealousy would have moved them to compass my downfall and death were many. Moreover Umzilikazi had become suspicious of late, and was inclined to suspect each and all of his principal captains of designs upon his life and seat; and there were times when I fancied his suspicions rested strongly on Kalipe, the chief *induna* of the army, and myself—but mostly upon myself.

Yet, *Nkose*, this idea, terrible as it was, did not fill me with unmingled dismay. That I, but yesterday an *umfane*[2] and unringed, should now be in a position to be suspected of usurping Umzilikazi's seat, of aspiring to become King of the Aba-ka-zulu; *Hau!* This indeed would cause my veins to flow and my nerves to thrill with a strange proud tingling. Yet the other side of the picture was grim and dark, for from it loomed the stake of impalement—the death of the hot stones; or, at the mildest, the knob-sticks of the slayers. I remembered, too, the words which, in times past, had been spoken by Nangeza, my chief wife: "A man who is brave and cautious may climb to any height"—and, indeed, she suffered me not to forget them, for she was as proud and ambitious as ever, and was continually inciting me to supplant Kalipe. Then once I held the army in the hollow of my hand, what easier than——

But at this point I would stop my ears and cry upon her to hold her peace, lest she brought me—brought us all—to a far more fearful and lingering death than that which I extended my breast to meet when I claimed and won the King's assegai—as I have already told you, *Nkose*. But Nangeza had a plotting brain and would ever be first—indeed, had the King taken her to wife, she would never have rested until she had made herself King over him or—until she had been led forth to the place of slaughter. Moreover, I would do nothing against Kalipe, whose word and ways were as straight as his path when the King's enemies lay before him, and although he was much older than I he would never show any jealousy because I had been promoted nearly to an equality with himself.

---

[1] Head-ringed men, and privileged to marry—Mitford's note from another novel. The head-ring, also known as the *isicoco*, is the traditional and most prized insignia of the married warrior.

[2] 'Boy,' *i.e.*, technically, one who has not attained to the distinction of the head-ring.—Mitford's note from another novel.

"It is the weakness of our nation, Untúswa," he would say, "that we rend and devour each other like a pack of jackals; and every man plots, lest another rise to be a little greater than himself. Now, the man I would sooner see second to me, or even equal with me, is not the oldest, nor yet the richest man, but the bravest; and that man is, I believe, yourself, son of Ntelani, young in years as you are."

Thus spake Kalipe, and, indeed, he meant his words; and while this was so, and I had old Masuka on my side, I feared the grudges and jealousy of no man.

Now, it was in the mind of the King to abandon Ekupumuleni, and to move farther northward, partly for the reasons I have given, partly that the arm of Tshaka stretched far, and he was never quite certain that we were beyond the reach of it. So he ordered me to take a force of warriors, and make an expedition into the country with the ever-flowing streams, and to verify such reports of it as had come in.

My command was but a small one, comprising perhaps sixty or seventy men—the merest handful, remembering that those through whom our path lay were in countless thousands, and that small cause indeed had they to love us. Yet such was the terror inspired by the very name of the Amandebeli—or Aba-ka-zulu, as these people termed us—that though they were in swarming numbers, they fled from their kraals as our tiny *impi* drew near, and took refuge among the hills. We laughed and shook our spears at them in proud contempt, and taking whatever we wanted, passed on our way, for we were only the eyes of the lion this time, not his teeth and claws, wherefore we left them their lives and their cattle.

But this was not to last for ever. Day by day as we progressed the country became fairer, swarming as it did with great herds of game—elephant and buffalo and kudu—in the forest tracts, and vast quantities of eland and springbok and other game upon the rolling treeless plains. And the cattle which the people owned were round and fat; and the people themselves, though not warriors, were rich and happy. We looked at each other and laughed in our delight. Here was the country we would occupy. Here was the fair land of plenty we had fled from Tshaka's spears to gain. Here was the land wherein we would set up our new nation, and these people already here should be our dogs—our slaves.

Thus we thought, thus we spake, although we were but a tiny handful among tens of thousands. The cattle of these people covered the land—fat and sleek. It was well. They should be ours. What a nation ours should become!

So resolving, we continued our march, already the proud march of the conqueror. It was evening, nigh to sundown. We had slaughtered oxen at the last kraal we passed, and had seized women and boys to carry our meat for us. We were ascending a long rise, intending to rest in the valley beyond, where a river flowed, when, lo! the crest of the hill was crowned with spears—bright spears—a forest of them moving and extending in waves of light beneath the now sinking sun.

At the sight a deep gasp broke from every chest, and up went every man's head with distended nostrils. We snuffed battle even as a hound snuffs the warm scent of a buck. We gripped our shields and our weapons, and we massed together, halting to see what the enemy would do next.

"*Hau!* They are surrounding us," muttered some of the warriors in their deep voices—their eyes glaring like those of hyænas hungering for blood. "Shall we fall upon them, *Induna* of the King? Shall we fall upon them?"

"Not so," I answered, leaning on my shield and calmly taking snuff, though the wild expectation of battle and its delights caused my heart to beat and my pulses to thrill, for I was young yet, although so high up in a position of trust. "Not so. Let us see first if they are coming in to *konza* to the messengers of the Great Great One; but if they mean war, my children, by the head ring of Senzangakona, they shall have as much of it as they can stomach. Let no blow be struck until I give the word, but raise the song of the Great Great One, and advance in battle order. When I give the word we will walk through and through their ranks, leaving a broad path every way."

So each warrior, striking his shield with his knobstick, raised the war song of Umzilikazi—

> *"Yaingahlabi*
> *Leyo 'nkunzi!*
> *Yai ukúfa!"*[1]

---

[1] "That bull did not (merely) gore.
It was death."—Mitford's note.

And thus we paced up the slope slowly, and roaring the terrible battle-song, which had told the tidings of blood and fire and widespread death along our nation's track, and as the excitement spread over us we began to "see red," and the aspect of each warrior was so grim and ferocious, that those in front, hundreds though they were, hesitated before our unswerving advance, then halted and called for an *indaba*.

As we still advanced, singing loudly, we began to observe more closely those who opposed us, and all but hemmed us in. They were armed with spears, which seemed well made, with axes, and hard square shields. In aspect they were akin to the Bapedi and the people of old Masuka, but their faces were softer, as those of women, or of men who were not fond of war; their ranks, too, were loose and open, and in no order: indeed, I had little doubt but that, in the event of hostilities, we could carry out our original plan, and hew lanes through and through them. But now a voice called out to us—

"Who are ye, stranger people, who enter the land of the Bakoni? Who are ye? so few, yet singing songs of war?"

Our warriors shook their heads and growled like dogs. They understood not this language, but I understood it moderately well, having been at pains to learn from old Masuka both the tongues and customs of the people around, with all of which he was well-acquainted; and, indeed, it was because of my knowledge of these tongues that the King had sent me in command of such a small *impi*, which might easily have been led by a chief of far inferior rank.

"Of the Bakoni? Who is your chief, and where is he?" I cried in return.

"Ascend hither, strangers, then you may see and speak with him," came the reply.

Not a shade of hesitation did our warriors show as I made known this request. They advanced up the hill, marching in rank and singing, as proudly disdainful of the vastly overwhelming numbers in front as though safe at Ekupumuleni. Even the women and boys, staggering under their loads of meat, dared not leave us, although their own people were around them in force and we were but few.

We soon gained the brow of the rise, and spreading out on either hand in two long lines, their spears glittering in the sinking sun, we beheld the battle rank of the Bakoni warriors. But we beheld something more. Beyond the rise whereon we stood, beyond the small river which flowed at its base on the further side, was a wide rolling plain covered with cattle, and beyond the cattle lay the countless huts of an immense town.

Our eyes opened wide, and a deep-throated gasp escaped us. What a place to burn! What countless herds to sweep away! was the thought in each man's mind.

Behind this town rose a great hill, steep-sided, flat-topped, and belted by lines of cliffs. There were further hills beyond it, but this one stood out from all, seeming to stand by itself upon the plain. We almost forgot the near presence of a great number of enemies. These, however, now closed in around us.

"Draw near, strangers," said the man who had first hailed us, and who seemed to be a leader of some kind—"the Chief of the People of the Blue Cattle sits before you."[1]

I beheld, seated upon a leopard skin, a man just past middle age. He was a well-built man, tall and sinewy, and more martial-looking than any of his people. He was seated alone, a few councillors attending him several paces in the background, and save for a battle-axe, no arms were near him. He wore ornaments of gold, as we noticed did quite a number of the people, and the axe itself was profusely inlaid with gold.

"This people," I thought, "if not warlike, is skilful in making weapons. Good. It shall make weapons for its masters, the conquerors of the world."

"Greeting, Chief of the Blue Cattle," I said, taking up the title by which he had been named; and, indeed, looking upon the countless herds which were scattered over the plain, I noticed that the greater number were of a bluish-white colour.

He frowned, thinking I accosted him with scant deference, which was true, for we Amazulu, People of the Heavens, do not bend low before the chiefs of such tribes as this.

"Why do you approach me with weapons in your hand, stranger? Is this a custom among yourselves when approaching a chief?"

---

[1] The "blue cattle" (not a cerulean shade) have a light base coat intermixed with darker hairs, producing a bluish-white color; conversely, the black base coat of the "blue" wildebeest is intermixed with white hairs, giving it a grey coat with a silvery bluish tint.

"Our weapons were placed in our hands by the Great Great One—the Black Elephant, whose voice trumpets afar. Not until we return into his presence again do we lay them down," I answered shortly.

All this while I was keenly watching the chief's face, and I read therein a bragging nature, but a coward spirit underlying it. He, for his part, was noting our large stature and fearless bearing, our great shields and heavy-bladed spears, and I knew he was impressed thereby.

"What do you here, in my country, strangers?" he continued, frowning still deeper. "You enter it armed and slaughter our cattle, and seize upon our women and boys to act as your slaves," with a glance at the group behind us who had thrown off their loads to rest. "This must be explained."

"The explanation is short, O Chief of the Blue Cattle," I answered haughtily, standing straight and with my head thrown back. "We entered this, your country, as we would enter any country, at the bidding of the Great Great One, who sits at Ekupumuleni, the Black Elephant, who is King over the whole world and King over the Bakoni of course. This is the explanation, O Chief of the Blue Cattle."

At these words an enraged murmur arose from those immediately before us, and rolled along the ranks in a defiant shout. Still, with my head thrown back, I only laughed slightly.

"That is my explanation; now hear my advice," I went on. "Send back immediately your highest *indunas* with a large present of girls and cattle to the Great Great One who sits at Ekupumuleni. Then will he fix the terms upon which he will suffer you and your people to live, O Chief of the Blue Cattle."

To the first shout of rage now succeeded a deafening yell of exasperation as the people caught the gist of these proud words. There was a swift rush and the ranks tightened around us. Spears were shaken towards us, and eyes glared with angry menace. But my little band made scarcely a movement; a hand here and there would shift nearer to the head of the deadly stabbing assegai, or a shield would quiver in sinewy grip. That was all, yet upon every face there glowed the light of battle. A moment and we should be hewing our way through those broad ranks to the inspiration of our fiercely maddening war-cry.

But the chief's command availed to arrest the rush of his exasperated fighting men, which was well for him; else had he fallen that moment—for I had marked him as first victim, nor could he have escaped me.

"What is thy name, leader of this band of strangers?" he said.

"Untúswa, son of Ntelani, of the tribe of Umtetwa, of the nation of Zulu, is my name. Ponder it well, O Chief of the Blue Cattle, for in truth thou shalt hear it again."

Once more, a loud and angry shout arose from the warriors. Once more the words of the chief stayed the tumult.

"Look around, Untúswa, son of Ntelani," he said, rising for the first time. "Yonder is our town—one of many. Behind it rises a hill, which is flat on the top, whereon grows abundant grass, and springs flow. It could carry the cattle of a nation and the fighting men of a nation, and the force who would climb it might just as well think to climb the Heavens themselves, for it is fortified from base to summit. Behold these," designating the armed warriors, "these are but a handful among the fighting-men who obey my word. Yet I would quarrel with none, wherefore I will not suffer that violence should overtake you—even though you have offered insult to a mighty nation in the person of its chief. Depart now, ye strangers, in peace, while ye may. Farewell!"

"How is it called, this great and mighty town, my father?" I said, somewhat mockingly.

"It is called 'The Queen of the World,'" he answered proudly.

"Ha! That is good," I replied. "When the tread of the Elephant—Umzilikazi, the Great Great One, the Founder of Nations—shaketh yonder town, then the King and the Queen of the World will be mated? Till then, farewell, O Chief of the Blue Cattle!"

Then we departed even as we had come—slaves and all—no man hindering us. Yes, the name of Zulu was mighty indeed in those days.

CHAPTER II.

TREASON IN THE AIR.

STRONG as we felt in the might of our name and nation, we were too well skilled in the game of war to allow ourselves to be lulled into a blind security. Day after day, night after night, we kept a sharp look-out, expecting the forces of the Bakoni and their allies to fall upon us in overwhelming numbers. But they did not; which went to show that something of the terror of our name had travelled to the Chief of the Blue Cattle; nor, indeed, did I doubt but that messengers would follow shortly after us with gifts, and desiring to *konza* to Umzilikazi, even as had done all other nations within our reach.

At length we drew near to Ekupumuleni, and our hearts were light, for the thoughts of all of us were full of the richness of the country which lay awaiting our possession; and as we returned to the home of our wandering nation, the dryness of the land struck us as quite cheerless—not that it was so really, but only by comparison with the green, well-watered region we had just left.

Having sent messengers on to announce our arrival, we entered the great kraal, singing lustily the praises of the King. Umzilikazi was seated in his wonted place, at the upper end of the great open circle, and as we flung our weapons to the ground and, tossing our right hands aloft, roared the *Bayéte*, I could see that pleased expression I knew so well steal over his face.

"Greeting, son of Ntelani," he said, as bending low, I drew near. "Seat thyself, and tell me what thou hast seen and done."

This I did, and the Great Great One took snuff and listened. Then he ordered those women and boys whom we had taken as bearers to be brought before him.

Crouching low to the earth they came, those poor slaves, their eyes starting from their heads in fear. They had never seen anything like this—the splendour of our huge kraal and its shapeliness and strength; so different to their own town, which, though far larger, was utterly without shape or design—the stature and strength, and fierce bearing of our warriors, who had mustered in crowds to witness our return, and above all, the proud majesty of our King, and the roaring volume of praises which went up from every throat to hail his appearance. They bent low to the very earth, trembling with fear.

"It is good, it is good," said the King, eyeing them between pinches of snuff. "These are right well-made specimens, albeit somewhat light of skin. I ordered thee to take no captives, Untúswa, yet the *impi* needed bearers for its goods, and thou hast chosen the pick and flower of the girls. Ah! ah! Untúswa; thou hast ever an eye for all that is best in that way."

"*Yeh-bo Nkulu 'nkulu!*" I cried, delighted that I had pleased the King.

"I will choose the best, Untúswa. After that thou canst take the two that will suit thee; the remainder I will otherwise dispose of."

Then the King dismissed us, ordering cattle to be slain for us to feast on, and we departed from his presence uttering shouts of *bonga*.

When I gained my hut I found Nangeza, my principal wife, awaiting me with ill-concealed impatience.

"Welcome, Untúswa," she said. "And so upon the news you bring it depends whether we move onward or no?"

"Who am I, to seek to interpret the mind of the King?" I answered darkly, for Nangeza was ever trying to wring out of me what went on in the secret councils of the *izinduna*, and even in my private conferences with the Great Great One himself. This was all very well while I was unringed and a thoughtless boy, but now things were different. The less women had to say to such matters the better; but although I could see this now, Nangeza never could be brought to do so. She would show an evil temper at such times, and hint that she had been the making of me—that I had been ready enough to take counsel of her in times past, but that now I was somebody I thought I could do without her. Then she would bid me beware, saying that, even as she had made me, it might still be within her power to unmake me. Now of this sort of talk, *Nkose*, I began to have more than enough. Nangeza might be the *inkosikazi*[1]—she deserved that—but she should not be the chief, too.

She was now a tall, fine, commanding woman, and as fearless and ready of wit as she had been when a girl, yet with the lapse of

[1] Chieftainess. The principal wife of a man of rank.—Mitford's note.

time she had become too commanding—had developed an expression of hardness which does not become a woman. She had slaves to wait on her, and had little or no hard work to do herself. Moreover, by this time, I had two other wives, those two girls whom I had promised to *lobola*[1] for when they had surprised me and Nangeza together; and I had kept my word. They were soft-hearted, merry, laughing girls, who never dreamed that the second fighting *induna* of the King's army ought to take his commands from women; wherefore it not unfrequently befell that I preferred their huts to that of Nangeza, my *inkosikazi*.[2]

A woman of Nangeza's disposition could not be other than a jealous woman. She hated my other two wives. She had borne me one child, a daughter, whereas the other two had each borne me a son, and she feared lest I should name one of these as my successor, and as chief son, thus conferring precedence over any she might hereafter bear me. You white people, *Nkose*, think that we Zulus keep our women in the lowest subjection. Well, we do not allow them to rule us, yet now and again we find one who tries hard to do so, and gives a great amount of trouble before we can convince her that it is not to be done; and Nangeza was one of these. And of her I was even then beginning to have more than enough.

Now she sullenly acquiesced in my reticence, for I would not unfold one word of the King's counsels. But she gave me a very dark look and turned away muttering. Yet during my absence events of the gravest moment had been transpiring.

In the evening Umzilikazi sent for me. I found him alone in his hut, and as I sat opposite him it seemed as though I were once more the *inceku*[3] and shield-bearer, and that the dread ordeal which had terminated in the winning of my head-ring and the King's Assegai had been all a dream.

"What think you, Untúswa?" said the King at first. "Is it for good or for ill that we leave Ekupumuleni, 'The Place of Rest,' and depart for this new land?"

"It is for good, Great Great One. The land is a better one than

---

[1] The cattle-price paid by the bridegroom to the girl's parent.
[2] It is customary for each wife of a Zulu of rank to have a hut to herself.—Mitford's note.
[3] A king's household attendant.

this. There is more room in it for a new nation to become mighty and rich."

"Yet there are some who would remain here, some who shake a doleful head over the prospect of going farther."

"Those who shake their heads against the will of the King may happen to shake them off, O Elephant."

"Ha! Thou sayest well, son of Ntelani. They may happen to shake them off—ah! ah! they may."

Now Umzilikazi spoke in that soft and pleasant voice of his, and I thought that trouble was gathering for somebody. Then as his keen eyes, half-closed, were fixed upon mine, piercing through and through my brain, I did not sit at ease, for I had been absent many moons, and certain powerful enemies of mine had not. Then he went on, still speaking in that soft and terrible voice.

"There are those who have reason to love Ekupumuleni, for it is not too far from the land of their birth. Good. Ekupumuleni shall indeed be their resting-place—their resting-place forever."

Now I knew that ill awaited somebody, and strangely, too, at that moment, I remembered Nangeza's dark looks and words. Yet how could the shadow of coming ill affect me? I aspired to be nothing but a fighting leader! My mind was the mind of the King. I cared nothing for intriguing or plotting. I only asked to lead my shields against the enemies of the King. The occupation I favoured most was that of fighting.

Then Umzilikazi went on to talk about this new land, and of the chief and people who owned the blue cattle.

"There will be spoil for all, for all who deserve it," he said; "and these slaves you have brought back please me well. *Whau*, Untúswa! How is it that a man like you, and a fighting captain, has but three wives—only three?" he asked, laughing at me.

"I care not for such, Great Great One. I desire only to wield the King's Assegai in battle," I said.

"That is well. In a few days we shall see. Go now, Untúswa."

I saluted and left the King. As I passed the gate of the *isigodhlo*, or royal enclosure, which gate was only wide enough to admit one man at a time, I met my father, Ntelani, entering. Not a word had the King let fall on the matter of my father, and this meeting, which was a surprise to both of us, seemed an evil omen; for now that

I wore the head-ring, and had become great, and commanded the King's troops, my father was more jealous than ever, and hated me more. We exchanged greetings, and then in the darkness I made my way to old Masuka's hut.

I pushed the wicker door open and crept in. The old witch-doctor was awake, and, seated by his fire, looked more like a big black spider than a man, such a skin-and-bone old skeleton had he become.

"I have seen you,[1] Untúswa," he said, looking up.

"Greeting, father," I replied.

"*Au!*" he said, handing me snuff. "And have you brought back cow and calf from the land of the Blue Cattle, Untúswa? The cow, whose milk keeps the life in my old frame, is dead—a lion killed her."

"No cattle did I bring from the land of the Bakoni, father, though it will not be a long time before we go and take all of it," I replied; "but there is a red cow in milk among my herd. To-morrow she and her calf shall be driven in among your beasts, my father."

The old man looked pleased. He loved cattle, and although by now he was one of the wealthiest among us, yet he never lost an opportunity of adding to his herds; but if any man gave him a cow he did not ask for more; unlike our own *izanusi*, who were wont to go on asking and asking until they had obtained ten or twelve beasts. Now I, each time that I was enriched by increase in my herd, or took spoil from an enemy, never failed to send a head or two to old Masuka; but from me our own *izanusi* got nothing—wherefore they hated me. But the old Mosutu had been the means of saving my life and making me great; wherefore I grudged him not such gifts from time to time.

When the King had caused Isilwana, the head *isanusi*, to be killed, for failing to cure a man who was wounded by the poisoned arrows of the mountain tribes, he had desired to put Masuka in his place; but the old man begged permission to refuse, saying that his *muti*[2] would be of no avail if worked with others. So Umzilikazi, not sorry to set up a rivalry between the witch-doctors, had allowed him to go his own way; and since the rain-making, the old Mosutu had stood higher in the King's favour than ever.

---

[1] The polite Zulu hello, *Sawubona*, literally translated means "I see you."
[2] Medicine, or charm.—Mitford's note.

"That is well, my son," he replied, "but delay not to send the cow with morning light, for by nightfall it may be that she will never be sent."

"*Hau!*" I cried. "What mean you, my father?"

"You are brave, Untúswa, and I have made you great. It is a pity that such should die young."

"What mean you, my father?" I cried again, seeing a deadly meaning in his words.

He gazed at me for a moment, then bending forward spoke low in the Sesutu tongue, which by this time he had taught me; and as I listened my horror became greater and greater, for it seemed as though a wide and black pit of darkness yawned at my feet, and I must either spring over it or into it. Verily, the enemies at work within a man's kraal are more to be feared than any outside. I must warn the King this very night. Yet, was it too late?

"Even now I hear steps which seek thee, son of Ntelani," he ended. "Yet go to meet them. I know not if thou wilt return."

Obedient to the old man's injunction, I rose, and now I, too, heard steps in the silence of the night. With a heavy foreboding of trouble, I crept through the door of the hut, and stood upright.

"The King desires speech of thee, son of Ntelani," said a voice, as a man came in sight. I recognised him as one of the *izinceku* or household attendants, and I thought there was something of malice and mischief in his tone. But I lost no time in gaining the *isigodhlo.*

Now, the royal house was of great size, nearly twice that of the largest of any other. I approached, singing in a low voice the King's praises, to give notice that I was coming; then, disarming, I entered. The Great Great One was alone. A fire burning in the centre lighted up the interior brightly, and in its blaze I could see upon the royal countenance a look I did not like. But still less did I like what immediately followed.

"Thou dog and whelp of a dog!" hissed the King, as, with the rapidity of lightning, he dropped aside his skin robe and hurled a casting assegai at me. It grazed my head with a vicious "zip!" and buried itself in the side of the house, where it stuck quivering.

I did not move. Not a word did I speak, yet I felt that death and myself were closely shoulder to shoulder once more.

"Well, dog! Hast thou no word to say?" went on Umzilikazi, his hand gripping another casting spear.

"Yes, I have a 'word,' Great Great One. My life is ever in the hand of the King. But now I know of no reason why it should be taken," I answered boldly.

"No reason? *Au!* Can a nation serve two Kings, Untúswa, my dog?" he mocked.

"Now have the dreams of the Elephant been bad—now have the ears of the Great Great One been filled with dark and false things. Moreover, I know well that it was not really in thy mind to slay me, Father; else had yon spear been buried in something very different to the grass wall of the house," I ended, with my usual boldness, which was so great as sometimes to astonish myself nearly as much as it did those who witnessed it. But it was in the minds of men that I should never now be slain by order of the Great Great One, because I held the King's Assegai. Yet upon this I did not put over-much trust.

"You have a ready tongue, Untúswa, and a ready wit," said Umzilikazi, no longer wrathfully. "The word is true, and well said, for I could hardly miss a man at that distance, even though there are some who think it is time to find a new King."

These last words were spoken low. I had heard enough from old Masuka not to require to ask their meaning. Yet I spoke in surprise and disgust, at the thought that such a thing should be possible.

"What is your thought on the matter, Untúswa?" said the King softly, eyeing me with his head on one side.

"*Au!* that is not a question to ask of me, Great Great One; for was I not on my way hither to point out those who think thus?" I said.

He started eagerly.

"Can you do this, Untúswa? Can you point them out?"

"I can, Great Great One. Shall I silently call together the slayers? The pool beyond Ncwelo's kraal is not far, and the moon will not take long to sink now. In the morning its water shall be red."

"Ha! The pool beyond Ncwelo's?" muttered the King. "Wait. Call not together the slayers, for I will see these evil-doers with my own eyes, will hear their treachery with my own ears. You and I will go forth together, Untúswa; then on the morrow they shall behold their last sunrise."

"How many men shall I bring for safeguard, Father?" I said. "Ten, perhaps, or more?"

"No men shalt thou bring, Untúswa. Thou and I will go forth together and witness the doings of these wizards, these *abatagati*,[1] who meet at night."

I looked anxious, for this was a serious adventure. The risks were enormous. Of the exact number of conspirators we were in ignorance, but we, being only two, would be sure to find ourselves at a great disadvantage in the event of discovery. Again, if any harm befell the King, should not I be held responsible for it? So I said—

"May I not go alone and bring back word, Black Elephant?"

I fancied Umzilikazi looked suspicious.

"Not so, Untúswa," he said. "I will satisfy my own eyes, my own ears, and then—— Hearken now. Take thy weapons, for it is time to start. Walk in front of me until we are without the gates. If we meet any man, harm him not. But any man who recognises the King, with the first words of royal greeting which pass his lips, slay him instantly and without a word, be he whom he may. I would not be known to have moved in this matter."

Umzilikazi took a broad-bladed spear in his hand and a black shield, of smaller size than those used in war. It happened that I was armed in like manner, except that I had a large knobstick as well. Thus equipped, we started upon our adventure.

---

[1] Evil-doers; *tagati*, magic.

CHAPTER III.

THE CONSPIRACY OF NCWELO'S POOL.

WE passed out of the *isigodhlo* by a secret way, known to and used by the King alone. The night was not a dark one, for the stars were shining bright and clear, and a waning moon hung low down in the heavens. As we stepped rapidly forth across the open plain we could make out the dim outline of the great kraal lying silent and slumbrous. Suddenly the figure of a man rose up, right across our path.

Now we were facing the setting moon, and the man was advancing stealthily in the direction of the kraal, wherefore we met. His face was in darkness. Not so ours, however, and as he recognised the lion countenance of the Great Great One, thus walking abroad by night, he was seized with a mighty fear, and, uttering the *Bayéte*, he crouched low—hiding his face that we might pass him. And he had looked on the things of this world for the last time, for the words of the Black Elephant were fresh in my ears. This man had recognised the King—had spoken the royal greeting—wherefore, as he crouched, the blade of my broad *umkonto*[1] drove through between his shoulders, coming out far through his breast. So he died there in the night, uttering no further sound.

"That was well done, Untúswa," whispered the King. "I have but one word, and now there is one *umtagati* the less. Proceed!"

So we stepped forward again, leaving the slain man lying there; and as we held on our way, I leading, and gripping my spear, all on the alert lest we should meet others prompt to recognise the King, we heard before and around us the howling of hyænas and the yelping of jackals, with now and again the thunder roar of a lion at no very great distance, also a strange and unearthly wail, which could come from no beast—but only, it might be, from the sad ghosts of those slain, who were weeping over their own shattered bones above the place of slaughter.

---

[1] A long-bladed, short stabbing spear; Shaka was the first to arm warriors with this weapon alone. Lt. F. G. Farewell observed (1825) that Zulus "charge with a single *umconto*, or spear, and each man must return with it from the field, or bring that of his enemy, otherwise he is sure to be put to death."

"This is a night for *abatagati* indeed," growled the King. "Yet there will be more ghosts to weep, Untúswa, after our visit to Ncwelo's pool."

"*Gahle, Nkulu 'nkulu*,"[1] I whispered. "Yonder is Ncwelo's kraal. If his dogs hear us, will not their tongues be swift to put the conspirators to flight? Yonder by the shade of the trees must we pass, for they whom we seek will have eyes watching the plain in all directions."

"Lead on, Untúswa," whispered the King.

Some distance round, under the shade of the trees, had we to travel, for we dared not cross the open, though to do so were far more direct. *Au!* it was black where the light of the moon and the stars could not pierce, and we had to writhe our way as silently as serpents—indeed more silently, for twice the rustle of some great serpent uncoiling himself to withdraw slowly from our path, and his shrill angry hiss at being disturbed, caused us to pause in order to allow him to retreat.

At length I, who was leading, halted and held up a hand. It was not a sound that I had heard in front through the black gloom, but there had floated to my nostrils on the clear air of the night an odour. It was the smell of a horse. Now of horses among us there were but few—all belonging to the King—and at Ncwelo's kraal were none. The Great Great One perceived it too, for just then a shaft of moonlight between the tree-tops revealed his face, and upon it was the eager, smiling, terrible expression I had seen there more than once, but usually when leading us into the very thickest of the battle. Yet neither of us spake, and we resumed our way, though tenfold more cautiously than before.

Again I held up my hand. We were now where the ground ended. Before were several jagged pinnacles of rock; in front of these—air. We had made our way by a circuit to the high ground overlooking the back of Ncwelo's pool.

There it lay, the pool—its surface glistening in the moonlight, reflecting the stars—lying beneath us at a depth, it might be, of eight or ten times the length of a man; and the murmur of voices rose to our ears, together with the occasional stamp of a horse and the sound as of the shaking of a saddle. The grasp of the King's hand tightened on my shoulder, as we drew ourselves yet nearer to the brink of the rocks and peered cautiously forth.

---

[1] Gently, Great Great One.—Mitford's note.

"Listen, Untúswa," he breathed into my ear. "Mark well the voices, lest the darkness prevent us from seeing the speakers. Ha!" he added, "that, at any rate, is a voice thou shouldst know."

And there in truth, *Nkose*, Umzilikazi spoke no lie; for the voice was that of Ntelani, my father.

It was raised in reproof. Someone at that moment was striking a light—with the stone fire-makers the white men used at that time—and there arose to our nostrils the odour of tobacco being smoked in a pipe. But while this light still flamed we made out with the greatest plainness the faces of six men.

Yes, in that flash we saw them all, for they were immediately below us. Two were white men, with rough faces covered with thick shaggy beards. They wore large hats and clothing made of dressed leather, and were armed with knives and long guns. They were tall, big men, but slow and heavy of speech and aspect. We knew them in a moment for Amabuna.[1]

The other four were our own people: Tyuyumane, an influential *induna* and a relation of the King; Notalwa, the head of our witch doctors; Senkonya, another *induna*, and my father Ntelani. The latter was speaking:

"I fear lest the odour of *gwai* thus burned spread far into the stillness of the night, for none of us Amazulu use our *gwai* in such wise. Wherefore it will be known that white men are about."

But that Ibuna answered roughly that he cared nothing if it reached the nostrils of Umzilikazi himself, save that he uttered the King's name "Selekas," so badly did that people speak with our tongue.

The other, however, reproved him, which was well, for our people, traitors though they were, liked not to listen to that sort of talk.

"And now, Ntelani," went on this man, speaking softly and pleasantly, "if we help you in the matter, how do you propose to carry out the change?"

"Thus," replied my father, having paused awhile to take snuff and think. "Umzilikazi is great—he is a lion—a buffalo bull—an elephant. The young men are with him. The young men are all his

---

[1] Boers.—Mitford's note. Singular, Ibuna. White Afrikaans-speaking farmers of Dutch-French descent, the toughest fighters in Africa apart from the Zulu. Possibly onomatopoeic for their firearms: "People of the Boom."

dogs, for he gives them plenty of fighting and abundance of spoil. Moreover, he allows them to tunga¹ while yet children, and exalts them to be izinduna over the heads of their fathers. Their fathers are to be their dogs. He loves not old men as izinduna. He creates izinduna out of children like himself."

Now the King pushed me as we lay and listened, for both of us understood this speech, which was not even dark. Then my father went on:—

"Here is my plan, leader of the Amabuna. We must have a King, but when the Elephant who now trumpets is henceforth trumpeting in black night the warriors will demand a leader, and no man is there who holds their hearts like one, a lion-cub which I have bred, for he is fearless in war, and him they will have to reign over them. This wish they must have granted, if only to accustom them to the change. He shall be King—King for a day—ah! ah!"

And my father chuckled with malice as he took more snuff.

"But what if he will not? What if he remains faithful to Umzilikazi?" said the leader of the Amabuna; for that people talks plain, and understands not our way of dark speaking.

"Au! Will he not?" sneered my father. "I tell thee, Ibuna, that he would slay the King with his own hand but to sit in his seat, if only for a day."

Now, Nkose, my fury well nigh got the mastery over me. Such dangerous and fatal words uttered by my father in the hearing of the Great Great One struck dismay into my heart, for the minds of Kings are ever suspicious, and had not I been brought there half under suspicion myself? Besides, they were not true; for even were the chance to offer, I would not sit in the seat of Umzilikazi in his lifetime. For he had made me great, and, in reality, second only to himself. No thought of treason was in my heart, nor had there ever been since the time when, as a hot-headed and foolish boy, I had all but thrown away my life for the sake of a girl; but since then—au! had the whole nation turned against the King, I, even if the only one, would have kept faithful to him, would have given my life for his. Further, my father's intended treachery towards myself—towards the King and the nation—made my blood flow hot; for no promises of advantage on the part of these lying Amabuna would ever have

¹ "Sew"—the head-ring—i. e. marry.—Mitford's note.

deceived me, even could I see of what advantage they could be to us. I began to "see red." It was all I could do not to plunge down the rocks and slay Ntelani where he sat, even though he were my own father. And something of this must have shown itself—I know not how—for again that grasp of iron was upon my shoulder, pressing me down, and the King's voice breathed into my ear—

"*Gahle, gahle*,[1] Untúswa. Hast thou not even yet learned sound judgment, thou who art no more a boy, but a *kehla*, and the leader of warriors in battle? Give ear now while these creeping scorpions advance even further and further into the black jaws of death."

So we lay and listened, and presently we knew all there was to know, and, in truth, the news was great, for many things had been hatching within the womb of Time. We learned that Tshaka, the Mighty One, the Lion of Zulu, was no more, and that Dingane, a brother of that Elephant, had reddened his spear in the Great One's blood, and now sat as King in Zululand. We learned that the Amabuna were coming up out of the west—advancing in great numbers, with guns and horses, desiring the land which lay between the Tugela and the sea—and to obtain this, their leaders sought the aid of our nation, promising to set up as King in Zululand he who should aid them the most in their war against Dingane. But before this should happen, Umzilikazi must be sent to join his father, for great as he might have reason to dread the power of Dingane, these plotters knew that he hated that of the Amabuna still more, and that by no inducement whatever could he be brought to listen to their promises, still less to trust in them.

All this we drank in as we lay there among the rocks, listening to that dark midnight plot—all this and more: how the old men were dissatisfied, because of the favour shown to the younger ones—yet this was necessary, *Nkose*, for ours was a young nation, which had to carve out its own place with the arms and assegais of its warriors, most of whom were young. So we lay in the black midnight stillness, listening to these *abatagati* squatted around by the rock-hung pool, and the dismal howling of beasts far and near seemed to re-echo their foul and evil plotting. But at the last we learned something more. Should I, the son of Ntelani, refuse to be made King—for a day—ah! yes, only for a day—the *induna* Tyuyumane was to reign.

---

[1] Or *kahle*: gently, carefully, slowly.

And with this understanding the Amabuna rose to depart. As they swung themselves into their saddles the one who had spoken more pleasantly said:

"The day after the new moon then, Ntelani, an Elephant will fall into the staked pit from which there is no escape. Our people, with guns and horses, will be at hand. Is that so?"

"That is so, leader of the Amabuna," grunted my father. "*Au!* from the spear of a pitfall there is no escape, even for the Elephant." And the others laughed deeply as they assented.

"My father," I whispered, as the Amabuna rode off, "shall I not go down and slay yonder four?"

"Not so, Untúswa," whispered the King in reply.

"Shall I not then go and call forth an *impi* to eat up those dirty white jackals, O Elephant for whom no pit shall be laid?"

"Not so, Untúswa. Ha! It is the whole nest of foul birds that shall be destroyed—not two only, that the remainder may take alarm and escape."

After the Amabuna had gone, those four traitors sat there in the darkness and talked more freely, and in the course of this *indaba*[1] it was arranged that Tyuyumane should sit in the seat of the Great Great One. But, first of all, on the day after the new moon, when the Amabuna should be at hand with their horses and guns, it was settled that I was to reign for a little while, only to accustom the younger warriors to the change; then I was to be sent to travel the road of Umzilikazi. All this these four fools talked over among themselves, little thinking what ears were drinking in their words—little dreaming what a sharp and fiery throne awaited Tyuyumane—and, indeed, all of them. Then the moon sank down, and darkness lay upon the face of that wizard pool, and silently the conspirators rose and were gone.

"Ha! Untúswa," whispered the King in mockery, "soon will the nation cry thee the *Bayéte*. How now? Dost thou not feel already great?"

"Mock me not, Black Elephant," I pleaded; "mock me not that I am begotten of Ntelani, who is the very chief of fools. If the fooleries, which we have just heard seem to the mind of the Great Great

---

[1] A meeting to discuss serious affairs (*u-daba*), to chat and gossip (*dla indaba*), or to give a report.

One true, then let him slay me as I stand. If not, suffer that I slay their utterers."

And, dropping my assegai—the King's Assegai—I turned my breast to the Black Elephant, even as on that day when I stood expecting the death-stroke in the sight of all the nation.

"Not yet, Untúswa, not yet," was the answer, uttered softly. "Lead on now, that we may return before these *abatagati* smell that the Lion has been on their track."

Now, as we took our way beneath the blackness of the forest shades, it seemed to me, *Nkose*, that I was standing with one foot upon the point of an exceedingly lofty pinnacle, which point pierced more and more my foot, and yet on each and every side, was the dizzy height of death. For now came back to me those plotting and foolish dreams of the days when my principal wife, Nangeza, and myself were making love without permission, and breaking daily the stern law of our nation. Then we had talked over the possibility which lay before every man who knew not fear, and who dared stake everything on fate, and how no man was more fitted to aspire to the rule of a warrior race than such a born warrior as myself; and, although now I had come to see the foolishness of such dreams—for I loved Umzilikazi as a dog does his master—and, further, was happy enough in my position as second fighting *induna*—yet it might be that Nangeza, who was ill-disposed to me now by reason of her evil and over-reaching temper, had whispered abroad such old tales—adding insidiously to them, as the manner is with women—and these might have reached the ears of the King—as what indeed did not?—and, taken with what he had just heard, might mean my downfall. Yet I could do nothing, save to trust in my steady and faithful services to the King, and the weight and general soundness of my counsel; for, young as I was, the Great Great One took counsel of me oft, though secretly—oftener, indeed, than of older *izinduna*, such as my father Ntelani, or even Mcumbete, who of all his counsellors was the most trusted.

Suddenly the King's hand fell upon my shoulder again, pressing me down gently but firmly to the very earth. Not a moment too soon, for as we lay crouching there, over us passed the four conspirators—right over us, so that had they trodden but a foot's breadth to one side they had touched us. They were now upon the edge of the brush, and we could see their forms clearly outlined against the stars. Moreover, each held his broad assegai in his right hand, for the man who wanders at night does well to be prepared for peril at every step. As for me, I desired nothing better than to have at them then and there; but that restraining grasp relaxed not on my shoulder, and the will of the Great Great One was sufficient. So we let those traitors go for the moment, but better had it been for them had we stricken them down in the darkness as they walked.

We regained the *isigodhlo* by the same secret way, and perceived of none. But before dismissing me for the night the King whispered a few orders. And then I knew that the morrow would witness terrible things—that, for some at least, it should bring forth that which might well make them wish they had never been born.

CHAPTER IV.

THE "SMELLING-OUT."

ON the morrow, ere yet the sun was up, heralds went running throughout Ekupumuleni, crying aloud that none might venture away from the kraal on pain of death. Others, again, ran swiftly to the cattle outposts and outlying kraals, ordering all men to assemble immediately at the royal place. But before this I had already despatched several armed parties, picked warriors of my own regiment, who should form a belt round the kraals at a great distance, so that, being distributed in pickets, none might pass.

Now a great fear fell upon all the people when these ominous preparations became known; and this deepened, as presently it got noised abroad that the King's dreams had been bad, for it was certain that a great witch-finding impended—greater, indeed, than had been known since Ekupumuleni was erected. An uneasy feeling of restlessness and suspicion had been astir for some little time, and now men whispered to each other with their blankets over their heads, fearing lest their words should fall upon the wrong ears.

Throughout the morning people continued to stream in from the outlying places, men and women, for children were not cited; the former carrying no weapons but sticks only. But all the warriors of my own regiment, to the number of several hundreds, were fully armed. Kalipe, also, the other war-captain, had as many of his own men under arms. The bulk of the people, however, were, as I said, unarmed.

"*Au!*" cried Nangeza, as I went into my hut to put on some of my war-adornments, "I think, Untúswa, this reminds me not a little of the morning following upon the death of the sleeping sentinel, Sekweni. They say, too, that this morning a man was found outside, not far from the gates, with his heart cleft in twain by the stroke of a broad *umkonto*—a broad *umkonto*, Untúswa. Ah! ah!" she jeered, letting her eyes rest with meaning upon my royal weapon, which was seldom out of my grasp. "Art thou not afraid, Untúswa? for the glance of Notalwa seeth far, and his tongue is long."

"I know yet another tongue which is long, Nangeza," I answered. "Tell me, thou fool, hast thou ever seen me afraid?"

"Once only, when I told thee thou mightest yet be King. Ah! ah!" she mocked.

I turned as I was departing and looked her full in the face.

"A warning, Nangeza!" I said. "There is a greater than Notalwa, and a long tongue is a worse thing than dangerous. It is wearisome. The King is not fond of those who wag their tongues overmuch, claiming to be in the counsels of his *izinduna*. Have a care, Nangeza!" And with these words I left her; yet not without seeing that she was alarmed.

Now, by the time the sun was at his highest in the heavens, the great kraal, Ekupumuleni, was packed full of people, and all were in a brooding and breathless state of dread; for the rumours which filled the air were as the early rumblings of a mighty storm brooding over the face of the world. It was known that the witch-doctors were making *múti*. It was whispered that the King's sleeping visions had so shaped that vast and unmentionable wizardry had been at work. It was known further that a man of the House of Ncwelo had died in blood, wandering abroad in the night. Things looked dark for the House of Ncwelo. None doubted but that, before the sun went down, some, if not many, should walk in the darkness of the Great Unknown.

All the morning, from every direction, people came flocking. Ncwelo's kraal to the number of nearly a hundred, Janisa's clan, who were in charge of some of the cattle outposts, and the followings of many petty chiefs. All these took up positions in the circles within circles ranged around the inside of the great open space. But belting round the whole, hemming in all in a ring of iron—a fence of spear blades—were two half-moons of warriors fully armed, those of my own particular following, and those of Kalipe. And at the high end of the kraal were two companies of slayers, or executioners, bearing thongs and heavy knob-sticks.

Seated among the *izinduna* awaiting the arrival of the Great Great One was my father Ntelani, the same morose and dissatisfied expression upon his face. But upon that of Tyuyumane, the King's relation, I thought I could detect a lively expression of fear—also upon that of Senkonya—and I laughed behind my shield, for I was in full dress as a war-captain.

"Ah! ah!" I said to myself. "The Great Great One was right. These *abatagati* are about to weep blood. No swift and merciful death in the darkness is to be theirs."

Now the King came forth attended by his shield-bearer, and all the nation assembled there bowed low and thundered out the *Bayéte*. But the countenance of the Great Great One was gloomy and stern, as his gaze travelled over the enormous bending crowd. He advanced to his usual place, at the head of the open space, and seated himself. And then the *izanusi*, bedecked in all their hideousness of skulls and entrails and streaming blood and rattling bones, came dancing and howling before the King, and clamouring to be let loose upon the wizards who had bewitched his dreams.

Notalwa was at their head. He was arrayed in a cloak of quagga-skin vividly striped, and was crowned with the lower jaw of a sea-cow cunningly joined with the upper part of a lion's skull, the whole painted red and surmounted by cranes' feathers. For my own part, I laughed to myself at the sight of this cowardly boaster, who had never shed blood, save that of some wretched *umtagati* whom he had smelt out, trying to render his appearance terrific. So, too, did several among us war-captains. But the bulk of the people saw terror in him, and groaned loudly.

This hideous band began to dance before the King, sweeping the ground and air with wands tipped with giraffe tails, as they circled round, and howling—

"Great Great One! Black Buffalo Bull! Elephant who bears the world! give the word, that we may name the *abatagati!* Thou whose glance is brighter than the sun! give the word that we may consume them with lightning! Hou! Hou! Hou!"

With these and such-like bellowings did the *izanusi* rave for long; but the King sat and took snuff in silence, as though they were not there at all. At last he said—

"Away from me, ye jackals! ye who are impostors, and no *izanusi* at all! Still your howlings; for there is a greater than you, who shall find out quickly what ye never shall."

I had my eyes upon Notalwa's face, and saw that he feared. The others fell back in awed silence, for there was that in the King's eyes, in the King's glance, which meant death, and nothing less. And then old Masuka advanced to take their place.

His little bowed, shrivelled figure was undecked by gauds of any kind, but his eyes were keen and bright, and searching as ever. He was attended by three others—young men of our own people, whom the King had appointed to him to be instructed in his magic; for Umzilikazi was too clear-sighted to arouse disaffection among our own people by leaving the chief magic entirely in the hands of strangers. Besides, he wanted to set up a rival band to that of Notalwa.

"Hearken!" said the King. "This morning a man was found who had died in blood in the night—had died in blood under the very shadow of where I sit. Who is he that arrogates to himself the right to slay where that right is of one alone? Who dares take life without my decree? Here has been *tagati* of the most deadly kind!"

These words were taken up by a trumpet-voiced *imbonga*,[1] and rolled forth aloud, that all the nation might hear. And the people heard, and the shivering that went through those crouched circles was as the shaking of the forest leaves just before a gale.

"Find him!" said the King, with a sweep of the hand.

The three who were learners of Masuka's sorcery sprang to their feet, and began to intone the witch-finding chant. Then they ran softly hither and thither, striking the ground with their tail-tipped wands. But the old Mosutu himself remained rigid and motionless where he had first been standing.

The three witch-finders, running lightly, entered among the people, for lanes had been left between the densely-serried ranks. As they advanced down these a dread silence lay upon all. Tens of thousands of eyeballs rolled white in chill apprehension. There alone, gloomy, and with lowering brow, sat the King, terrible in his fell and destroying wrath. Even I, who was in the counsels of the Great Great One, felt a shiver of awe; remembering, too, the words my father had let fall in the conclave of the midnight conspirators.

Down the ranks went the witch-finders, chanting, and twirling their rods. And behind them came a grim and fearsome company— the whole body of the slayers, namely—the fierce light of expectancy upon their dread faces, as each held his thong ready, grasping in a cruel grip the heavy knobstick.

Ha! The witch-finders have halted, and their singing rises shrill

---

[1] Professional "praiser," or herald.—Mitford's note.

and loud. A man is touched with the fatal wand. In a moment a
thong is about his neck, and two of the slayers are leading him forth
to the great gate—are leading him forth to the place of slaughter—
to die! Two more now are touched! They also are led forth in like
manner immediately behind the first. A great gasp, like a sob, sways
the multitude; and in dead silence a way is opened out for these ill-
fated ones, passing through to their death. Then, as the people take
up once more the chorus of the wizard song, an *imbonga*, standing
at the King's side, names aloud those who have thus looked their
last upon the sun. But the progress of the *izanusi* continues, and by
the time they have gone half through the ranks some thirty men
have been named: and now we can see these stringing up the slope
outside the kraal, in the direction of the place of slaughter—they and
their slayers—and, in the dead and awesome silence which now and
again falls upon the immense crowd, can hear the dull crashing of
broken skulls, and the distant and hollow groans, as the great knob-
sticks of the executioners are already beginning their fell work. And
still the line of doomed men is ascending to the hill of death; and
far above, like a gathering cloud in the heavens, the white pinions
of vultures are wheeling and soaring, impatient to begin, for such a
feast as this great destruction of evil-doers has never yet been theirs
since they began to follow our migrating nation for their food.

By the time the witch-finders had made the complete round of
those gathered together, upwards of fourscore men had been smelt
out, and the remaining body of slayers, with disappointment upon
their fierce countenances, stole envious looks out towards the place
of death, where the crash of knobsticks and the hollow groans of
the doomed had almost ceased. Not a cry, however, floated from
thence, for no women had been among those named. All were warriors; and the warriors of our race faced death in those days without a
cry, albeit the groan which often followed the crash of the knobstick
was the voice of the parting *itongo*, or spirit, not of the body which
had contained it. And of those who had been named a number were
of Ncwelo's kraal; others were of the houses of other chiefs, including that of Senkonya; some few, indeed, were of my own particular
fighters. These last, on being touched, were immediately disarmed
by their brethren, and turned over to the slayers.

Now, when the three witch-finders had completed their task,

and returned once more into the presence of the King, an immense sigh of gladness went up from all the people—a very heave of the bosom of a whole nation relieved; and with one voice all broke forth into a fierce song of thanksgiving that so many *abatagati* had been removed from their midst. But I, if nobody else, knew that they were crying aloud their thanks too soon. For among those thus named was no man of any great distinction, albeit a petty chief or two. I knew, however, that the greater number of them were of the families of chiefs, some of great note. There was to be yet another stage in this grim game, whose stakes were the lives of men.

"Ye have done well, sons of the stranger's magic," said the King, as the three young *izanusi* returned to his presence, their eyeballs rolling, and their mouths still dropping foam after the frenzied excitement attendant upon the discharge of their dread office. "Well have ye done; and the wizard spells of those ye have named soar aloft to the heavens beneath the wings of yonder vultures?"—with a glance in the direction of the hill of slaughter, upon which already multitudes of the great white pinions were beating down. "Still the blood which has been shed is not dry. Who am I, that others claim the right to slay—here, at my very gates? *Hau!* I am no King!"—and now the tone was fierce and bitter, and those who listened trembled once more. "I am a servant—a slave—lower than the lowest of the Amaholi—until those who shed this blood at my gates are made known. Wherefore, now, Masuka, hasten to rid us of them, so that we may sleep in peace once more. There are yet those who have not been within touch of the wand."

A dead silence of eagerness and awe fell upon all the people at these words. For the only ones who had not been within touch of the witch-finder's wand were the *izinduna* grouped at the side of the King, and the *izanusi* themselves. Could it be that from these more victims were to be chosen? A flash of anxiety was to be seen on the faces of more than one of the councillors; and I, from where I stood, a little way down the circle of armed men, saw just such a shade of fear flit across that of Tyuyumane. My father's lined features, however, only puckered into a contemptuous grin. But before Masuka had time to obey the King's behest, Notalwa rushed forward howling that now was the time for him and his "dogs"—that the stranger's *muti* had been tried, and that now it was his own turn.

Kalipe was standing near the Great Great One, and as the head *izanusi* thus bounded forward he advanced a pace, and I could see that he held his broad *umkonto* gripped, and in readiness. So, too, did the picked warriors ranged at his back; and I, who knew what underlay all this, was likewise prepared to spring up, and deal forth death. But Umzilikazi changed not a muscle, as he sat playing with his broad-bladed spear, similar to the one which he had bestowed upon me. Yet in his eyes burned a soft and cruel light, as he met the glowering glances of Notalwa and the *izanusi*.

"Patience!" he said, softly and pleasantly, waving these back. "Proceed, Masuka."

The old Mosutu muttered a few words to one of his young assistants, who started off in the direction of the magician's hut, and presently reappeared, bearing upon his head a large bowl of burnt clay. This was lowered to the earth, and now I knew that something terrible would be manifested; for I had already looked into that bowl myself, and terrible things had been shown me, which, indeed, came to pass, as you know, *Nkose*.

The bowl was half-filled with some black yet shining, liquid; and over this old Masuka crouched, spreading forth his skinny and clawlike hands; now chanting high, shrill snatches of a strange song, now muttering incantations in an unknown tongue. Then he looked up.

"Draw near, Black Elephant, thou ruler of the world," he said. "Look in the face of this *múti*, and say what thou seest."

Umzilikazi rose, and, advancing with majestic step, stood, and with head slightly bent, gazed downward into the bowl. All the people held their breath for awe.

"I see a face," he said. "Yes; it is the face of a man having a ring on. Hither, Mcumbete! Look with me. Whose is the face?"

The old *induna*, his brow clouded with anxiety, advanced to the side of the King.

"*Hau!*" he cried, with a start of amazement. "It is indeed a face, Great Great One. It is the face of Ncwelo."

A deep murmur of awe went up from all who heard. Ncwelo, though a chief of some influence, was not an *induna*. His place at the head of his people was near me. Glancing at him, I could see that his look was that of a man who knows himself to be already dead.

"Look again, Mcumbete," said the King. "I see another face. Whose is it?"

"Ha!" cried the old *induna*, trembling with awe. "It is the face of Senkonya."

A cruel smile played upon the King's lips as he bade him look again.

"It is the face of Ntelani, Great Great One," almost yelled the old *induna*.

"Look again, Mcumbete, look again," laughed the King.

"I see now Tyuyumane," faltered the old man. "Ha," he went on, with a gasp. "Now I see a head, and it is wreathed in snakes—a head, a face. It is the face of Notalwa, the chief of the *izanusi*."

The terror-stricken countenance, the shaking limbs, of the old *induna* were too true, too real, for any suspicion of make-believe. There was a silence of indescribable awe upon all who heard, all who beheld. It was broken by Notalwa.

Uttering hideous yells, the head *isanusi* leaped in the air, dancing and roaring, bellowing forth all his incantations and wizardry. Stripping off his zebra robe, he gashed himself until his body streamed with blood, mouthing out wild predictions as to the fate that would speedily befall our race for supplanting its own sorcerers in favour of the magic of a stranger. But the King, with a frown, bade him cease his bellowing, for he might early need all his magic for himself. The others named sat still as stones, but their demeanour was various. Upon the face of my father Ntelani, was the set drawnness of despair, but it was the courage of a dogged despair; fierce, fearless to the last. Senkonya, too, looked as one who had already tasted death, but Tyuyumane, ah! his look was that of one who had tasted death a hundred times over. He was a tall, strong man, with a sullen and evil face, very near in blood to the King—indeed, it had been whispered, though cautiously—that he was an elder son of Matyobane. Now he showed signs of strong and restless fear. His glance rolled to right and to left, as though seeking means of escape. But behind each of those thus named had stealthily closed up a group of armed warriors.

And now the attention of all was diverted to old Masuka, who had fallen into one of his trances, and was mouthing wildly. Then he began to speak. He told of a pool, overhung by rocks, and whose

waters reflected the stars and the waning moon. He told of the
assembling of men by stealth, and of the tramp of horses, of the
talking together of men who wore head-rings, and of men who
wore large hats. Then he described so exactly the *indaba* which we
had witnessed—the Great Great One and I—that it seemed he must
have been present concealed on the spot where we had lain and
listened to it. But all this he told in a very low, and scarcely audible,
voice, only to be heard by such few as were immediately bending
over him, among whom was myself, for the King had beckoned me
to his side. Then, when he had finished, he lay as still as though
dead, and the faces had faded out of the *múti* bowl, whose contents
were as smooth and shining as before.

"I think we have heard enough," said Umzilikazi. Then turning
to the *izimbonga*, he bade them cry aloud to the people to depart, but
that, until the third day after the new moon, none should venture
beyond the chain of the furthest cattle-posts. And the people leaped
gladly to their feet, shouting the *Bayéte*, for their hearts were light
again. Death had passed through their ranks, yet there were still
many left.

As for those *izinduna* who were named last, few at that time knew
what their fate was, or what became of them, nor yet of Notalwa,
the head of the *izanusi*, who lay at first pretending to be dead. But
I knew; likewise did I know that every one of those who had gone
forth that day to the hill of slaughter was concerned in the treasonable plot which had for its object the death of the King. Yet, because
of its mystery, and the witch-finding on such a large scale, and the
slaughter of so many warriors as *abatagati*, a great fear rested upon
all the people for many days. And the marvellous power of Masuka
as a magician was in the minds of all; for, of course, none knew that
the Great Great One and I had witnessed that dark and treasonable
midnight gathering; nor, indeed, that any had.

CHAPTER V.

THE BOER LAAGER.

IT was our custom, *Nkose*, when a man was smelt out as *umtagati*, that his whole family and kraal should be eaten up too; but Umzilikazi, who loved not killing for its own sake, except in war, forbore to observe this custom in its entirety. He spared the relatives of those who had been named, allowing their wives and children to live, only exacting a fine of cattle from each house. But the case of Ncwelo he regarded as the worst of the lot; for Ncwelo occupied a position of trust at an important outpost; and this position he had turned to account by hatching treason; wherefore, immediately upon his being named, a party of armed men was sent out to put every one of his house to the assegai—even to his very dogs—and to sweep off all his cattle into the royal herds. The same fate fell upon the house of Notalwa; but, as regarded the others, the Great Great One was of opinion that sufficient example had been made.

Now, although it meant death to whisper a word as to what had become of those five principal evil-doers who had been named, yet my chief wife, Nangeza, would give me no rest on the subject; for herein was a mystery, and, being a woman, she must needs have a finger in it; so, thinking I would tell her, she tried all sorts of devices, such as creeping up to listen whenever I talked with another *induna*. At last, losing patience, I smote her; for, although we Amazulu do not beat our wives overmuch, as you white people say, yet there are times when hard wood is the only means of staying a woman's tongue. Besides, Nangeza was becoming altogether too troublesome, and already the young warriors would laugh among themselves, and put their hands to their mouths and say, "*Hau!* Untúswa is mighty in battle; a fighter who strikes hard. But—a chief? *Hau!* A woman is chief over him." Now, I thought things had gone far enough in this direction, wherefore I smote Nangeza.

She snarled like a she-leopard first struck by the spear.

"Good, Untúswa! Thou hast struck her through whom thou art made great. Thou shalt weep for it in blood one day."

I felt minded to kill her, and make an end of it all. But I refrained, and went to the huts of my other wives, instead, and made merry with them. "Now," I thought, "I will take ten, twenty, wives. So will Nangeza, perchance, find her match among all these."

The day of the new moon drew on, and all the fighting men of the nation were called up to Ekupumuleni, all, save such as were out in small parties spying for the Amabuna, and this especially to the south and westward. For several nights there was war-dancing, and all the regiments were doctored for battle; yet, against whom they were to be sent few among them knew, and those who did know told not. Finally came in two swift runners, one a little after the other. The Amabuna were drawing near, with many waggons and horses and guns, drawing near to take over our nation, to proclaim the traitor, Tyuyumane, King.

The night was rendered hideous with the howlings of the *izanusi* making *múti*, because of the new moon, and in the morning we started from Ekupumuleni, strong to the strength of nearly our whole army. No war-songs were allowed to be sung, and all shouting and noise was forbidden. In silence we meant to steal upon and enclose this formidable enemy, who was as the on-sweeping locust-swarm—resistless, numberless, devouring.

Half a day's march beyond Ncwelo's kraal, our runners came in to say that the advance guard of the Amabuna was at hand—ten horsemen, armed with long guns, and with them nearly as many servants of a yellow colour, also mounted and armed. Then the King, who accompanied the *impi*, called me aside, and together we ascended a bush-crowned hill, whence we could see for a distance around.

For a great way the country was grown with bush about as high as a man's head, with here and there groves of forest trees. Now, from where we lay we could see at a long distance off the waggons of the Amabuna creeping onward, drawn by their long lines of oxen, and behind them herds of cattle, feeding as they travelled. But between all this and ourselves horsemen were riding—men similar to the two whom we had seen at that meeting of traitors by Ncwelo's Pool. They were advancing in a double line, little knowing whither—advancing carelessly, to greet the new King, Tyuyumane—to enslave, as they thought, a conquered nation. Umzilikazi's eyes glowed like those of a lion whose fangs are already in the throat of the giraffe.

"See there, Untúswa!" he whispered. "Now the game begins. Ha! ha!"

"The Amabuna had arrived immediately beneath us, chattering carelessly in their ugly and head-cleaving tongue, which sounds to us as the croaking of many crows, and smoking *gwai* in their wooden pipes. But we could see what they could not—the low-lying, crouching shapes of hundreds of dark forms, writhing, crawling like serpents, among the long grass and thick bush around. Just then, however, the horses began to sniff uneasily, and throw forward their ears, as though they knew that an enemy lurked close at hand. The horsemen soon saw this, and halted; but at that moment there advanced towards them a man—one of ourselves. It was Notalwa.

Now, upon what followed, the King and I looked with eagerness; for Notalwa, being only a witch-doctor, and no warrior, the Great Great One had judged him the best-fitted to play this part, which was to detain the Amabuna in converse while our *impi* surrounded and stole in upon them the more completely—promising him, in the event of failure, the most terrible death by torture ever yet devised; and this evil-doer, being a coward and no warrior, had caught eagerly at a chance of saving his own forfeited life. So now he greeted the Amabuna, saying that Tyuyumane and the other traitors were behind him, and would be up in a very short time, for that now the deed was done, and the sun might soon blacken his face for a dead King.

But while he was yet speaking, one of the servants of the Amabuna caught sight of the gleam of a spotted shield in the bushes, and cried aloud his discovery. And then, further concealment being useless, our warriors rose in masses, and poured forward upon the Amabuna, still in complete silence, for all shouting had been strictly forbidden, lest it should travel to the ears of those with the waggons and the herds, who, being warned, might escape.

When they saw how entirely they were hemmed in, the thought of the Amabuna was no longer to dismount, but to fight their way through. They discharged their long guns into the thick of our onrushing warriors, many of whom fell; and then, using them as clubs, strove to hew their way through the ranks of our shields.

But their horses were utterly terrified, and plunging and squealing, were almost beyond control. The leader of the Amabuna, whom

I recognised as one of the two who had taken part in the *indaba* at the pool, was a mighty man in battle. He swept his clubbed gun, hither and thither, and men seemed to fall before him like grass before an advancing fire. But, as fast as they swept down our warriors, others would rise in their places. A line of spear-points barred the way at every turn, and soon the horses, disembowelled, hamstrung, were of no further use, as they sank down, uttering wild screams of agony and terror; and their riders, thus dismounted, were struck by countless spears the moment they touched the ground. *Hau, Nkose!* In far less time than I have taken to say these words those Amabuna and their servants were all dead men. Even their horses were cut to pieces; for when we "see red," we Amazulu spare no living thing.

All, did I say? *Hau!* I should have said all, save one; for the leader of those, our enemies, who was a strong, fearless man, a fine fighter, had somehow or other succeeded in breaking through our lines. He was mounted on a powerful horse, which was wounded: we could see that. We could see also that the man was wounded, for he swayed in his saddle as he rode, and seemed to keep his seat only with great difficulty. But, wounded though it was, the horse was going swift as the wind. Although the most fleet-footed of our warriors were streaming in pursuit, he was leaving them farther and farther behind.

"Hurry now, Untúswa," said the King. "Push on thine own men, and send word to Kalipe, to form up the whole body of the army. Run not, so as not to arrive breathless, yet march as rapidly as possible, and strike yon evil-doers while yet surprise is in their midst. Strike them hard, and spare none; for these Amabuna are as a devastating plague of locusts in whatsoever land they appear. Go!"

I saluted hurriedly and already was speeding down the hillside. The warriors had formed into rank, awaiting the commands of the Great Great One. Quickly making known the word to Kalipe, we started, eager to pour forth the blood of this accursed people, before whom other nations go down, like trees before the storm, never to rise again.

We were not long in coming upon the waggons of the strangers—not far behind the man who had escaped—for, as we drew near, we could see them bringing their waggons together, so as to form a square enclosure. But most of their cattle were still outside.

We could see them, too, as they moved hither and thither—large men most of them, with hairy faces, and clad in the tanned skins of animals; indeed, their wide leather breeches made a swishing sound as they walked. We could make out their women, too, helping to fortify the camp, as hard as the fighting men; and many a grunt and smothered burst of laughter went up from our young warriors at the sight of those, for their women looked even as sacks, and yet more devoid of shape, and their faces, looking out from great bonnets, were ugly. Yet they worked hard, pushing at the wheels of the waggons, and talking in their harsh and unpleasing tongue.

Now we consulted hurriedly together, Kalipe and I, and sent forward a strong body of the fleetest-footed of our warriors, that they should drive off the cattle. These dashed forward with wild yelling, and soon we saw them in among the herdsmen, spearing right and left. The Amabuna behind the waggons opened fire upon them; but, beyond killing a good many of their own cattle, the fire was harmless, for our people were sheltered behind the beasts as they swept them away.

Meanwhile we had been forming up, in shape like a half-moon; and, as the bellowing, plunging mass of horns and hides and lashing tails and eyeballs wildly rolling, receded in clouds of dust, we were already close upon the fortified camp of the Amabuna. The waggons seemed to spout forth flashes of fire, the dust jetted up beneath our feet where the bullets struck. Our men, too, began to fall; for as we drew nearer we were in the most deadly range, and the long guns of the Amabuna shot both strong and true.

Now we raised the war shout, and our moon-shaped formation extended its horns until the waggon-fort was completely encircled with our men. We rush forward! *Hau!* it is as the breaking of the sea upon the shore as we pour over the waggons. But those within shoot into our faces. The foremost of our ranks drop back. That blaze of fire, the tearing of the shot, daunts them.

"Turn not!" I cry. "Who will be named coward! On, on! the eye of the Black Elephant watches his children. Which of them shall it behold flee?"

Flourishing aloft my shield, I leap over the tongue of a waggon. Others pour after me. Ha! we are within the enclosure. Then a gun is pointed full at my chest, and, as the flash spurts forth, I see through it the countenance of the evil Ibuna, who spoke ill and roughly of the King.

But though I see the flash, the bullet passes over my head unhurt, yet it hums into the thick of those behind, and there is more than one yell of death. Now I spring upon this great Ibuna, but before I can strike him my assegai—the King's Assegai—is dashed from my hand by a clubbed gun. It has been done by one of their women—a great, ugly, toad-like witch, with grey hair. But immediately half a dozen spears enter her body, and she falls yelling. At the same time, under cover of my shield, I seize the great *umkonto* again, and close with the leader, hand to hand. He has a knife—no time has he to load—and we are at too close quarters for the long gun to be clubbed again. He aims now a furious kick at me. Ha! is it thus that such vermin fight? Then I leap upon him, and with one mighty stroke my great assegai lays him open from the throat downwards.

"*Hau!* dog of the Amabuna," I cried, as he fell, "dost care now that the smoke of thine ugly carcase should reach the nostrils of the King?"

Now was a terrible medley of Amabuna and children of the Great Great One. The air was black and heavy with smoke, and the jarring crash of weapons, and the thunder of the shock, as our *impi* came, thick and fast, pouring over the waggons on all sides, and a forest of tufted shields was dancing in the smoke, and blades tossed redly on high, reeking with the stream of life. And against the vaporous gloom could be seen the outlined faces of our warriors, the children of blood, as, with teeth bared, they threw their heads back and howled like hyænas because they could not get enough to slay, could not get at it quick enough. And the Amabuna fought—yes, they fought—and when it came to the last their women fought more fiercely than the men; yet all were brave. But what could they do against us, against our might? Driven hither and thither, broken up into handfuls, they stood back to back, men and women alike, sick with wounds and the flow of their own blood, that ran in streams; yet they struck and struck. Ha! our spears were blunted that day, and reddened indeed, and our pealing yells of rage and victory rent the skies again and again!

All were slain. We spared none. Their women also we killed, for not even among the younger did we see any who were fit to spare and take before the King, so evil-featured and unwashen and shape-less were these. The children, too, were slain, having their brains dashed out against the waggon-wheel, or flung into the air to be caught upon the spears of the warriors as they descended again.

The battle was over now, for none were left to fight. Our war-riors, like wild beasts who had tasted blood, were rolling their eyes hither and thither in search of more life to destroy. But there was none.

Then something seemed to move in one of the waggons. There was a wild howl, and a rush. My brother Mgwali was first. Plunging his hand beneath some sacking, he drew out the body of a little child.

It was a girl-child, and as Mgwali plucked it from its place of shelter, and held it aloft by the back of its clothing, I could see that it was yet unhurt. But it was terribly frightened. Its great blue eyes were starting from its head, and its long hair, like shining threads of sunlight, streamed down over the dark shoulder and arm of Mgwali, dabbling in the blood which yet lay undried upon him.

"Hau! Throw it up, Mgwali!" cried those who stood by, gripping their assegais ready to receive its little body on the blades. But before this could happen I leaped to the spot.

"Hold!" I roared, extending my stick. "Hold!"

The young men snarled, like hungry dogs reft of a bone. But they dared say no word, knowing that he who disputed my orders in the field of battle tasted death that moment. Still Mgwali held the child aloft, gazing at me in wonder. But at a further glance from me he set it down.

"See!" I said. "This is not a child of the Amabuna. It has the look of a child of a race of kings!"

The little thing sat on the ground, staring at the ring of grim faces and bloody weapons, trembling, and too frightened even to cry. And there was a look about it which moved me to spare its life. Its eyes were blue as the heavens above, and its soft skin and pink cheeks, and red, flower-like mouth marked it off as quite a differ-ent race to the leather-skinned herd we had just slain. So I began to speak it fair and soft, and found that it understood a few of my words, and, lo! it crept over to me, and began to hide behind my shield, hoping to shut out the fierce faces of the warriors who stood looking on, uttering many a deep-throated gasp of amazement. And well they might, *Nkose;* for here was I, the fiercest fighter of all that blood-stained *impi*—I, who had slain with my own hand as many of the foe as any other could boast of—and yet here was this little thing, with the eyes of heaven, and hair like a stream of sunlight, shrinking up against me for protection and shelter, as though I were her father. In truth, it was strange.

Not now, however, was the time for indulging in any further soft-ness of this kind; so, placing the little one in the care of Mgwali, and making it known that whoever should attempt to harm her should pay the penalty with his life, I went to muster the warriors, who were busy plundering the waggons. Great stores of *gwai* were there, and sacks of corn and flour, and all manner of things which were good. Such, however, were spoil for the Great Great One, to whom, of course, we had despatched runners immediately, announcing our victory.

Now we mustered our ranks to return in triumph to the King. *Whau!* we had lost many. In heaps our slain lay around—for the long guns of the Amabuna shot quickly and true. And there, in the midst of their waggon-fort, lay the ripped corpses of the Amabuna; and already the vultures were gathering in clouds overhead. Then as we marched, black and terrible, to the place where the Great Great One awaited, with the thunder of one loud and mighty voice, the warriors sang—

> *"Ningepinde nimhlab 'Umzilikazi,*
> *Leyo 'Nkunzi mnyama,*
> *Leyo 'Búbese mninimandhla!*
> *Ca-bo! Ca-bo!"*[1]

---

[1] "Not again shall you stab Umzilikazi,
    That Black Bull,
    That Mighty Lion!
     Oh, no! Oh, no!"—Mitford's note.

CHAPTER VI.

THE BURNING OF EKUPUMULENI.

THE spoils which were taken from the waggons of the Amabuna pleased the King greatly. The waggons themselves were useless to us, because none among us understood how to make the oxen draw them. So a party of men was ordered off to burn them, having first removed all the iron parts which might be of use. But what pleased the Great Great One most was the number of long guns and the plentiful supply of powder and ball which we took; and this, indeed, some of us did understand the use of moderately well. Howbeit, it was long before we became skilled in the use of them, and by that time, *Nkose*, nearly all the powder and ball was expended. But the tiny captive, with the eyes of heaven and hair like the crest of the sun, the Great Great One said I had done right to save. Yet, as he knew not what to do with her, he ordered that I should be a father to her for the present, adding that, as the last time I had spared one from the slaughter it had brought good to him and the nation—meaning the case of old Masuka—so now, perhaps, the same would hold. Now, I was right glad of the King's decision, *Nkose*, for I had already begun to look upon this little one as child of my own. So I made her over to the youngest of my wives, Fumana, who took care of her and loved her greatly.

Now, although we had made an end, utter and complete, of those Amabuna who came against us, and of the *abatagati* among ourselves who had plotted with them, yet the mind of Umzilikazi was not at ease. For he knew something of that people, had heard how they swarmed in such numbers over the country to the westward as to leave no further room, but were crowded out, and ever moving onward to seize upon new lands. Even then, as we had heard, they were plotting to seize land from Dingane, and if, as might befall, the Zulu power was worsted, and the House of Senzangakona forced to seek out other country, might not we have the remaining strength of Dingane falling upon us any day, even as we had fallen upon and swept aside those who lay in our own path? Further, although

of those Amabuna whom we had eaten up, not one was left alive
to carry back the tidings to his own people, yet, sooner or later,
such tidings would reach them, and then we might expect their
vengeance. Now, if those comparatively few whom we had slain—
some score and a half of families—had fought so fiercely and dealt so
much death amid our ranks with their long guns, what sort of foes
would their kinsfolk prove, assailing us in force and unhampered
by women and children? Or they might form a temporary alliance
with Dingane; and then how should we stand against the combined
strength of two such terrible and formidable foes?

All these considerations were debated gravely by the King and
a secret council of the *izinduna*, of whom I was one, and it was
decided to abandon Ekupumuleni and the surrounding country, and
to march upon and seize the fair lands occupied by the People of the
Blue Cattle, upon which I had reported. Howbeit, the real reason for
this decision was not to be talked about, a good and sufficient reason
for the people at large being that the land upon which we meant to
swoop down was better than that wherein we now dwelt.

It took time to send round to all the cattle outposts and muster
the nation at large, but this was done at last. The cattle and the
movable property was sent on in charge of the women and slaves,
and for several days the *izanusi* were busy making *múti*, and doctoring us all for our new undertaking. Then came the last night we
were to spend in Ekupumuleni, and through the hours of darkness
the wild howlings of the *izanusi* sounded at intervals; for it was no
light thing thus quitting the place which had been our home for so
long a time.

But with dawn of day, when all men turned out fully armed—for
a muster of our whole fighting strength had been ordered to march
out from Ekupumuleni in fitting state—a shiver of amazement, and
horror, and dismay ran through all. And well it might. For in the
middle of the great open space had been reared four stakes, and,
impaled upon each, quivered the trussed-up body of a man; and the
groan of horror and of fear deepened, for in the agonised, distorted
features of those four all men recognised the traitorous *izinduna* and
the head witch-doctor, Notalwa.

This, then, was the secret of their fate, which so far had lain in
dark and terrible mystery. They had been kept for such an end.

Five chief traitors had there been; yet here were but four! The first astonishment over, men looked at each other—their eyes asking in mute surprise where was the fifth? And of those who thus marvelled none wondered more than myself.

On the centre stake, raised half the height of a man above the others, was the body of Tyuyumane. On either hand of him were impaled Ncwelo and Senkonya, and, a little in front, Notalwa. Where, then, was Ntelani? Where, then, was my father? Well, wherever he was, it was not there.

The stake of impalement is a terrible thing, *Nkose*, and was seldom used among us—only once, indeed, since we had gone out from Zululand, and then in the case of three chiefs who had come in to *konza* to Umzilikazi, and had departed, laughing at their promise. Now, however, by the hideous fate to which he had adjudged these ringleaders of the conspiracy, it was clear that the King intended to strike terror into all who might at any future time be tempted to travel the same road.

They were still alive, those wretches—for a man may live a day or more in that torment, and these had not long been on the stakes. And as we stood gazing upon them thus suffering, several *izimbonga* came running forth from the *isigodhlo*—roaring like lions, trumpeting like elephants, bellowing like bulls—shouting the praise and the royal titles of the King. And from the whole army, ranged on either side of the open space in two immense half-moons, these were taken up, and re-echoed again and again.

But Umzilikazi, advancing down the centre, with his head thrown proudly back, halted, and held up his hand.

"Cry not to me the *Bayéte*, my children!" he said, in clear and ringing tones. "Cry it to your King, Tyuyumane. Behold him, yonder—your King, Tyuyumane!"

Bitter and biting as serpents were the words, splendid the gesture, as the Great Great One waved a hand towards the chief of the impaled traitors, who was raised higher than the rest. An awestruck murmur ran through the ranks. None knew what to do; for the humour of a King is of the nature of fire, in that it is not a thing to be played with.

"What? Have ye no word, my children? Have ye no greetings for your King, Tyuyumane—your new King, who reigns from a high seat? See, I will set you the example."

Then going before the stake whereon writhed Tyuyumane, the
Great Great One mocked him, crying—

"Hail, Tyuyumane! Hail, new King of the Amazulu—ruler of the
world! Is thy seat high enough? Is it soft enough? Ha! Praise him, ye
izimbonga! Cry him the *Bayéte*, ye warriors!"

The impaled wretch gave a quivering heave, and his lips curled
back from his jaw, baring the teeth, which were locked together in
the agony of his torment. It was a fearful sight, for though ruthless
in the heat of battle, yet at this moment we saw not red; and these
sufferers, though deservedly thus punished, were of our own blood.
Yet none pitied overmuch Notalwa, for the *izanusi* were hated and
feared by all.

"We leave thee in peace, Tyuyumane," went on Umzilikazi, still
mocking. "We go out from thee, because a nation cannot own two
kings. We leave thee, but will *konza* to thee from afar. We leave
thee our royal dwelling, Ekupumuleni. We leave thee in the midst
of thine *izinduna*,"—with a wave towards Ncwelo and Senkonya,
between whom he was impaled. "We leave thee, too, our head *iza-
nuzsi*, Notalwa, and we go forth, homeless and scanty in possessions,
to seek a new home. Thou, who art weary, need travel no further.
Ekupumuleni, 'the Place of Rest,' shall be thy resting-place forever.
Ha! *Hlala gahle*, Tyuyumane! Rest in peace!"

With this mocking salutation, the King turned away, and, preceded by the *izimbonga* shouting in praise of the royal justice, he
paced for the last time, and with great state, through the principal
gate of Ekupumuleni, and, mounting his horse, which was awaiting
him outside, signed that we should commence our march. Then, as
the immense array of armed warriors, in full war adornments, filed
out of the great gate, spreading forth over the plain as the waves of
a dark sea, once more was raised the song of triumph which told of
our victory over the Amabuna:

> "Ningepinde nimhlab 'Umzilikazi!
> Ha—ha—ha!
> Ca-bo! Ca-bo!"

And soon the mighty kraal which had been the home of a warrior-
nation for so long a time was quite deserted—given over to those

four grisly figures, writhing there upon their stakes in blood and agony.

But scarcely had the rear of the last column passed out through the gates than flames and smoke were seen issuing from four points of the kraal at once. The King had given secret orders that it should be thus fired; and the blaze, once kindled, leaped from dome to dome of the thatch huts, running along the dry thorn fences with a crackling roar like the volleys from the guns of the Amabuna; and now in a marvellously short space of time the immense circle of Ekupumuleni was wrapped in huge sheets of flame; and in the dense smoke-clouds which rolled down upon the whole of its area, before towering aloft to the heavens, the bodies upon the stakes were completely swallowed up. And then all cried aloud in praise of the mercy of the King, who had thus shortened the just suffering of those traitors by the swift death of suffocation, while rendering them such a noble tomb as the ashes of a royal dwelling.

Such then was the end of Ekupumuleni, the Place of Rest; and again as we resumed our journeyings, again as we swept northward upon our devastating way, our path might have been read by the line of the vultures in the heavens, by the track of wild beasts through the brake and the grass, running side by side with us, well knowing who should supply them with plentiful and easy prey.

Now none knew why the King should have been minded to spare my father, Ntelani, for that the latter had been spared all now knew. Yet he was cut off from all fellowship with his equals, and was forced to accompany our march, sullen and sad, unarmed, and in the midst of a guard consisting only of slaves. Some thought it was because he was the father of him who wielded the King's Assegai; others that he was reserved for an even worse fate; but all wondered he did not take his own life rather than live on thus—he an *induna* of high degree, now forced to herd with Amaholi and the lowest of the people.[1]

The little blue-eyed child whom I had taken from among the Amabuna had by now quite lost all fear of us, and would laugh and play as merry as the merriest of our children. My two younger

---

[1] A direct allusion to an incident in R. Moffat's *Missionary Labours* (1842): 539-542, previously cited in *The King's Assegai*; Zulu warriors should prefer "death to dishonour."

wives cared for her greatly; indeed, I think they loved her more than
they did their own children. But Nangeza, my *inkosikazi*, looked
upon this little one with a scowling brow. It would draw ill upon
us, she used to declare, to bring into our midst a child of such a
race. However, beyond frowns and growlings even she dare not go;
for the child had been given into my charge by the King, and to
harm it meant death; nor was Nangeza tired of life just then. This
little one, too, feared nothing, not even the King himself; and often,
when Umzilikazi was moving abroad, and all were bowing down
before him with words of *bonga*, she would dart away from those
who would have restrained her, and run out all alone, and, standing
before the Great Great One, throw up her tiny hand in the air, and
cry aloud the *Bayéte*, her blue eyes laughing up into the King's face.
And he would talk softly to her, and presently send round a couple
of white calves or two or three goats for her to play with. And we
named her Kwelanga, from "Kanya Kwelanga," the "Light of the
Sun," because her hair, all bright as of gold, seemed to reflect that
light.

So our nation journeyed on, and more than one moon had
waxed and waned. And there was a brightening up of spirits among
the warriors, and talk and songs of war; for now we knew we were
drawing near the country of the People of the Blue Cattle, the land
of richness and promise, the land which should be ours.

CHAPTER VII.

UNTÚSWA'S EMBASSY.

WE had halted some days at a convenient place to hunt. The King was in high good humour, for the land with each day's progress fell off in no wise from the report I had made upon it.

"In truth, Untúswa, thou art a wise man as well as a brave one, though young in years," he said one day, as we sat beneath the shade of a great tree, taking snuff; for Umzilikazi, with a number of his body-guard, and three or four *izinceku*, had gone on in advance of the remainder of the nation, intending to hunt before the game was scared out of our path. But the game we sought was fierce and dangerous game—the lion, and the elephant, and the buffalo—and in the slaying of such none was bolder or more skilful than the King himself. I was the only *induna* of the party, and, indeed, it seemed to me that Umzilikazi liked to find some reason for keeping me about him, even as when I was a boy and unringed.

"It seems to me," he went on, after I had uttered my thanks for his word of approval, "it seems to me that we are drawing near to the country of the Chief of the Blue Cattle, yet the choicest of those cattle have not travelled our way, nor have their owners sent to beg to be allowed to live. How do you explain this, Untúswa?"

"The Bakoni are a nation of fools, Great Great One. Their warriors are numerous, but they do not look much of warriors. They, in their ignorance, fear not the might of the all-devouring Amazulu. Give but the word, Father, and the day we sight their town, there shall not be a man left."

"Thou art a lion-cub, indeed, Untúswa," said the King, with a laugh. "No. I have another mind in this matter. I will not destroy these people, for I think to make use of them—that is, I will give them one more chance. I will send to their chief, that he delay not to come in and place his neck beneath my foot. But who to send? None but these slaves speak with the tongue of those people—and who can trust a slave?—and Masuka is too old, and to me too valuable."

This last the King said rather to himself than to me, yet I understood his meaning.

"Send me, Father," I said. "I am able to converse with these people, and who better can explain the mind of the King in such a matter?"

"That is so, Untúswa. But it is like sending thee to thy death; for, if these people are wallowing in their folly to the extent of refusing to *konza* to me, it is as likely as not they will slay my messenger. And it is not a very great death for a fighting captain."

"When a man dies in the service of the King, any death is a great death," I answered. "Send me, Black Elephant."

Umzilikazi took snuff a moment and pondered.

"I will send thee, son of Ntelani," he said. "Who now is there to bear thee company, for thou must go alone, with one other, and four slaves to carry thy game. I will not that an *induna* of the King go before the chief of a numerous nation unattended."

It was, as the King had said, a dangerous service. The Bakoni, I knew, were relying on their numbers. It was extremely probable they would put me to death in the first instance, and, at any rate, certain that they would do so later, when they realised that our *impis* were actually drawing near to sweep them off the face of the earth. Yet I felt sure that the Great Great One had some reason in sending me; and, even had I not, never was I known to think twice when ordered to any post of danger. I was the only *induna* with the King there in our advanced camp, but among the royal body-guard was that aforementioned younger brother of mine, Mgwali, son of the same mother as Sekweni, who was put to death for suffering himself to be overpowered at his post. Him now I named to the King.

"It is well," said Umzilikazi. "Go now to this chief named Tauane, which appears to mean in the tongue of his race, 'A Young Lion,' and say that not many days off draweth near an old lion, whose roar is louder—that unless I behold the usual tribute, brought by himself in person, before we are within a day's march of his town, he and his people are already dead. Go!"

I stood before the King, cried aloud the *Bayéte*, and strode off. I armed myself with my great war-shield, several strong assegais, and a heavy knobstick. Then I took in my hand the King's Assegai, and sent for my brother Mgwali.

"Pick out four of the slaves, load them with such things as we need for a long march, and follow me. It is the 'word' of the King!"

I stepped forth from the camp with my face turned northward. Before I had gone far I heard a sound of singing, and footsteps behind me, and immediately I was overtaken by my brother, and behind him the four Amaholi bearing loads.

"Whither are we bound, son of my father?" he asked, now that he had time for speech. I told him.

"Whau! It is like the King sending two men to take a whole nation by the beard!" he said, with a joyous laugh. "Yet, Untúswa, I am glad to be one of those chosen, for know that I am tired of my own hair, and would fain wear the ring instead of it. Moreover, thou sayest that these Bakoni maidens are fair."

"Thou shalt soon see for thyself, Mgwali. Yet it may be that a grimmer embrace awaits us both in their town. How likest thou that, son of my father?"

"I care not. Hau! Ibúbese!" he cried, hurling an assegai with the quickness of lightning at a long, yellow gliding shape, which had darted from a thicket in front of us. But the lion uttered a quick, frightened yelp, and made off unhurt. The spear had fallen short.

"No more of that—no more of that!" I cried, in anger. "We are on the King's service, boy. No time have we to stop and hunt. Our game lies yonder, and it may be yet more dangerous than the slaying of lions."

Not many days had we to travel before we drew near the Great Place of the Bakoni; and, from the commotion which our appearance excited among the inhabitants of such outlying kraals as we passed, we felt pretty sure that the news of our approach had already been conveyed to the chief. And such, indeed, was the case; for on the last rise, which should bring us within sight of the town, we were surrounded by two large bands of armed warriors.

"Delay us not," I cried haughtily, with a wave of the hand, as these made as though they would have drawn up across our path. "Delay us not. We carry the 'word' of the Black Elephant to the Chief of the Blue Cattle."

We did not halt, we did not slacken our pace. We marched right into the midst of that company of armed men as though none were there. They gave way in silence, but formed up on either side of us in the manner of an escort, and in this order we drew near to the town—not exchanging a word, though we could hear the slaves behind, who bore our burdens, whispering to each other excitedly. Thus we entered, and as we did so the same thought was in both our minds. How, and in what manner should we depart from it again?

The plain for some distance outside the town was dotted about with people: women in groups, men with weapons in their hands, children herding the sleek, blue-coloured cattle, but all gazing with unbounded curiosity upon two men walking alone into their midst as though kings over them, and such indeed we felt.

In those days, Nkose, I was at the very height of my strength and manhood. Now I am old and wrinkled, but I am not short. Then I was of a largeness of limb in proportion to my lofty stature. My body was a framework of hard muscles, and indeed there was not a man in our nation who could overcome me in strength or surpass me in agility, in which my brother, Mgwali, was somewhat my inferior; yet even he was a giant in comparison with the people among whom we now were, though in other matters than strength and stature they seemed far from being a race of fools. Indeed, I have thought since that the King may have had such a contrast in his eye when he sent me to represent him among these people.

If this place had struck me as large before, it now seemed doubly so. In among the huts, too, were strange circular stone walls, here and there, looking like old and strong buildings, for their strength was immense. The huts were without end; they were built of grass, rising to a point, and were neat and clean. We were conducted to one, and bidden to rest, for that the chief would confer with us on the morrow.

"That may not be," I said decidedly. "This night must the 'word' of the Great King be spoken. To-morrow may be too late for ye, O people of the Blue Cattle."

"E-hé!" assented my brother.

Our escort looked at one another, and their looks were blank. However, they invited us to enter the hut, saying that food and drink should be brought us, and that meanwhile my words should be carried to the ears of Tauane.

We had finished the piece of beef which had been sent us, and had drained the large bowl of tywala, when messengers arrived to announce that the council of the nation would be convened at sundown, and that the "word" to be returned to our King would then be made known to us.

At the appointed time we set forth, Mgwali and I, fully armed, and bearing our shields. As we walked behind our guides, I noted the intense curiosity which our appearance was inspiring, and laughed to myself. For I heard the bystanders, especially the women, comparing our stature and fierce aspect with that of their own people, and saying if we were representatives of that horrible race—of which they had already begun to hear—then, indeed, they were as good as dead. Moreover, while not appearing to do so, I took note of the high fortified hill, which lay a little way back from the town, and thought I could find a way up it—wherein, however, I might have been wrong.

The men of the nation were gathered in an immense half-circle, like the formation of one of our *impis* when throwing out flanking "horns." They sat at the upper end of a great open square, and in the bend of the half-circle were grouped the principal councillors and chiefs, and, a little in advance of the rest, clothed in the skin of a maned lion, and wearing ornaments of gold, sat the chief, Tauane. Behind were several huts of much larger size than any of the others.

Although those immediately in front of us were not armed, yet the ranks on either side showed a perfect glitter of spears. The shields were square, and not made of oxhide, like ours, but of wood. We knew at a glance that, were our death intended, we should stand no chance whatever. Two men, however brave, however well armed, would be nothing among these.

"Greeting, Chief of the Blue Cattle!" I said, as we drew near. "Remember you the name of Untúswa, son of Ntelani, and an *induna* of the Great King? It is a name I promised you should hear again."

Tauane frowned, and I could see his gaze rest meaningly on our weapons. These we had gone so far as to hold in our left hands only, extending the right, open and in greeting. Further, he expected we should have bent down before him; but I, an *induna of* the King, a Zulu of pure blood, and coming of a kingly house, thought myself an immeasurably greater man than even the head chief of such a large and wealthy tribe as this.

"Is the nation gathered to hear my message, the 'word' of the Great Great One?" I asked, without further ceremony.

"Speak it, stranger," said the chief shortly.

"This it is, then, Chief of the Blue Cattle, and councillors and people of the Bakoni. The 'word' of Umzilikazi, the Great King—the Black Elephant, whose tread shaketh the world—is short, even as the measure he meteth out to they who think to defy him. This it is:—'Go, now, to this chief, Tauane, the lion-cub, and say that not many days off there draweth near an old lion, whose roar is louder than his own—that unless I behold the usual tribute, brought by himself in person, before we are within a day's march of his town, he and his people are already dead.' Such was the word of the founder of nations, the eater-up of disobedient peoples, O Tauane, and councillors of the Bakoni."

I was not sure, *Nkose*, that that moment was not my last. Such a chorus of rage went up from the armed ranks as I delivered my message as might have been heard a great way off.

"To death with him!" they roared. "To death with the man who wears the black ring! Let him be burnt in the fire!"

But of all this I took no notice. I even gave a slight laugh, as I stood, with my head thrown back, looking down upon Tauane.

"Such is the word of the Great Great One," I repeated, slowly.

"Have you ever done a bolder act, stranger?" said Tauane. "Hear you these? They howl for the blood of him who has insulted their nation and chief. Have you ever done a bolder act?"

"I have, indeed—an act which has won me the *isicoco* I wear—also this"—holding forth the King's Assegai. "If they howl now, what will they do when the 'word' of Umzilikazi, the mighty King, is not obeyed. Never does he send forth his 'word' twice. Now, when wilt thou *konza* to the Elephant, O Tauane? The sooner the better!"

The howl that went up now was terrible to hear. The dense lines of armed warriors sprang to their feet and hurled themselves upon us, spears uplifted.

Mgwali and I stood back to back, covered by our shields. We would die like Zulu warriors, but before we did so the King's Assegai should cleave in twain the heart of the chief. This Tauane knew, and made furious signs to his people to forbear. But they would not listen, and it seemed that in a moment more we should fall beneath the weight of the corpses of the Bakoni whom we would carry with us to the Dark Unknown, when there arose a new and sudden tumult out beyond the lines of those who would have slain us.

Up the open square men were running—fleeing as before some great and unknown terror—calling out wildly and looking back as they ran. Every hand was stayed, each uplifted weapon lowered. Away, over the plain, dust-clouds were moving, and soon we could descry among them the advancing horns of driven cattle. Our hearts leaped. Soon we expected to behold the avenging spears of our nation. The King had repented him of our errand of peace. Our army was even now hurrying to sweep this rebellious people from the land.

"Arm ourselves, men of the Bakoni!" cried the fugitives. "Foes are at our gate! Three days have we fled before them, such of us as are left to flee, with what we could save of our cattle. Yonder they come! They will soon be here!"

Now in the disturbance which followed, the Bakoni thought no more of taking our lives. Wildly the fugitives urged that all should at once take refuge in the hills, for that a strange and mighty race was advancing like a devouring swarm of locusts, its warriors as countless in number as the destroying insects themselves. They had received warning in time and had fled; had received warning from the remnant of those who had already been devoured. But those around us laughed. Look at their strength; at their armed might! Whom did they fear? Had they not behind them, too, an impregnable fortress?

The eyes of all were directed to the fleeing cattle. But as these drew near, urged on by their drivers, no further dust-cloud beyond them betokened the advance of a pursuing enemy. If there had been such, he had prudently drawn off on finding himself too near their great town, the Queen of the North, decided the chiefs and councillors of the Bakoni. They little knew—ah, they little knew!

During this disturbance we two had quite recovered our proud and disdainful calmness. We stood watching what went on as though in it we had no lot or part. At last, when it had quieted down somewhat, Tauane spoke:

"It will be well to retire to your house, ye two strangers. On the morrow will be decided the answer that shall be sent to your King."

CHAPTER VIII.

THE SCOURGE.

THE morrow came, but with it no answer to the King's "word." The day was spent by the Bakoni in sending forth scouting parties to look for the rumoured enemy, but these returned bearing no further news, and the chiefs and people of this doomed race felt safer than ever.

No council was convened in the evening and now, feeling sure that no answer was intended, I sent an angry message to Tauane, saying that I would give him till the middle of the following day, and that unless I had his reply by then I should depart; that his chance of safety would have gone by, and that when next he saw me it would be in the forefront of the destroyers.

We did not sleep much that night, my brother and I. We feared even to eat the food supplied to us until we had first caused one of our slaves to partake freely of it. We talked together in a low voice and made our plans.

Morning dawned. We stepped outside our hut, and, lo! all things looked as usual. Women were passing to their ordinary work. Cattle were being milked—those fine blue cattle of which these people were so fond. Young men lounged about, scarcely armed, laughing with the girls, and old men sat taking snuff and chattering. As we stood before our door, their attention was drawn to us, though their remarks were uttered too low for us to catch.

"Of a truth, some of these Bakoni maidens are good to look upon!" murmured my brother, as a string of girls, calabash on head, stepped by.

"Peace, boy," I answered sternly. "What have we to do with such, we who bear the 'word' of the King?"

Taking a rod, I planted it upright in the earth. We stood watching it; but no message came from the Chief of the Blue Cattle. The shadow thrown out by the rod was now scarcely twice the length of a man's finger. Then I directed Mgwali to cause our four slaves to gather together their loads, for the time for departure had arrived. Only three, however, appeared. The fourth was not to be found. Clearly he had deserted. This looked badly.

The sun had reached his highest. The rod which I had planted in the earth cast no shadow now.

At a word from me we stepped forth, my brother and I together, the three remaining slaves but a few paces behind. As we passed through the town we noticed some of those strange-looking stone walls we had seen on our first arrival. These were about the height of a man's head—though, in places, higher—and were built in a round formation, seeming to encircle a second enclosure. We noticed just then that the outer wall was entered by a narrow opening just wide enough to admit the body of a man.

But now all our attention was turned upon ourselves, for we were suddenly encompassed by a crowd of armed Bakoni. These, flourishing their weapons, ordered us, in angry and jeering tones, to return to the hut we had occupied. Oh, those fools, who thought to dictate orders to the second *induna* of the army of the Great King!

We did not even halt; but, instead of assailing us, a number of them rushed upon our slaves, and speared them under our eyes. *Hau!* They fell, those unfortunate Amaholi, simply cut into strips. What happened then, *Nkose*, I scarcely know. I saw red. We both "saw red." The thunder of our fierce war shout frightened them as though it was the roar of a lion in their midst. I heard and felt the hiss of the King's Assegai as it rushed through the body of the warrior nearest to me, splitting it nigh in twain. Then, as a buffet from my great shield sent another staggering, he, too, was devoured by the dark-handled spear. *Whau, Nkose!* I know not how many we slew. Leaping hither and thither, roaring like lions, we hewed our way; yet we were but two, and they were hundreds. They yielded before us, only to close up again immediately. *Au!* They had never seen Zulus in battle before. But even Zulus, being but two, cannot go on fighting all day against the might of a whole nation, and surrounded on all sides. We might kill a number, but our death was certain at last.

Now, of death we thought not at all, for in battle it is not our custom to think of aught beyond how many enemies we could kill. But to me came the thought that I would like to live, if only to assist in destroying the whole of this den of jackals. And I saw the means of attaining to that purpose.

"The wall, Mgwali!" I cried. "Through them—to the wall! We can hold that. It is our only chance."

I spoke in Zulu, which they understood not. During the conflict we had been drawing nearer and nearer to the wall. Now, as we turned to face it, we were confronted by a double line of Bakoni. Their shields and spears were ready. We could not hope to break through them.

"Leap, Mgwali, leap!" I growled, feeling the searing burn of a spear blade grazing my shoulder. Covered by our shields, we gathered our legs under us, and leaped. *Au!* we could leap in those days. Right over the heads of the lines of our foes we flew, and immediately, and before they had time to recover their amaze, we had gained the shelter of the stone walls.

Not too soon, though, for we had only just time to turn and receive them, as a crowd of our enemies flung themselves against the opening. Then the King's Assegai had meat to eat. *Au!* in a moment the opening was so filled up with bodies that they alone formed a defence; and, as I have said, the opening was narrow, and would only admit one man at a time.

The Bakoni fell back, yelling shrilly in their rage. We two were covered with blood from head to foot, and our spears were dripping. My brother had a deep spear-cut in his leg, from which the blood was welling in a manner I did not like. Both of us had other wounds, but slight, though a blow from an axe, which had been hurled at me, and which I had just warded off my ear, catching it on the elbow, had come near disabling my right arm. We put our heads above the wall and laughed at our cowardly enemies.

"Ha! dogs—jackals!" I cried. "Have you fought enough? We have not. Come now, and have some more. We are but two, you are a nation. Does the whole nation of the People of the Blue Cattle fear two men? What then will it do before the hosts of the Great King?"

And we took snuff, laughing loudly at this army of cowards, who dared not come within a certain distance of us.

"Wait there, black baboons! You are in a trap, ringed ape!" they cried, jeering at our darker colour. "You are trapped, like the *tshukurau*[1] in the pit. We will spear you at our ease!" And a few assegais came whistling past our heads.

Then they hurled their spears up straight in the air, so they should fall back on our heads. But we only made houses of our shields, and

---

[1] Rhinoceros.—Mitford's note.

laughed louder than ever, as the spears came down, "zip—zip," like hailstones on the roof of a hut. We returned them to their owners, too, for we taught them that Zulu warriors, when it came to spear-throwing, had nothing to learn from any other race. This drove them back yet further, and we sat and rested, and sang the war-song of the King.

Our plan was to remain there until dark, then to make a dash through their lines, and this we had little fear of failing to accomplish, wherefore we felt no great concern now. But what puzzled us throughout was that Tauane should have treated the King's messengers with violence, remembering how impressed he was upon our first visit to his country; and not until afterwards did we learn the true reason, which was this.

During the time he had been in our midst, the slave who had deserted us had learned that, great and formidable as our nation was, still it was a fugitive nation—that behind it was a greater, from whose vengeance we were fleeing. This he had imparted to Tauane, destroying in the minds of that chief and his councillors the terror which our name and appearance had at first inspired. A fleeing nation could not be a very formidable one, they reasoned, looking around upon the wealth and strength of their own settled and numerous people; and, accordingly, they resolved to meet Umzilikazi's demands with quiet defiance, detaining, meanwhile, the persons of his messengers. Ah! they little knew, those poor fools—they little knew!

Time went by, and, secure behind our stone walls, we felt as though we should like to go to sleep. But we dared not do this—at any rate, not more than one of us at a time. We saw the people gathering, till it seemed that we were beleaguered by the whole Bakoni nation. To those who had first assailed us came other companies of warriors; and behind them women and children, all gazing eagerly at the "two black baboons," as they called us, in a trap. Then a new move seemed to be taking place among them. A number of people were staggering under huge loads of reeds and dry bushes. We started up eagerly, for now we saw their plan. They intended to burn us out.

A wild yell of delight went up from the whole assembly as these loads of combustibles were borne forward from all sides. We had no means of stopping them. We had hurled back, generally with effect, nearly all the assegais which had been thrown inside the walls; besides, even had we not done so, the bodies of those who approached were so hidden by the loads they bore or pushed before them that they were quite shielded. Amid yells and shrieks of laughter the burdens were placed in a ring, close up against the walls, while more were fetched. It seemed that we were, indeed, as these dogs had said, like trapped rhinoceros.

The walls were of hard stone, and, of course, would not burn. But the mass of that flaming, glowing stuff was so enormous that the heat and smoke would be enough to smother us many times over. We took counsel together, and thought hard.

As I said, before, *Nkose*, the construction of these walls was that of an inclosure within an inclosure, even like the plan of our own kraals. The centre space, ringed round by the outer wall, was large enough to contain perhaps threescore men, not standing very close together; the outer ring was only wide enough to allow one to stand at a time. There was just a single chance of escape.

The outside wall was now surrounded by a high fence of dry stuff—higher than a man's head; and, amid a roar of delight from the thousands who were watching, we saw blue columns of smoke curling up from the circle all round. At the same time red tongues of flame shot forth, crackling shrilly as they licked among the dry thorns and grass. In a moment the heat became unbearable, engirdled, as we were, within a ring of flame; and the dense, choking volumes of smoke swept in upon us, blinding us completely.

"If we would not see the end of our lives, we must get within the inner wall, son of my father," I said.

Mgwali uttered not a word. A great cloud of smoke beat down upon us, and, taking advantage of its folds, we climbed over the inner wall. As we did so the smoke-cloud parted, and in the flash of a glance we could see that the place was surrounded by a dense belt of Bakoni warriors, many ranks deep, watching the place in motionless attention, their spears and axes ready for us when we should attempt to break through, as they were sure we must. No; there was no escape that way.

Once within the inner wall, we found we could breathe more freely. The smoke rolled in its thick, choking fumes, but by crouching low to the ground we could still find air; but what air there was we knew was going: our senses were going, our heads grew hot, and our brain was throbbing as though to burst. Then there came for the first time a faint puff of air, followed by another less faint. We could see the sky above. The wind was rising. The smoke-clouds were dispersing. From that peril we were saved.

And now, as we crouched low in our place of refuge, it seemed to us that the voices of the multitude without had taken a different tone. We listened with wide ears. There was a hurrying to and fro of thousands of feet—of eager feet, of frightened feet. Then, raising our heads cautiously above the top of the wall, we peered forth.

The place was still engirdled by a ring of smouldering, glowing ashes, the heat from whose red caverns almost blinded us at first. The smoke had nearly all dispersed, and the whole of the plain stood revealed to our gaze. But the dense belt of armed warriors which we had last seen encompassing us had broken up, and its attention was but little given to us at all.

Every eye was bent upon the distant sky-line, which was bordered by a range of hills. From these the dust was now whirling in clouds, sweeping on rapidly towards us—nearer and nearer—and behind it still, black columns of smoke were mounting to the heavens. Our hearts were ready to burst with wild delight, for well did we know the meaning of this. But our enemies gazed upon it in blank and chill dismay, with hearts turned to water; for its meaning they, too, began to read, as was made clear by the wild hubbub of voices, some panic-stricken, but all eager, all excited. Then, with shrill shrieks, the women and children took flight in every direction.

On whirled the great dust-clouds, spreading over the plain afar on either hand, and through them appeared the tossing heads and horns of thousands and thousands of cattle, the sleek blue-coloured herds of the Bakoni. The ground rumbled like approaching thunder beneath their furious hoofs as they streamed madly forward. And behind them now was visible something else—a vast array of naked figures and of tufted shields, the blue gleam of wavy lines of spears. Regardless now of the danger from those around, we sprang on the wall and danced and shouted, jeering at those who just now were threatening us—the strength of a nation against two men!

"Ho, dogs! jackals! cowards!" we cried. "Flee now to your burrows. Yonder is the army of the Great King—the hand of the Great Great One, stretched forth to avenge his messengers."

The immense herd of cattle had now divided, and was streaming off in the distance to right and to left, leaving in its place that mighty array of the conquerors of the world sweeping forward upon this doomed people who had been mad enough to defy their wrath.

"Ho, Tauane! young lion!" I shouted, as the chief passed close beneath. "Yonder is the lion whose roar is the loudest. Go, tell him what has been your treatment of his messengers."

The chief heard, but made no answer as he hurried away, and we could see him and his war-captains disposing their warriors in battle array. And, indeed, they made a brave show, being more numerous than our own, and as well armed. But who can withstand the rush of the Zulu lion?

From our high position we could take in the whole of that battle. Battle, did I say? It can hardly be called a battle. In spite of the dense and well-armed array confronting them, our warriors did not even slacken their pace. Coming on at a swift but steady run, covered with their great shields, their heads bent slightly forward, their eyes glaring like red coals, the air thrilling with their fierce war-whistle or hiss, as it really was, the aspect of the King's host was so terrific that the Bakoni, for all their numbers, began to hesitate and look wildly around, thinking of flight. But no time was allowed them even for this. Our people were upon them. The crash of shields was as the thunder of the storm-driven billow striking the shore. Whole lines went down, and, pouring over them, the warriors of the Great King delayed not a moment. The Bakoni could not stand a second time. Their battle rank was broken— rolled up as one might roll up a newly-stripped hide. With wild, shrill shrieks of despair they turned and fled headlong.

Then the roar that went up from the ranks of our warriors was as the roar of an army of lions. Fleet-footed, they pressed on the disordered masses of the flying foe, hewing them down like corn, yet still preserving their own order of battle. The panic which had seized upon the Bakoni was complete. They were slaughtered as they fell, slaughtered like stricken sheep, and over them poured the destroying lines of their devourers—slaying ever, slaying and slaying—showing no mercy; for these people had rejected the King's mercy with scorn and insult. The day of mercy was now past.

CHAPTER IX.

THE LIVING BRIDGE.

WE waited no longer, Mgwali and I. We leaped from our shelter, waving our shields and shouting the King's war-cry. We had to dash through the glowing ring of ashes which still smouldered redly around our place of refuge, but if it burnt us we knew it not, for we were not in the mind to feel hurts. But, as we dashed forth, black and terrible, to take our share in the slaughter, we found ourselves in the thick of the flying Bakoni.

In the very midst of them we were, hemmed in so close that, we had but to move our hands, and with each thrust a man fell, as a slain bullock when the point of the assegai is placed behind his shoulder, and in this manner we swiftly cleared a ring around us. At first they saw nothing, looking neither to the one side nor the other, as they fled, their heads stretched out before them. But when they did look up, and beheld Zulu shields right in among them, Zulu spears rising and falling, they shrieked aloud in their terror, fleeing even more wildly than ever. Thus we, being but two, were carried along in this flying rout—killing, killing, till we were well nigh weary. Never a weapon was raised against us; no resistance even did they attempt. So great was the fear which was upon them that they allowed themselves to be slain like cattle, and Mgwali and I slew and slew, and laughed aloud.

We had gained the further edge of the town, and now we thought it time to get out of the crowd and rejoin our people. So we worked our way clear without difficulty and turned our faces toward our approaching countrymen.

Then as we were among the huts once more, another great mass of Bakoni suddenly appeared, fleeing for their lives. We sprang forth to meet them, sounding our shrill war-whistles, but these valiant warriors, seeing Zulu shields thus suddenly in front of them, halted, and, turning, strove to flee back the way they had come. But their rear ranks, panic-stricken, crashed against them, forcing them on; yet the fear of the enemy they had seen in front—for they could not

have noticed that we were but two—was so great that they would
not advance, and the whole of that armed crowd stood shouting
and shrieking, crumpled back in the most deadly confusion, not
knowing which way to run. At last, turning off from their original
course, they streamed wildly out upon the plain, we two pursuing
them and laughing as we had never laughed in our lives.

But they had not far to run, for the further "horn" of our army
had swung round here, and blindly they rushed upon the lines of
Zulu spears, even as they had intended, but a brief while back, we
should rush upon theirs. A half-circle of tufted shields, and of blades
now reddened and reeking, hemmed them in. The air quivered with
the shrill buzzing war-whistle. *Whau, Nkose!* before a man could have
counted fifty, there was not one of those Bakoni left alive. Then a
mighty shout of laughter arose from the slayers.

"Ho, Untúswa!" they cried. "We thought these dogs had
devoured thee. And, thou, Mgwali! Ha! we have been paying them
for your deaths. Greeting, sons of Ntelani! Greeting!"

Thus clamoured my comrades. But I made no reply. Up went
my right hand, my weapons dropped upon the corpses of the slain
Bakoni, and I cried aloud the *Bayéte*, for I saw that I was standing in
the presence of the King.

Umzilikazi was on horseback. He had led the first onset in person;
but, finding with what a craven and cowardly foe he had to deal, he
had dropped back in disgust, ordering his children to stamp out the
lot, save such as it was customary to spare.

"Welcome, Untúswa!" he exclaimed. "I thought you dead—that
these cowardly dogs had slain him whom I had sent as my voice. Yet
here you meet us—you and the boy yonder—driving hundreds of
armed men before you like so many cattle!"

"No praise is due to these dogs that we still live, O Great Great
One, for they have killed our slaves, and rushed upon us to kill us,
but we fought our way to yonder wall, whence we defied their
whole nation. Then they heaped fire around to burn us out. Behold,
Elephant, it is still smoking!"

The King's glance rested upon the stone-wall, and a flash of eager
interest lit up his eyes.

"Ha! I have an idea!" he cried. "It is good. Go now among your
shields, son of Ntelani. They wait to welcome you. We will make an

end of these people, who laughed at my offers of mercy."

Shouts of greeting hailed my return, as I sped along the ranks, for I was well liked by the fighting men, especially the younger ones, and none had expected ever to behold me again. I joined for a moment in counsel with Kalipe, and then we surrounded the town. We fired the huts, and the flame spread from thatch to thatch, till, before long, it gave forth so great a heat that we could hardly endure to remain at our posts.

But, as the flames began to spread, there came rushing out terrified figures, thick and fast—men, women, and children; all such as had not been able to escape to the fortified hill, which Tauane had so proudly pointed out to me. They came out, only to be met by a ring of blades. They were slain, speared through again and again, and flung back into the flames, all save such few of the young girls who seemed fair enough for captives; yet even of these not many were spared, for our people "saw red," *Nkose*, as the custom with us is when there is battle and blood-shedding, and at such times every living thing is slaughtered. Besides, we were doubly exasperated against these, who had dared offer violence to the King's ambassadors, and mercy was a fire of which no spark was kindled in any of our breasts that day.

Leaving the burning town when there remained no more to slay, we formed in columns, and marched to the fortified mountain. But by the time we reached it, the sun was sinking, and the King gave orders that the army should rest. The mountain was surrounded, so that no living thing thereon might escape, and, great fires being kindled, we went into camp. But, first of all, the King ordered a slaughter of cattle to take place. *Whau!* that was a sight! They were driven up—hundreds of beasts of the fine blue-coloured cattle—and ringed in by the slayers. *Hau!* then began a scene! Not all fell at once to the assegai: many escaped. Maddened by the blood, the terrified beasts, their horns clashing and eyes glowing, broke through the ring, and their frenzied bellowing mingled with the deafening whistles of those in pursuit as, with heads lowered, and tails aloft, they scattered over the plain in all directions, some bristling with spears which had been hurled into their bodies. But all, or nearly all, were slaughtered at last, and soon the fires were hissing and sputtering with huge red quarters. Then, as we devoured the blue cattle, we who engirdled the hill united around our fires in one grand war-dance, and the chant of the King's war-song was more terrible than the thunder of heaven, and, indeed, if those upon the hill, awaiting their fate in the morning, did not die of fear, it must have been that they had no room left for any more fear. And away over the plain a dull red glow hung above the ashes of the burnt town, whence would the night wind ever and again sweep up a whirling shower of sparks.

Not much did we sleep, for we passed the night in dancing and feasting. Then in the grey of dawn we stormed the mountain, sur-rounded as it was on every side. We had to ascend with some care, yet so eager were our young men that several lost their lives through being crowded over the edge of a cliff rather than pause to allow passage to their fellows. They had tasted blood. All were eager to begin killing again.

A long, low wall lay right across our march. Over this they poured before the word could be given to restrain them, and yells of surprise and pain went up from those who did. For on the other side the ground was staked with spear-heads and spikes of iron, and upon these writhed the bodies of the too eager soldiers. So close together were these spikes that if a man succeeded in freeing himself from one, he was immediately impaled upon another. Moreover, in the struggling and confusion each thrust his fellow down, and thus unknowingly impaled him. Numbers died in this way.

The ascent at this point was steep and rough. Above and in front rose a great cliff, which had to be surmounted by a long gully pierc-ing its face and winding round by a gradual ascent beyond our view. We could see the tracks of cattle, fresh and plentiful, leading up this, and if cattle had been driven by it, why then, indeed, it was a broad and open road for the soldiers of the King.

With shouts of rage, which spoke ill for those above when we should reach them, the warriors wrenched up the blades and spikes, and having thus opened a passage, poured onward and upward. We soon gained the entrance to the gully, and now we could hear the sound of voices above and the lowing of cattle. Then, as we turned the corner of this passage, and were expecting to rush on to the summit with a roar of victory, lo! the way was barred by another stone wall.

Right across our path it stretched, from cliff to cliff, and the defile was there so narrow that scarce fifty men could walk in a line. But this time no man was eager to spring over that wall, fearing the ground might be staked on the other side, and this, indeed, was the case, and with longer and sharper iron points than the place we had already passed. Moreover, these points reached back almost as far as a spear might be thrown.

I gave orders to demolish the wall, but no sooner was the first stone torn up than a volley of rocks was showered upon us from above, killing several. So narrow was the passage wherein we stood that our whole *impi* could have been slain piecemeal by this means.

As the rocks came crashing down upon us, I noted that the brow of the cliff, on the side whence they fell, overhung. I gave the word then for the warriors to quit the centre way and press themselves closely against the base of this cliff, and when this was done the stones crashed out harmlessly, not being able to fall upon us as we stood. The bulk of the *impi* was in the background and beyond reach of the falling rocks.

Now, this check concerned me greatly. The only way of ascending further was to tear down the wall and pluck up the stakes; yet every time this was attempted a shower of great stones fell from above, killing more of our people than these cowardly jackals had been able to slay face to face in the open field. Standing beneath the shelter of the over-hanging cliff, I thought hard. Then my heart leaped and my blood thrilled wildly. I had lighted upon a plan.

"Come hither, son of my father," I called, "and carry my word to the Great Great One."

Now, whether Mgwali liked or not being sent back from the front of the battle that I knew not, for he made no sign thereof, and herein he was wise; for, were he ten times the son of my father, he who should have disputed my orders at such a time would have spoken his last word. For a few moments I whispered in my brother's ear; then, as I bade him go, he sped away down the mountain side, running and leaping with the speed of a buck.

So we rested beneath the shelter of the cliff for a space, taking snuff, and laughing at the attempts made by those above to reach us with the stones. Once, indeed, they caused some of their oxen to leap out from the height, in the hope that these might crush us, but they were disappointed. We roared with laughter as the crushed beef fell before us, harming nobody, and rolling down the slope in many a shattered and bleeding mass.

At length, as the sun rose clear above the far horizon, striking blood-red upon the iron walls of the great cliffs, a multitude of persons was seen coming up the slope. A loud exclamation of astonishment arose from the warriors as in these they recognised prisoners whom we had taken on our march, and some few of the Bakoni who had been spared in outlying kraals. They were panting and breathless, but they dared not hang back, for they were urged on by the spears of a number of our people behind, foremost among whom I described my brother, Mgwali.

"Now, my children!" I cried. "Behold your bridge! These shall carry us over the spike-studded ground!"

A roar of delight, of admiration, went up from the *impi* as my plan became clear. Forced onward, the exhausted groans and despairing shrieks of the driven herd, the human herd, mingled with the loud yells of their drivers. As the foremost of them swept past us a shower of rocks from above crashed down upon them, splattering us with their blood, yet even then they dared not waver, for the spears of the breast of the *impi* had now closed up behind them, goading them on, ruthlessly slaying those who fell exhausted. On they rushed, several hundreds of them, surging over the wall.

But the frantic shrieks of those who fell first upon the spikes availed nothing. The remainder poured over them, for they had to do it—being there for that purpose—and fell in their turn, and others behind them, and so on, until not one of the sharp blades which so thickly studded the ground was visible. All were buried within and beneath the bodies of those we had driven over them. Then, as I gave the signal, the whole *impi* charged forward, trampling over this shrieking mangled mass of human beings. But we were on clear ground again. My plan had succeeded. I had thrown a bridge over that terrible gulf of spear points—a *bridge built of the living bodies of our captives!*

As we sprang to the clear summit of the mountain we beheld outstretched before us a broad table-land, grassy and level, and at the further end a rocky cone. This space was alive with cattle and fleeing groups of fugitives, striving to gain that end, for the mountain was only to be gained by two sides. We did not shout now. With heads bent and eyes glowing, each warrior grasping his spear in readiness, we swept across that level summit. Wildly those doomed ones fled—fled for the only side still open; but here they rushed upon the spears of Kalipe, and were driven back, so that they were now hemmed in with blades. *Au!* then we began to kill! We slew and slew until we could hardly raise our arms; but what I was keenly on the alert for was the chief, Tauane; for Umzilikazi had specially ordered that, if possible, this man should be taken alive.

Wearied with killing, I shouted to the groups of screaming Bakoni still alive, both men and women, who now lay upon the ground, begging hard for their lives:

"Where is Tauane? Where is the Chief of the Blue Cattle?"

They hesitated to reply. Immediately our assegais set to work again. Then some of the women screamed out:

"Yonder he is, Lion. There, among those."

I followed their glance. A group of men, terror-stricken, sat huddled together, their looks wildly imploring that mercy they knew it would be useless to ask. Already our warriors were bounding upon them with uplifted spears. But I ran forward and ordered them to forbear.

"Greeting, Chief of the Blue Cattle!" I cried aloud in a great mocking voice. "Greeting, young lion, lord of thousands and thousands of spears. What was my 'word' but this day? That the next time the Chief of the Bakoni saw my face it would be in the forefront of the destroyers; and it is so. But how do I again behold the chief of so many spears and shields? Is it armed and fighting to the death? Not so. It is crouching low, and weeping even as these miserable women!"

"*Xi!*" cried the warriors in contemptuous disgust, the sharp click sounding in chorus like the cracking of sticks. "*Bayéte, Nkulu 'nkulu!*" they mocked. "We *konza* to thee, young lion, who roars louder than the Lion of the Amandebeli."

Thus they jeered the fallen chief, and amid their shouts of laughter I gave orders that he should be tied with his right hand to his left ankle, so that he could walk only with great difficulty. This I did, *Nkose*, because he was contemptible as a pitiful coward. Had he been a brave man, although he was doomed, I would have spared him insult; but for a chief, the chief of a nation, to crouch among the women and whine for mercy—*au!* he deserved all that befell him.

"Now," I cried, when I had set aside those whom I judged should be taken alive to the King, "as for these, they shall have a choice of deaths. Yonder the cliff is high, and the way thereto is smooth and level. Hold! give them a fair chance. Go now, ye that remain of the nation of Bakoni! *Hambani gahle!*"

The warriors roared aloud at this jest. Those of the vanquished who were left alive started to run, doubtless hoping to find a way of escape. But there was none such, for the cliff went down in a smooth wall to a vast depth. Then I gave the word, and the young men leaped forward in pursuit, and in a moment that sunny cliff brow was red with death. Every one of the Bakoni had been forced to spring from the height or was speared.

CHAPTER X.

THE MYSTERY QUEEN.

WHILE the young men were thus amusing themselves, *Nkose*, I ran my gaze over the faces of the prisoners whom we had spared, and as I did so it fell upon a countenance which made me start and grip my assegai. The man who owned this face met my glance, and shook with fear. And well he might; for, in spite of a plentiful besmearing of red ochre, I knew that face and he saw that I did—knew it for the face of the deserter, the slave Maroane.

"Spare me, father," he murmured quickly in the Sechuana tongue. "Spare me, and I will tell you something that will be worth knowing—something which the King would give me my life ten times over to know."

"Speak, dog!" I said. "Speak or die!"

But he would not. He talked swiftly and low in the Sechuana tongue, which none of our people understood, urging me to go apart with him for a space.

Just then the mountain-top was covered with our warriors, for Kalipe's *impi* had now joined mine. All were in a state of the highest excitement and delight. Some were resting, some were dancing, some singing, some jeering the prisoners, others caring for wounds they had received, but the hubbub of voices was enough to make a man deaf. In the commotion I managed to get Maroane apart unobserved.

"Now, slave, thy last hour has come," I said. "What are thy tidings?"

"Spare my life, father, and they shall be yours," he said. "Only promise me my life."

"Hearken, dog," I growled, fingering the point of my spear. "If what thou showest me is worth thy miserable life, then I will not take it. But speak, or I slay thee here. That is my 'word.'"

He knew it was. He knew that I was not one to speak twice.

"Come with me, father," he said. "But—come alone."

We threaded our way through many a noisy and boisterous

group who jeered and threatened the man in front of me, reckoning him one of the Bakoni. But I restrained them, giving an order here, and a word of advice there, in my capacity of second in command. All thought I was going on a round of inspection, and then thought no more about anything at all. The while Maroane had been craftily leading me the complete circle of the mountain-top, and now we had gained the rocky cone which arose from the further end. Then, as we passed behind it, and the people were lost to view, Maroane bent down suddenly in the grass and dragged out by the heels the dead body of a man. Another, too, he dragged forth, then turned panting to me.

"In here, leader of the King's might," he said.

I looked in amazement. Under the bodies which he had removed was a hole slanting downwards into the earth, partly hidden in the long grass. The slave explained that these two had been purposely killed by their own people, in order to conceal this opening with their bodies.

Now, I had already known what it is to walk in darkness through the heart of the earth, as you will remember, *Nkose*, when I followed Gungana into the cave of the *Izimu*, or Eaters-of-Men. But for such places I have no liking, wherefore I growled:

"And what will I find, dog, when I have left the light of day?"

The fellow's eyes shone with excitement.

"The Queen of the *múti* of the Bakoni, father. She is beautiful," he whispered. "And, indeed, my life is well worth this secret."

"Ha! lead on, dog," I said. "But beware that thou beholdest not the end of this spear-point through thy chest."

I trod in Maroane's footsteps in almost complete darkness for a little way, and while I did so I pondered. What was going to be revealed? I was ever eager to look into strange mysteries—a longing implanted in me, I think, by old Masuka. And now I heard a wild, sweet voice singing, and it seemed to me the words were in the Zulu tongue.

Now it grew light, and in a moment we walked out from the darkness of the underground passage, and stood in the light of day.

It was a marvellous place, like an enormous bowl hollowed out in the face of the cliff. The rock sloped gradually outward, and above it a narrow belt of blue sky, but overhead the vaulted roof of the cliff. The floor of this place was of solid stone. It was a marvellous hiding-place, for from beneath the face of the cliff showed no sort or sign of a break. Why had not the craven Tauane sought refuge here? But perhaps even from him was the secret hidden.

This strange rock-nest was occupied by one human being—a woman. As I sprang into her view a low sharp scream of terror escaped her, and, covering her head, she sank down at the further end of the place; not, however, before I was able to see that she was of most beautiful and shapely build. She expected instant death. Yet she begged for mercy, and the voice that came from beneath the beaded robe which covered her was marvellously enthralling. She begged that her life might be spared, or taken as quickly and painlessly as possible. That she was terrified could hardly be wondered at, for my appearance must have been terrifying in the extreme. I had borne far from the smallest share in the slaughter of the Bakoni, and now, weapons, shield, and person were covered with blood. As I leaped into view she at once took me for the first of the slayers. But the words with which she appealed to me were spoken well and fluently in our own tongue.

"What is this?" I said. "The tongue of the Zulu in the mouth of a stranger?"

"I know you, son of Ntelani," she said, without looking up from her crouching attitude. "I have seen you more than once, messenger of the King."

"But I have not seen you, stranger, who speakest with the voice of the west wind. Uncover now, that I may do so, before we return to the King."

"To the King? To Umzilikazi?" she uttered, in a tone as of fear. "That may not be. Look now, son of Ntelani, and say whether I am to fall a spoil to the King."

Throwing off the beaded robe, she stood upright, and now I saw that my first glimpse had told me no lie. She was tall—tall as Nangeza—but never did I see more perfect proportions and rounder, firmer limbs. She, like Nangeza, was light of colour; but, unlike Nangeza, there was a softness, a sweetness in her face, and in her clear eyes, which was enough to befool any man, being young, who looked. She wore the short beaded petticoat and gold ornaments of the Bakoni, but her hair was gathered up in the *impiti*, or reddened cone, such as is worn by Zulu women.

Now, for all my bragging to the King that I cared not about women, I was, in those days, just as great a fool as others of my age, and although in a general way I did not care to add to the number of my wives, yet, when I came upon such a woman as this, I was apt to leave my reason and ordinary sense so far behind that a long journey would be required to pick it up again. So when this one—revealing herself thus suddenly—threw out those words about falling a spoil to the King, my reason started away—to hunt game perhaps; and the thought that ran through my mind was that I would, by some means, keep her for myself.

"Who art thou, sister?" I said; "and how art thou called?"

"I am called Lalusini, and my Zulu blood is as pure as thine own, son of Ntelani. Perhaps purer."

"*Hau!*" I cried, bringing my hand to my mouth in amazement. "Here is a marvel! Then how camest thou here, Lalusini, whom this dog just now named Queen of the Bakoni *múti?*"

"In that he told no lie, Untúswa," she answered, with a glance at the slave. "But the tale is overlong to be told at such a time."

My attention being recalled to the slave, I turned to look at him. He was crouching on the ground behind me—eyes, ears, mouth, all wide-open, looking scared somewhat; and, indeed, he would have looked more so could he have read what was passing in my mind. For I had resolved that this woman should belong to me alone; and that this should be so I must leave her here—and, indeed, her first words had seemed to point that way—for such an one as she, did Umzilikazi once set his eyes upon her, she would be taken into the *isigodhlo* at that moment. But the secret of this hiding-place was known to three of us—Maroane being the third—and I felt that it was shared by just one too many.

"I saw thee, Untúswa," she went on, "thee and another. I saw thee, the chief of two men, laying down terms to an armed and angry nation. I saw thee again—thee and another—in the ruined walls; two men keeping back swarms of yonder dogs; and my heart went out to thee, and to the days when I dwelt among my own people. Yes, my heart went out to thee, thou great, brave fighter; but if it were better that it should go out to the King——"

This she spoke in a low voice, but with a look that shook my pulses, and made me mad. I swore then that she should not be delivered up to the King, but should remain hidden there, and belong to me, and to me alone; and my words seemed to please her. I promised to return shortly, but now I must depart, or the warriors would be wondering at my absence.

"Lead on now, dog!" I said to the slave. And it was the last word his ears ever heard, for when we had passed through the dark passage, and gained the outer air, I seized him by the ankle, and overthrew him; then bringing my knobstick down upon the back of his neck, I laid him dead before he could utter a sound. No second blow was required. The secret of the hiding-place was now shared by two only.

It is true, *Nkose*, that I had made a half-promise to spare his life, but to do so now would be to throw away my own. Nor could the dog be relied upon to preserve silence. He had betrayed me once, and deserted to the Bakoni; he would certainly not hesitate to betray me again—this time to the Great Great One himself.

But as I returned, and mixed with the people, I told myself that I was indeed the very king of fools. Had I not thrown away my life before for the sake of a woman, and to-day this same woman was an element of great trouble and disturbance in my life? And now, here I was, older, and with plentiful experience, doing exactly the same thing again! For to secrete captives or cattle taken in war was one of the most deadly offences in the eyes of the King. Its penalty was death, and more than death, for it was usually death by torture. And this deadly offence, I, Untúswa, the second fighting captain and trusted *induna* of the King, had deliberately committed; and all for the sake of a woman! In truth was I the very chief of fools!

Yet, at the time, I did not so name myself; for as we returned in triumph, with the captives in our midst, streaming down the mountain-side, and singing the war-song of Umzilikazi, I, for once, thought but little of warrior-pride, for my mind was back in that strange hiding-place, and in my ears was still the music of the voice of her whom I had found there. A spell indeed as of witchcraft had she cast over me; and now, as I walked among the triumphant warriors, I seemed quite outside of their rejoicings. It might be witchcraft, I told myself, but it was witchcraft that rose above the fear of death.

The plain beneath was covered with the blue cattle of the Bakoni, and, huddled in groups, were the women captives, frightened and sad. Other captives were there—men—and these had a set, still, stony look, for they reckoned themselves as already dead. To these were added the others we had brought down from the summit of the mountain—that fortified mountain which Tauane had boasted was able to defy the world. Yet we had ascended it so easily!

"Ha, Chief of the Blue Cattle!" I said mockingly. Behold thy fortress! Behold the lion who roars louder than thee! Thou art already dead, thou who wouldst have done violence to the ambassadors of the Great King!"

"Perhaps not," he muttered, more to himself than to me. "Perhaps not. It may be that I can tell the King that which is worth my life."

Now, *Nkose*, my heart stood still within me, for these were exactly the words of Maroane the slave. To how many was known the existence of Lalusini—the secret of her hiding-place? Had I dared, I would have slain Tauane with my own hand, but this was impossible. He was the King's prisoner. Walking in the midst of the other captives, no colour had I for slaying him, and had I done so I should have drawn down upon myself the darkest suspicion. True, there was no direct proof, as yet, that I was aware of the secret, but the King's distrust would be aroused and my undoing would then be a certainty. And, over and above all this, the thought that Lalusini might be reft from me filled my mind with a fierce and savage dread. I felt capable of slaying the King himself rather than that should befall.

Then the whole army mustered in two immense half-circles, and the tufted shields and waving plumes, and the quiver of assegai-hafts made a noise like that of a mighty wind shaking a forest, and amid the thunder of the war-song, the King appeared, preceded by several *izimbonga*. These were roaring like lions, trumpeting like elephants, bellowing like bulls, wriggling like snakes, each ornamented with the skin, or horns, or teeth of the animal he represented and which constituted the King's titles.

Umzilikazi was arrayed in a war-dress of white ostrich-feathers and flowing cow-hair. The great white shield was held over him by his shield-bearer, but he himself carried a shield made of the skin of a lion, and a broad-bladed dark-handled spear similar to the one which

he had given to me. It was not often the King appeared in all the
war-adornments of a fighting leader, and now that he did the mad
delight of the warriors knew no bounds.

"Elephant who bears the world!" they roared. "Divider of the
sun! Black Serpent of Night! Black Bull, whose horns bear fire! Lion
whose roar causeth the stars to fall!" were some of the phrases
of *bonga* which arose; and, indeed, the King himself could hardly
command silence, and then not for a very long time, so great was
the excitement.

"Come hither, Untúswa," said the Great Great One. "Thou shalt
be my voice, for I talk not with the tongue of these dogs. Bring
forward the dog who names himself a young lion."

Tauane was brought forward. Deeming his obeisance not low
enough, one of the body-guard seized him by the back of the neck
and forced his face down on to the very earth before the King.

"Down, dog!" he growled. "Down before the Founder of Nations,
the Scourge of the World!"

And in fierce, threatening chorus the warriors echoed the
words.

Having contemplated with a scornful sneer the grovelling
captive, Umzilikazi said—

"Speak now with my tongue, Untúswa. But wait. Let old Masuka
be sent for. Two tongues are better than one."

Now I saw myself again undone, *Nkose*, for in turning that language into our own I thought not to render it all, and therein lay
safety. But the old Masuka would certainly render it word for word.
Still, my snake was watching over me then, for a message came
from the old *isanusi* that he was making *múti*, as befitted so serious
a time. This answer, which no other man among us would have
dared to send, unless he were more than tired of his life, seemed to
satisfy the King.

"No matter," he said. "Thou wert my tongue before, Untúswa,
when I despatched thee to offer favour to this dog who calls himself
a lion. Thou shalt be my tongue now."

CHAPTER XI.

THE END OF TAUANE.

As the King thus spoke, *Nkose*, I felt safe again, for old Masuka might not arrive before I had finished interpreting, and when that time had come I felt sure that the moments left to the captive chief of the Blue Cattle would be few indeed.

"So, brother!" said the Great Great One, speaking in that soft and pleasant voice which was the most terrible of all, "so, brother—who thought to rule the world? What bad dreams disturbed thy night's rest to cause thee to make a mock of my messengers?"

This I put to Tauane. But he made no reply save a murmur, waiting for the King to continue.

"I offered thee life, and thou didst choose death; death for thyself and thy people. Go, ask such as remain of the tribes and peoples which have lain in and around our path—ask if the son of Matyobane was ever known to send forth his 'word' twice?"

Still the chief made no reply, save for a murmur. But there was a light in his eyes as of hope, for Umzilikazi's voice was soft and pleasant, and therein he read mercy. Ha! we knew better than that—knew that for such a purpose the King's voice had better have in it the roar of thunder.

"Not only didst thou turn a deaf ear to my offer of thy life and the lives of thy people, O Chief of the Blue Cattle," went on Umzilikazi, "but to my messenger, Untúswa, thou didst offer violence, to him and to those who were with him. But for my arrival in time, he who was the tongue of the King would have been slain; slain by thee and thy people. What hast thou to say, Chief of the Blue Cattle?"

This I put to Tauane in glee, for I had not forgotten how they had smoked us like bees within the stone walls; how, but for our prowess and their cowardice, we should long since have been slain; how that we in our capacity of ambassadors should have been sacred, but, instead, had been set upon and assailed by these dogs of Bakoni. He urged eagerly in excuse that for what had happened he was not responsible, that he had been unable to control his people, which,

when I had rendered into our tongue, raised an exclamation of derision from all who heard it; for to us the idea of a people refusing to
listen to the voice of its chief, or any man remaining a chief who was
unable to compel the implicit obedience of his people, seemed the
most ridiculous thing in the whole world. If he thought to save his
own life by throwing the blame upon his people, why then, never
made any man a greater mistake, for never was cowardice in any
form a way to the favour of Umzilikazi.

"And that is all thou hast to say, thou treacherous and cowardly
dog?" said the King, dropping his soft and pleasant voice and pointing his spear at the captive chief.

"Not all, O Black Elephant," was the answer; and now I felt on
my own trial, for, if he mentioned the secret of Lalusini's existence
and hiding-place, how could I suppress it, or turn it into something
else? I knew that none of the *izinduna* or others seated near by
understood that language, yet many of the Amaholi, or slaves, did;
and although these were in the background, I knew not how far
Tauane's voice might reach.

"There is yet more I would say," he answered. "It is whispered
that the great nation before whose irresistible bravery our race has
gone down is followed by a hostile nation greater even than itself,
before whom it flees. Now, O King, our weapons are good, and
there are still some of our warriors left. Let them therefore *konza* to
the Elephant of the Amandebeli, so when the Lion of the Zulu roars
in pursuit behind, he will be met by many more spears than he had
expected."

This offer of alliance was so ludicrous that the warriors listening
could not restrain their shouts of derision.

"Lo, a fighting bull! a lion indeed! *Hau!* listen to the trumpeting
of the elephant!" they jeered, mocking the unfortunate chief. Then
the King spoke, and again his voice was soft.

"Ha! That is what thou hast to say, Chief of the Blue Cattle?
A noble alliance truly! An alliance between the elephant and the
cricket, between the serpent and the frog! Ha! a people who in their
armed hundreds are driven backwards and forwards like cattle by
two men—only two! A people who in their armed thousands, and
with fire to help them, are kept at a distance for half a day by two
men—only two! Such are they who would fight side by side with

us! Say now, chief of a nation of old women—if thy spears in their thousands could do nothing against two Zulu fighting-men, and that during half a day, how would they think to stand against a whole *impi?* The ostrich who vanishes beyond one sky-line when a man appears on the other is preferable as an ally to thee and thine. We want not such."

So great were the murmurs of contemptuous hate which went up that I could hardly make myself heard as I rendered the King's speech. It seemed to me, watching the countenance of Tauane, that hope had now left it, to be succeeded, however, by a rekindling gleam.

"I lie beneath the foot of the Elephant," he said; "but there is that, which, if I am suffered to go untrampled, the Elephant would gladly know."

I looked around. No sign of Masuka, and it seemed to me that none within hearing would understand this tongue. Now the moment had come, now was Tauane about to try and purchase his life by disclosing Lalusini's secret and mine, and I was resolved that he should not. Yet it was a terrible thing to stand before the majesty of the Great Great One, and deliberately deceive him—a terrible thing! But I turned the speech of Tauane into a mere prayer that he might not be crushed beneath the foot of the Elephant.

"The house of the Great King should be full of beautiful women," he went on; "yet the most beautiful of all is not there."

Yes, the air was getting hot now; but I rendered the words so as to mean that the most beautiful women of the Bakoni *had already* fallen to the King's possession.

"The blood of the most beautiful of all is that of the Amazulu. There flows in her veins the pure blood of kings," he continued.

"They are beautiful as those of the Amazulu, almost worthy to mingle with the pure blood of kings," I translated.

"She is the Queen of the hidden mysteries of the Bakoni; beautiful as the mate of the Great King should be, and she has yet to be brought to the Elephant of the Amandebeli."

"Some even are skilled in the hidden mysteries of the Bakoni, and all have been delivered to the Elephant of the Amandebeli," I put it.

"The secret of her hiding-place is known to me alone," he said. "She is there, safe and unharmed, awaiting the arrival of those who shall lead her before the King. She is of the Amazulu, and is called Lalusini."

I started inwardly. Ha! The name! I might play tricks with the remainder, but the name! It sounded so plain—stood forth so unmistakably Zulu among the wretched monkey-like speech of these people, that I saw, or fancied I saw, a spasm of astonishment come into the King's face. Then I saw light.

"*None have been hidden away in secret hiding-places,*" I translated; "*all have been delivered safe and unharmed to those who should lead them before the King. They are worthy mates for the Amazulu or the Baqulusini.*"[1]

Thus, *Nkose*, did I make use of the similarity between these two words, deeming that the King, if he detected any difference, would attribute it to the difficulty these people had in pronouncing Zulu words; and, in fact, he must have done so.

"And is this all thou hast to urge in favour of thy miserable life, rebellious dog, who barks at my messengers?" said the Great Great One, haughtily.

"*And is this secret, indeed, known but to thee alone, and to no other? Not even to a dog?*" I put it.

"To me alone; not even to a dog, Black Elephant," said the chief. But his answer I turned into: "*This is all I have to urge, O Black Elephant. If it is not enough, I must even die.*"

And now I felt safe. Nor could I help smiling to myself, for the words I had put into the mouth of Tauane were the words of a brave man, whereas the chief of the Blue Cattle was the greatest of cowards when face to face with death. And, indeed, I deserved gratitude from him, for in any case he was as good as dead; and it was better to die with the words of a brave man on one's lips than with the grovelling whine of a coward.

Yet, just then, the laugh disappeared from my mind, for, looking up, I beheld drawing near old Masuka. Bent double, tottering with age, he crept along, and squatted, just a little apart, behind the *izinduna*.

"Now," I thought, "if the King chooses to converse yet longer with Tauane through the old Mosutu, then, indeed, I am undone."

But the Great Great One seemed in no mood for further *indaba*.

[1] Or Abaqulusi. A mountain clan inhabiting Northern Zululand.—Mitford's note.

Signing me to approach, he whispered a few words, and seldom or
never have a few words sounded more welcome. Springing up, I
passed round my orders to the warriors, and in a moment Tauane
and those that remained of his people were seized and bound with
thongs.

Then the King spoke, and his tones never were softer:

"Yonder is a round wall within another. Within those walls two
men, fighting-men of the Amazulu, fought throughout the shining
of yesterday's sun—fought against a twofold enemy, the whole
might of the People of the Blue Cattle and against fire! And one
of these two men was the tongue and mouthpiece of myself. This
day, again, those walls shall witness a merry strife, but it shall not be
against such great and overpowering odds. The remaining fighting-
men of the People of the Blue Cattle, who still number a great many
more than two, shall, to-day, strive within those round walls. But
they shall fight there against one enemy only—one enemy instead
of two—wherein I am more merciful than they. And that enemy
shall be fire! Go now, ye who remain of the warriors of Bakoni!
go now, and fight where my two warriors fought. Fare ye well,
Hambani gahle!"

The wave of the hand with which the King concluded was our
signal. The warriors hailed the Great Great One's words with roars of
acclamation, and, throwing themselves upon the prisoners—nearly
a hundred in number—began dragging them off to the round stone
walls, which stood up from the plain some little distance off, amid
the smoking ruins of the town of the Bakoni. Others, fleet-footed,
had run on in advance, and by the time we arrived at the ruins had
gathered and piled up a dense ring of brushwood and dry grass. The
prisoners, bound, and shrieking and kicking, were flung within the
inner wall, where they were heaped up, one upon another, a tossing,
struggling mass.

"*Gahle—gahle!*" I cried. "Not so fast! The chief must crown the
pile. It is only due to his rank."

The warriors laughed, and went on flinging in the wretched
Bakoni.

"Ha, Tauane," I said, speaking in his own tongue, "it is not good
to shake weapons in the face of the King's messenger. And know
this. Not to thee alone is the secret of the Queen of the mysteries of

the Bakoni known. Through the darkness of the earth, to an outward chamber in the cliff, like unto the place of an eagle's nest, there lies hidden she in whose veins runs the pure blood of the Amazulu, even the blood which is fit to mingle with that of kings. I know the place beside thyself—I alone."

He stared at me with a strange, wild expression.

"Thou and the King—yes," he muttered.

"Not the King—I only," I jeered. "Not the King; thy words did not travel so far."

"Yet he would have given me my life!" he said, in a bewildered way, looking giddily around. Then, as it seemed to burst upon him how he had been tricked, he began to scream aloud the story; but none there understood a word, and before he could say many words I had seized him by the neck. At a sign from me others seized him too, and, swinging him up, bound as he was, flung him right over the two walls, where he fell upon the living struggling mass of all that remained of his followers. Now fire was put in, and the great piles of dry stuff crackled and flared, and the flames and smoke drove across the bodies of those who had taken the places of myself and Mgwali, and were now suffering the death to which they had destined us. And, as the flames roared upward to the heavens, in a great circle our warriors formed around as near as the heat would allow them to draw, and the thunderous stamp of the war-dance drowned the wild shrieks of the last of the victims due to the insult and outrage offered to the King's messengers. And that was the end of Tauane, the chief of the Bakoni, of the People of the Blue Cattle.

That night, when the fires were lighted, the King ordered a great dance of the *Tyay'igama*, or "calling of names," when those named by their captains for deeds of valour should have an opportunity of recounting their claims to such distinction before the King and the whole nation. And, among others, I "named" my brother, Mgwali, who, in his manner of setting forth his deeds, when dancing alone amid the circle of warriors, reminded me not a little of my own performance when I was "named" by Gungana on a like occasion. However, the King "pointed at" him, and thereby he obtained permission to *tunga*. Yet his admiration for the female captives we had taken from the Bakoni was destined to bring him some disappointment; for the King exacted that, being young, he should choose his bride from among the girls of our own nation. For so jealous was Umzilikazi on behalf of keeping the old Zulu blood pure and strong, that, as yet, he would hardly ever allow a young man to take to wife captives or girls of an inferior race. And when the *Tyay'igama* dance was ended there was a great slaughter of cattle—the blue cattle of the Bakoni—and the night was spent in feasting and singing. And in the morning we moved on further away still from this place of death. And behind us, where the abodes of the destroyed race had been—although the houses had long since burnt out—yet above the smouldering cattle-kraals the grey smoke still went wreathing up; and, high overhead in the blue heavens, their pinions dazzling white in the sun, like flakes of driving snow, floated clouds of vultures. For in those days the march of our conquering and destroying nation might ever be followed and marked out by two things: a cloud of smoke and a cloud of vultures.

CHAPTER XII.

"YOU—AN INDUNA?"

MANY days went by before I was able to return and visit Lalusini in her strange hiding-place, and herein I found that it was not always an advantage to be great. For Untúswa the *induna* was a man of such consequence that, did any one meet him wandering abroad, heads would be turned to see whither he was going, whereas Untúswa the *umfane* and unringed might go where he would and nobody would be at the trouble to so much as wonder concerning his business. Howbeit, I was ever known as a great hunter, and keen in the pursuit of game; wherefore, on this ground alone, I found opportunities of wandering afar.

I climbed the mountain of death, and there, indeed, so plenteous had food been that there were not enough vultures and crows and jackals to devour it all; for more than half the dead bodies were untouched, and lay, shrivelled and withered, just where they had been slain. For it is our custom, *Nkose*, to rip the bodies of those who fall beneath our spears, in order that they should dry up and spread no disease; and, remembering how we "ate up" whole nations in those days, the custom was a wise one. Carefully I took my way across the flat summit, stepping in and out between the skulls and fleshless ribs, and fearful lest I might be seen from beneath, whether from far or near. But when I gained the cleft in the ground, and began to descend into cold darkness, I felt a strange feeling, for all was silence, and I wondered whether I should indeed find Lalusini still there. So I began to sing, and presently I heard that soft voice answering, as I had heard it at first.

And now, as I stood once more within this strange retreat, looking upon the beautiful and splendid form and into the shining eyes of her who dwelt in it, all thoughts of the danger I had incurred had fled as the morning mists when the sun mounts high. No longer did I call myself the king of fools—oh, no! I was the very *induna* of wisdom, so my feelings told me. I sprang forward to seize her in my arms, but she repulsed me very decidedly—though laughing.

"Not yet, Untúswa, not yet. The time has not yet come," she cried. "But—are you come to fetch me for the King?"

And her eyes full of mockery, were laughing at me.

"The King? *Hau!* Not so. An *induna's* wife only shalt thou be, Lalusini—not the wife of a King."

"Ah, ah! An *induna's* wife? But I love not old men, and *indunas* are always old."

"Not so, Lalusini. But yesterday I was only a boy, and unringed."

"Ah, ah! son of Ntelani! You—an *induna?* You?"

And again she made the rocks ring with the music of her laughter.

"I?—yes, I," was my answer, given with dignity, for my pride was ruffled. "I am only the second *induna* in command of the King's army. Nothing very great. But a small thing. Laugh on, Lalusini; laugh on!"

But she did not laugh. Something in my words seemed to turn her suddenly grave. "Ah—the chance! The chance at last!" I heard her murmur. "I, too, am somebody," she said. Then, turning to me, "Yes, Untúswa, I am somebody who is great—greater than any man among the Aba-ka-zulu; greater than Umzilikazi himself. And it may be that the day will come when you, too, shall be greater, son of Ntelani—greater than the King yonder."

"*Hau!* We are talking in a ring!" I cried, but her words troubled me. "How now didst thou come among the people of the Blue Cattle, Lalusini?—for it seems to me the time has come for me to hear that tale."

"The time has not come—not yet—but it will. And now tell me of the end of the Bakoni, for I think there must be few still alive."

"Few, indeed," I said. "But Tauane—was he the only one to know of this place?"

"The only one—he and the slave who brought you hither. What of them?" And her tone became quick and anxious.

"The slave, or what is left of him, lies above our heads. He got no further than the entrance hither when last I passed out through it. For Tauane, he is as the ashes of last season's burnt grass."

And then I told her all about the end of the prisoners, how the chief would have sold the secret of her hiding-place to save his own life, and how I had so misinterpreted his words as to prevent him from doing so. Lalusini's eyes beamed with delight.

"Ha! You deserve to be an *induna*," she said, "and a great one. The big, brave, strong fighting-man is frequently a fool in matters requiring head. But you, Untúswa, are no part of a fool. You have both the head and the strength. Lalusini—Baqulusini!" she repeated. "*Whau!* that was crafty indeed. But the King, did he have no suspicion?"

"He showed none," I answered, in just the shadow of a cloud. "Yet how will I finally bring you in among ourselves? The name will bring back the King's recollections."

"Perhaps I will never go back among yourselves," she answered. "There is a people into whose midst I will one day return, and there I shall be great indeed, and you through me. Come now, Untúswa— let us return to that people together."

"*Hau!*" I cried, with a very dissatisfied shake of the head. "That which is distant is ever that which is uncertain." For this proposition startled me. It reminded me too much of past foolishness. Once before I had sacrificed my chances as a warrior, had deserted my people, and had thrown away my life with both hands, all for the sake of a girl, and had found the position so little to my liking that I had willingly exchanged it for certain death. I had not found the death I expected, but life and great honour; yet that was a marvel, and such marvels do not occur twice within the experience of any one man. Now, I desired Lalusini greatly, but I desired her as a favourite wife of the King's *induna*—not as the mate of a disgraced runaway. Wherefore her proposal found but little favour in my eyes; and, indeed, I thought she had made it only to try me.

Then we talked of other things, of Tauane and the nation we had destroyed; but of her powers as a sorceress she would tell me nothing, or how she had come among that people. And I sat and listened to her talk, for I was young in those days, and the sound of her voice was to my ears as the rippling of water in a sun-dried land. I know not how it is among you white people, *Nkose*, but among ourselves, when we are yet young, we are ever as fools in such matters; when we are older—ah, then it is different.

While we talked, her eye fell upon my broad spear—the King's Assegai—and, reaching for it, she examined it knowingly.

"Worthy to be wielded by Tshaka himself," she muttered. "A splendid spear! A royal weapon," examining the haft, which was dark-red then, although it is now black with age. "Truly a royal weapon!"

"And a royal weapon it is," I answered, "for I had it from Umzilikazi's own hand."

"Ha! And how was that?" she asked eagerly. But I looked knowing and laughed.

"Nothing for nothing, Lalusini," I said. "Tell me thine own tale; then thou shalt have that of the King's Assegai. And I promise thee that it is a stirring one."

But she would not. Nevertheless, I told her my own tale, or a part of it. At the mention of Nangeza she looked up quickly. "How many wives have you, Untúswa?" she asked.

"Only three. But my *inkosikazi* is more trouble than any thirty ordinary women, for she wants to be chief over me, too."

Lalusini laughed.

"And that is Nangeza for whom you deserted your nation and incurred death under its most terrible form?" she said.

I answered that it was.

"And you want me to go and be second to your *inkosikazi*, Untúswa!"

"Not so, for you would ever be my favourite wife."

"Until you found some other Mystery Queen hidden in a mountain cave," she said, mocking me. But I took snuff and answered nothing, for a man who undertakes to answer everything a woman says is like one who begins to swim across a flooded river: he knows where he goes in, but cannot tell where he may get out, or if ever—at least, so it is among ourselves; I know not if it is the same among white people.

"And the King?" she said. "How many wives has he?"

"That question is hard to answer. A great many does he possess, yet he cares not for any of them, neither does he love women over-much. A woman, he says, is like the grains of the *umbona*,[1] which is tender and nice when young, but soon grows hard and tooth-breaking, and needs much pounding to turn it once more into any use at all. Thus has the King often spoken when we have been talking together."

How Lalusini laughed, and it was good to hear her laugh, even as to hear her talk.

"*Yau!*" she cried. "I do not think I will enter the *isigodhlo* of Umzilikazi."

---

[1] Maize.—Mitford's note.

"But what if no choice is allowed you?"

"But there will be. There is that by which Umzilikazi dare not wed me."

Now I cried out in wonder, yet was my mind relieved.

"There is," she went on. "And—I am greater than your King, son of Ntelani."

"Then must you be of the root of Senzangakona[1] himself, for there is but one who is greater than our King, and that is Dingane, who now sits in the seat of Tshaka."

This I said jestingly, and then, seeing that the shadows were getting long, I rose and, going to the entrance of the place, I dragged in the carcass of a buck I had slain on my way; for, besides what game I could bring her, Lalusini had no food but dry corn. Of water she had abundance, for a little clear spring trickled down the rock at the further end of the place, losing itself in a dark cleft; but only at night could she make a fire, for then alone there was no risk of the smoke betraying her, and the light—of a small fire, at any rate—was quite hidden from without.

"*Au!* it must be lonely here at night," I said, looking upward at the great gloomy rock-roof. "Do you not hear the ghosts up above, wailing among the dry bones wherein they dwelt when alive?"

"I fear not such things, Untúswa. What I fear more is that yonder stone may not be heavy enough to keep out a lion I have heard upon the mountain the last two nights. He was snapping and growling among the bones, and I feared he might try to force his way in here."

I examined the hole, which was only large enough to admit the body of a man creeping on his hands and knees. This hole Lalusini used to stop at night by rolling a stone against its mouth, yet the stone did not fill up the entire hole, but only enough to render it too small for the passage of any large body.

"It is safe," I said, testing the weight. "Nothing large enough to be harmful could force an entrance, yet I must try and slay that lion. And now, Lalusini, I must return, for it will be dark by the time I arrive, and our people like not those who wander overmuch in the night-time."

We took an affectionate leave of each other, yet Lalusini would

---

[1] Father of Tshaka, the founder of the Zulu military dynasty.—Mitford's note.

not at that time tell me anything of her own tale, and I made my way back to the top of the mountain. And all the way homeward my mind was full of her whom I had left, and I pondered much and oft about the greatness she had hinted at, and how such was in store for myself, too, as though she were the chieftainess of some mighty nation—and mighty indeed must it have been were it greater than our own, as she had said it was. But most of all I pondered as to how I should ever be able to bring her in among ourselves so that the King's suspicions should not take the right road.

Thus thinking, and alternately singing to myself, I got over the ground at a swift pace, yet by the time I entered the hut of my chief wife it was quite dark. Nangeza was seated within alone. As I entered she looked up with a frown upon her face; and, indeed, a frown was more often to be found there than a smile in those days.

"Welcome, great hunter," she said mockingly. "And, where is the game?"

"I have none," I answered shortly, for I was in no humour to be worried by this woman's evil temper.

"None?" she echoed. "Yet there are blood spots about thee, Untúswa."

There were. In dragging the buck down through the hole into Lalusini's hiding-place I had become smeared with blood, and this I had forgotten to wash away.

"I slew but two small bucks," I said. "One I ate in the middle of the day. The other I gave to old Masuka."

"Didst thou take it to him in the *isigodhlo*, Untúswa? For there has the old Mosutu been since the sun was at its highest, and is there still. Yet I saw thee from far off over the plain, and certainly thou hast not been to the *isigodhlo*, which is far beyond this house," she answered; and her tones were jeering, and her eyes shone with evil fire, as those of a snake.

"Enough!" I cried. "Enough of this!" And, bending down to the side of the hut, I took up a stick, and advanced towards her; for I was furious. "I have never beaten thee, Nangeza, but hadst thou belonged to any other man, I think by this time not a whole bone would remain within thee. Now, of thine evil temper have I had more than enough; also of thy tongue."

She retreated back as far as she could to the side of the hut—her eyes flashing, her lips drawn back from her gums, like those of a wild beast. But it was time to put a stop to this, or soon the second fighting commander of the King's army would be under the command of a woman.

"Beware, Untúswa!" she snarled. "Beware! I made thee! Yea, I! And I will unmake thee!"

"*Whau!* if any one made me, it was not thou, but the King, and old Masuka, perhaps." And then, as I saw her looking around for a weapon, I——well, I gave her no opportunity of either finding one or losing one; and, I think, *Nkose*, my *inkosikazi* went to sleep that night feeling as though she had been rolled down the rocky side of a very high mountain; while I went to the huts of my two other wives, and we spent a great part of that night in singing, and jests, and laughter. But the fault lay with Nangeza's evil and inquisitive temper; and, more still, with her attempts to rule me, as though I were the woman and she the *induna* of the King. Wherefore, from the intolerable weariness which she had put upon me, I sought the company of my other wives, that they might cheer and amuse me, which, indeed, they were very glad to do.

Now, on the morrow, Nangeza went and complained to the King as to the punishment I had given her; but she might have spared herself the trouble, for Umzilikazi only mocked her, telling her that she was fortunate indeed in having to deal with me, and that warriors were not to be ruled by women, but the other way round. Then he bade them drive her from his presence. And afterwards he would often laugh with me about this matter; but from that day Nangeza hated me with a surpassing hatred, and set herself to work to bring about my ruin and downfall by some method or other, even though it should cost her her life.

CHAPTER XIII.

"THE PLACE OF THE ALLIGATORS."

DURING this while, since we had "eaten up" the Bakoni, we had been living in hastily run up huts. Many, indeed, had not even these, but lived and slept in the open. But now the King gave orders that we should remove a day's march further, and there build a large kraal.

The site of this was a pleasant open plain, well grassed, and sprinkled with mimosa and other bush, and watered by a good-sized river.

The slaves and women were set to work; also the young regiments; the great circles were marked out, and in a few days there stood a noble kraal, built on the Zulu plan; the great open space ringed in by a double thorn-fence as high as a man's head, between which stood the rows of round-topped huts, and the *isigodhlo*, or royal enclosure, at the upper end, partitioned off by a fence of fine woven grass. This kraal was of greater size than Ekupumuleni, and the surroundings far pleasanter, for there was abundance of grass, well watered by streams which never ran dry; and the rolling plains and dark forest belts were swarming with game. The river, too, was plentiful with sea-cows and alligators, which last the King would not allow any man to kill; so that they soon increased in numbers and boldness to an alarming extent; indeed, from this it was that our new kraal took its name, for it was called Kwa'zingwenya, "the Place of Alligators." And when it was completed there was great dancing and singing, and the slaughter of cattle and general feasting, for here we intended to make our home, at any rate for a long time to come.

Now there was another reason why the place should have been named as it was. It happened one day that the King was strolling along the river bank, I being in attendance on him, when we came upon the high brow of a cliff falling sheer down into a deep, still pool. As we looked over we beheld several small dark objects floating upon the surface of the water. They were the heads and noses of alligators.

"Ha!" cried the King. "I have an idea, Untúswa, and I think it is not a bad one." Then, turning round, he called to a boy who was herding calves not far off. The lad drew near, and, seeing who had called him, his knees began to tremble and his eyes to start from his head in his terror and awe of the Great Great One. He prostrated himself to the ground, and his tongue nearly clove to his mouth as he stuttered the *Bayéte*.

"Rise up, child," said the King, "and go quickly and bring hither yonder calves. Delay not—yet stay; call those within sight to help thee."

The lad sped away, and soon, in obedience to his calls, about a dozen other boys came up, and, making a half-circle, drove the entire herd, to the number of about twenty well-grown calves, up to where we were standing, the King and I, leaning upon our sticks.

"Make them leap," said Umzilikazi. "Make them leap."

But this was not so easy, for the calves were big, and, their instincts of danger warning them, they all bunched together, nor would they suffer themselves to be driven to the edge of the cliff, notwithstanding the yells and sticks of the boys who strove to drive them; and, indeed, I myself had to seize two of them and drag them to the brink, and even then I only pushed them over at the greatest risk of falling after them myself. Then the whole herd followed with a mighty splash, which echoed like thunder from the face of the rock.

The splash subsided, the surface was dotted with the heads of the animals swimming for the other side; and then the pool was in a boil, and the calves, swimming quietly before, heaved themselves up in the water with frantic bellowing as the alligators rose to seize them. They were dragged under wildly, to reappear again but for a moment, and soon the surface was dyed red, and the tranquil water lashed into foam; and the wild bellowings of anguish mingled with the snap, snap of bony jaws, followed by a hideous crunch; and as the long, grim, ugly bodies turned with their struggling prey, we could see that these alligators were of enormous size. It was over at last, save here and there a livid head, or a mangled quarter, or other fragment floating on the surface; but the shakings of the water, and the long strings of red bubbles which came streaming up, showed that the hideous brutes beneath were tearing and devouring their welcome, though unexpected, prey.

"Hau!" cried the King. "That was a good thought of mine. Now we have a new way of disposing of evil-doers, Untúswa. Not long have the alligators taken to dispose of twenty large and well-grown calves; not long would they take to dispose of a man, or of twenty men. In truth, it was a great idea!"

To this I agreed, of course. But, looking into that horrid pool and its bloody surface, where even now two or three of the alligators were reappearing, turning their eyes upward as though looking for more, I thought of the secreted captive and the hiding-place away on the mountain, and wondered if my death would come to me down in that horrible hole; and the thought, *Nkose,* was not a nice one.

"Go now, children," said the King, waving away the staring and terrified boys; and go they did, for I believe they thought they were to be thrown in after the calves. "The idea is great; yes—great!" continued Umzilikazi, in high good humour, as we walked back. "They shall be kept there, those alligators, and from time to time I doubt not but we shall find them some food."

During this time, *Nkose,* I have neglected to speak of my father, Ntelani. Him the King had still suffered to live—I think, because he desired to spare two such brave fighters as Mgwali and myself the disgrace of being henceforth the sons of nobody; for had our father died the death of a convicted traitor we could nevermore have been known as his sons. But, though his life was spared, Ntelani was adjudged to spend it in a state of banishment. He was allowed to erect a small kraal, and here with such of his wives as chose to cleave unto him, and just enough cattle to keep him and them alive—but only just—he dwelt, soon sinking into a state of premature old age and foolishness. Indeed, he passed out of the life of the nation, and his voice from its councils.

Once settled in our new country, the King lost no time in establishing cattle outposts and military kraals, of which latter I was appointed administrator, being held responsible for their order and efficiency. We fighting *indunas,* too, were required to form new regiments, levying upon the youth of the nation at a far earlier age than had hitherto been customary among us; but our losses during our wars were beginning to form a serious gap, and the King preferred, where possible, to recruit our fighting strength among our own blood, rather than among that of our miserable, poor-spirited slaves. But these youths made up in martial ardour what they lacked in years, for they were continually worrying the Great Great One, through us *izinduna*, to allow them to go forth—it mattered not where—and wet their spears. But Umzilikazi would dismiss them, laughing, and bidding them be patient; yet at their importunity he was not ill-pleased. However, they little knew there should shortly befall that which would give all their fiery mettle as much outlet as it could take care of.

Just then I was very busy, travelling from kraal to kraal, inspecting, and, at times, reviewing, the regiments, numbering the cattle and possessions of the King and the nation—for here, in this land, we intended to dwell, and already the women—who preferred peace and plenty to wandering and war—were making the land re-echo with their songs of gladness, as they laid out new gardens for their corn and melons, and daily saw the cattle milked at the same place. And the chiefs and heads of other tribes—learning of the fate which had overwhelmed Tauana and the Bakoni—hastened to come in and *konza* to Umzilikazi, realising that the tread of the Black Elephant of the Amandebeli stamped far, and that from it there was no escape.

It happened that I was returning from one of my rounds to make my report to the Great Great One. The morning was yet young; indeed, the sun had only just risen, and the forest path along which we travelled—I and Mgwali, who accompanied me—was bright with a golden network of sunshine through the leaves, and joyous with the song and whistle of birds and the chatter of monkeys. We were drawing near a pile of rocks, overhung with forest trees and trailers. Suddenly, my brother, who was walking behind me, touched my elbow.

"Do you hear nothing, son of my father?" he whispered.

I listened long and hard. I was about to reply, "Nothing," when I heard the sound as of a voice—the voice of a man murmuring—even as the voice of one of our *isanusi* engaged in making *múti*. Now, there were caves in those rocks, *Nkose*, caves which were not unassociated among ourselves with *tagati*; wherefore, with the instinct of a warrior in the presence of evil, I gripped my broad assegai, and stole silently forward, eager to see through this mystery—if mystery there was—Mgwali pressing close behind me. The murmuring of

the voice sounded plainer now; then we heard a low musical tinkling, as of the ringing of a bell.

Whau! Here was a strange thing. What could such sounds mean,
here among the rocks and caves? The voice, too, was murmuring
in a strange language; soft, though not so soft as ours, yet immeasurably softer than the croaking tongues of those inferior peoples
which we had destroyed or enslaved. Stealthily we drew nearer,
and, peering out through the trees, this is what we saw.

A great slab of rock outhung from the cliff, forming a shallow
cave. In the mouth of this a man was standing, his back towards us.
He was clothed in a great cloak, red in colour, and bearing a broad
crossed bar down its entire length, while showing below it was a
long white garment which seemed to cover him from neck to foot.
His movements called to our mind those of our own *izanusi* when
sacrificing cattle to the ghosts of our fathers on solemn occasions;
yet not. But this could be no *isanusi*, for he was a white man! Still he
must be an *isanusi* of some sort, for he was undoubtedly engaged in
offering sacrifice. In front of him and further in the cave was a great
block of stone or a ledge in the rock formation—we could not deter-
mine which—and upon it were two little pillars tipped with flame.
Moreover, upon this the man's words and actions seemed centred,
for upon it was something else, which from there we could not
see. But here, if possible, was a more surprising thing. Behind him,
bending low, knelt another man—a dark man, one of ourselves, and
of the same race, for he wore the ring upon his head, and his other
adornments were as ours. He, too, seemed in some way to be assist-
ing the other, for his movements were much the same, and a few
words would now and again drop from him as though in reply to
the one who was sacrificing. *Hau!* it was wonderful! In rigid wonder
we stared, not knowing what was to come next.

But a dead silence had fallen upon these two now, and the murmuring had ceased. Then the tinkling of the bell rang out once
more, and the *isanusi* in the red cloak, having bent low, straightened
himself up, raising both hands high overhead, and in his hands there
flashed forth a Something—a Something upon which a ray of the
newly-risen sun now glinted with dazzling whiteness. And the man
behind—the black man—bent prone as one dead—even as a man
might lie who awaits the sentence of the Great Great One himself.

Whau, Nkose! I know not how it was, but something seemed to cloud the brain of Mgwali and myself, binding us to the spot, staring at this strange and marvellous mystery, so unlike aught we had ever beheld before. We watched, confused by what followed, but of it we have but small recollection, save of one thing. The white *isanusi* turned full towards us, more than once, still murmuring, and, while we shrank in dread lest he should be putting upon us the spell of his *múti*, we took note of his face and that keenly. It was the face of a white man, very dark and burned as though by many suns; but it was a strong face, that of a man to whom, we could see at a glance, fear was unknown. The eyes were black and piercing as those of an eagle, and a long, thick beard fell low upon the breast, its dark masses plentifully streaked with grey.

We stood watching this marvellous performance, we two fearless and armed warriors, and yet there was that in it which laid upon us a kind of awe. At length it came to an end. Then we saw the white man extinguish the fire upon his stone of sacrifice and wrap up carefully in coverings such things as had been upon it. But our astonishment was greatest when we watched him take off his outer cloak of red and then the long white garment which was girded around him. We saw him then in a large loose robe of black, and this he did not take off.[1] The other dresses, however, he carefully rolled up in coverings, and while he was doing this the man who was with him—the *kehla*—lighted a fire, and set upon it a joint of game to roast, evidently the quarter of one of the smaller kinds of buck.

Few, indeed, *Nkose*, were the white men, except Amabuna, we had seen in those days, and that this was not one of those we felt certain. Mgwali was the first to recover from his astonishment.

"*Whau!*" he grunted. "I know not how yon *isanusi*—white though he be—dare come here and make *múti* without leave from the Great Great One. It may be *tagati*."

"No hurt lurks beneath such *múti*, son of my father: of that I feel sure," I answered. "But I think it is time to have speech with these."

---

[1] From Untúswa's description, it seems certain that he and his brother were witnessing an open-air celebration of Mass; and the strange white man would appear to have been a travelling missionary-priest of French nationality—probably a Jesuit.—Mitford's note.

"*Yeh-bo*," assented Mgwali, grinning. "And I think that quarter of meat roasting yonder seems too large for only two men. *Au!* but the smell of it is good."

We went forward, and as we discovered ourselves but small was the surprise shown by these two strangers. The head-ringed man, who was attending to the fire and the roast, returned our salutation in the usual form, not heeding us much. But the other, speaking with our tongue, though haltingly, said:

"Welcome, my sons! Draw near, and seat yourselves; for our morning meal is nearly ready, and there is enough for all."

Mgwali's eyes glistened, and his mouth broadened into a grin; for he was younger than I, and hungry; and, in truth, the meat smelt good. He uttered a word or two of emphatic assent, and made a movement to comply. But I, remembering my dignity as an *induna* of the King, still stood. Then I said:

"First tell me, O white stranger, by whose leave you have entered this country, and made *múti* in the land of the Great Great One by whose light we live?"

"By whose leave?" he echoed; his face brightening up. "Ha! By the leave—nay, by the order—of the Great Great One in whose light we live." Then, seeing that I frowned, and looked suspicious, he explained. "I will not pretend to misunderstand you; but I came into the country of your King by favour of even a greater than he."

"*Hau!* You are joking, my father!" I answered, with a sneer, though my first thought was that he was speaking of Dingane. "Yet such words uttered here are dangerous, and would mean death to him who uttered them. Where, now, is he who is greater than Umzilikazi, the Mighty Elephant? Our young regiments are consumed with a longing to wet their spears; and there, I think, is the chance. Where is he who is greater than our king?"

"*Pezulu!*"[1] replied the stranger, simply, pointing upward to the heavens.

Then I partly understood. I had heard strange tales of certain men among the whites who taught that a great, though invisible, King sat above the blue of the sky, and caused the sun to shine and

---

[1] Up above.—Mitford's note. "Pezulu," "Pezoolu" is currently spelled "Izulu." The prefix *ili-/i-* is a noun marker for a person and *zulu* derives from the Zulu word for "heaven," one of the titles of the king: "heavenly one."

the rain to fall; whose might was such that beside it the might of Tshaka himself was less than the might of a child. This, then, must be one of them. Yet—the strange ceremonies we had witnessed?

"Wherefore, then, wert thou making *múti* yonder, beneath the rock, O father of the red *múti* cloak? To what end was this?" I asked.

"To the end that all good might fall upon your King, and his people, and his land. With that object and intention were we making *múti*, as ye call it, children of this nation," he answered, looking us fearlessly in the eyes.

And there was that about his glance which satisfied me that we might safely eat meat with him; nor did the ceremony which he and the other went through before partaking of it, and which was very like what we had seen during their strange act of sacrifice, avail to destroy this assurance. And, indeed, when, having finished, we rose up, to proceed at once to the presence of the Great Great One, we left nothing behind us but bones; for Mgwali had a fine appetite— nor came I far behind him in that way—and a quarter of buck is not quite too much among four men.

CHAPTER XIV.

THE WHITE *ISANUSI*.

WE were not far from Kwa'zingwenya, *Nkose*, when this meeting took place, and as we came in among the people on the outskirts of the great kraal the excitement was intense. All gazed curiously to see whom we had brought with us, and we could hear the cries of wonder which broke forth from the people as they beheld a white man. Yet, though they gazed in astonishment, they did not draw near and crowd around us to gaze, for such is not our custom as regards strangers.

Now, this white man and he who attended him, bearing their burdens, walked on contentedly by our sides, and as we entered the gates of Kwa'zingwenya I sent a message to the King, reporting the strange discovery we had made. Then, having taken the strangers to my own hut, where my wives speedily set *tywala* before them, I went at once to learn the Great Great One's pleasure concerning them.

"And the man is not of the Amabuna, son of Ntelani," he said, when I had told my tale.

"Not so, Black Elephant. He says he is of a race which comes from far over the sea."

"Ha! And the man with him, he is of ourselves?"

"He is, Father, and yet not. He is of the Abagaza."[1]

"*Hau!* Of the Abagaza? I would fain hear something of that people. See now, Untúswa, when these strangers are rested, I will talk with them here."

I saluted and withdrew. When I regained my hut the white *isanusi* was reading from a book softly to himself. *Whau!* I have seen many books since, but at that time never, and it looked wonderful. At last he ceased, and, making one of those strange turns of his hand such as we had before noticed, he closed the book and looked up.

---

[1] The People of Gaza, a kingdom covering what is presently southeastern Zimbabwe down to the southern part of Mozambique. Shaka's army earlier had failed to conquer the tribe.

Then I spoke the King's message, and he rose to his feet, declaring he was ready.

Umzilikazi was seated outside the *isigodhlo* as we drew near. The white man halted in front of the King, and, inclining his head slightly, raised his hand aloft and said, "*Bayéte!*" The Gaza, however, bent low to the ground, murmuring words of *bonga* even as one of ourselves. Him the King began to question first:

"Who art thou, who art of us and yet not of us? How art thou named?"

"Ngubazana, son of Tumela, of the people of Gaza, Great Great One," replied the man.

"And wherefore hast thou left thine own country—thou a *kehla*? Art thou an *induna*?"

"No *induna* am I, Black Elephant of the Amendebeli. I have left my country to follow my father here."

"And the feet of those who pursue thee? When a man forsakes his country, is it not that he may travel faster than the feet of those who run behind him?" said Umzilikazi, with meaning.

"None such are behind me, Serpent of Wisdom," replied the man. "In due time I return to my own country again, and to my wives. No evil have I done there that I should not return."

"Ha! Thy wives?" said the King. Then, turning to the white man—

"And thou, stranger? They say of thee that thou art an *isanusi*—though white—that thou wert making *múti* of a wonderful and unheard-of kind?"

"That is true, O King."

"And wherefore was this *múti*?"

"Let the King listen," answered the white man. "When the *isanusi* of the peoples of the Zulu offer sacrifice of cattle to the spirits of departed chiefs and kings, they do so to gain something. Is not this true, Great Great One?"

"It is no lie," answered Umzilikazi.

"When I offer sacrifice, it is of a different kind, for it is offered to the Mighty Ruler of the world who dwells above the heavens. The sacrifice which the *induna* Untúswa beheld me offering amid the rocks in the forest was also to gain something—very especially to gain something."

"And what was that?"

"The peace and welfare and happiness of the people—who dwell in this land, and of the King who reigns over them."

"*Hau!*" burst from all who heard these strange words. And for a space all sat gazing at this white man in silence, as he stood there in his black robe, which was torn and patched and soiled as with hard travel. His face was as the face of a good man, and in height he was not quite so tall as our warriors. Now he stood there looking round upon us all with the eyes of a friend.

"Thy words are good, white stranger," said the King. "But there is one thing that sounds strange to our ears, and that is that thou shouldst seek to gain us peace. For we are a nation of warriors, and what have such to do with peace? Would they not speedily be eaten up, even as these miserable peoples whom we have swept from our path? No; peace is not a thing to desire for such as we."

We who heard greeted the King's words with a shout of assent—I, especially, gripping my hand, as though I held the great Assegai, the royal gift.

"Yet peace is good," said the white *isanusi*, speaking pleasantly. "Under its shadow nations prosper and grow great."

"*Atyi!* were ever such words heard!" we cried, shaking our heads. "Grow great beneath the shadow of peace! *Ca-bo—Ca-bo!*" And we laughed scornfully.

"I think thy words please not the ears of my children, white stranger," said the King, with a grim smile. "It is war by which nations grow great—not peace—war, wherein they destroy all their enemies. The nation which does this is the greatest nation; and such is ours."

"*All* their enemies?" repeated the white man softly, with head slightly on one side and his eyes fixed upon those of the Great Great One. "*All* their enemies did the King say?"

"All—all whom they can reach."

"Ah! But what of those who would reach *them?* With every nation, however great, there is at least one other which it has cause to fear—at least one other which is stronger than itself, or which any day may become so."

Now the cry of anger, of disgust, which arose to our lips was checked, for beyond a lightening up of the eyes the King's face showed no sign that he had grasped the full meaning of this speech. For we knew—we *izinduna*—that in his heart of hearts Umzilikazi was uneasy on the subject of the Amabuna and Dingane, but especially Dingane. He knew that, sooner or later, the arm of Dingane would be long enough to reach him; and it was for this reason that such immense pains were taken to keep up the strength and efficiency of our army. Even then, nearly half of it was composed of slaves reared among base peoples. How should these withstand, in the day of trial, the pure blood and disciplined numbers of the *impis* of Dingane? We had overthrown Tshaka's *impi* among the mountain passes, but that was a running fight, and but for the cloud which descended upon the crests of Kwahlamba and rested there for days the end might well have been different, and to-day there might have been no new nation ruled over by the son of Matyobane. It was a dangerous speech to utter into the ears of the Great Great One, for a King likes not to be reminded that there may be a mightier king than himself. It was a speech which, coming from the lips of many a man, might well have amounted to a prayer for death.

"Nations are like lions," replied Umzilikazi; "the stronger drives out the weaker, that it may keep its hunting-grounds for itself alone. The weaker, in turn, drives out the weaker still; and so things go on, and ever will go on."

"Not so, Black Elephant. The time will come—has come in some parts of the earth—when the strong no longer drive out the weak, but both shall sit down side by side in peace. There is One who gave His life that this should come to pass, and that all should be turned into the way of the truth. And He who thus suffered death to save a world was the Son of a King—a King beside whom the might of the mightiest King the earth ever saw is less than the weakness of a child beside the strength of an elephant. For He was the Son of God."

"What was He like? How did He die, the son of this mighty King?" said Umzilikazi.

"Thus, ruler of a nation which loves war. Thus."

And the white *isanusi* drew from his robe something we had beheld sticking in it, and had deemed some portion of his *múti* and held it out towards the King. And we, too, all saw it. It was a black cross, and upon it, fashioned in some shining metal, was stretched the Figure of a Man.

A gasp of astonishment went up from every throat; for we Zulus, *Nkose*, are always anxious to hear something new. *Au!* This was something new, if ever anything was.

"Seat thyself, father of the red *múti* cloak," said Umzilikazi, after we had gazed awhile upon this strange object. "Seat thyself, and tell us the tale of this marvel. I would fain hear of the doings of a King whose house was mightier than that of Senzangakona."

So the white stranger seated himself there beside the King and told his tale; and a wonderful tale it was, and long did it take in telling. *Whau, Nkose!* It was new then, though I have more than once heard it since from the lips of white preachers, but never did they tell it as this man told it whom we found, my brother and I, making strange *múti* and offering sacrifice in the forest.

But there was one side of that story which pleased not any of us, which pleased not the King, and this was the teaching that all men should live at peace. We looked at one another, we war-captains, and shook our heads as we tried to imagine ourselves even more helpless than the cowardly Bakoni, whose ways were the ways of peace. We looked at the Great Great One too, though guardedly, at those parts of a story which set forth that there could be a mightier King than himself. *Au!* The tale was good, as a tale; but these were not teachings we liked to listen to, we chief men among a warrior race whose greatness lay in war.

"It is a great tale!" said Umzilikazi, when we had listened for a long time; "a wonderful tale. And now, my father, I would fain behold this making of *múti* such as my *induna* Untúswa witnessed unawares. I would fain see thee offer sacrifice. Shall we go forth into the forest, or can it be offered here?"

"It can be offered anywhere, Elephant of the Amandebeli, by one who is qualified to offer it," answered the white *isanusi*. "But it is a very high and holy act, and cannot be offered twice upon the same day except under certain conditions, but not at all if food has been partaken of on that day."

This answer satisfied the King. But there were some among us who murmured that the will of the Great Great One should thus be crossed, saying it brought back the day when old Masuka first came into our midst, who, being desired to make *múti*, refused, on the ground that the moment was not propitious.

Now, whether Umzilikazi was thus reminded, or whether his ears caught some of our murmurings, I know not. But he gave orders that the Mosutu should be called.

"Here is another *isanusi*, Masuka," he said, when the old man appeared, murmuring words of *bonga*. "He is white, but I am not sure he is not a greater than thou."

"I am not the greatest of my kind the world ever saw, Lord. Perchance there may be greater," answered Masuka, darting a quick glance at the stranger with his bright and piercing eyes. "But can he make fire out of nothing, Great Great One? Can he make the thunder roar forth balls of flame into a black smoke out of nothing? Can he make the countenances of the enemies of the King show clear in a bowl? Can he do these things, O Elephant?"

But the white man showed no dismay, no anxiety. There was nothing about him of the *isanusi* who fears a more powerful rival still. He looked straight in the old Mosutu's face, and in his own was nothing but friendliness.

"Not in such spells do I deal, old man of a stranger race," he answered. "The Great Great One whom I serve loves not such. Yet thou—the *múti* thou usest is not generally for ill, and thy divinations are in favour of right and justice and for the well-being and safety of thy King and adopted nation. While this is so may it go well with thee."

"Ha!" we cried, amazed that this stranger should thus describe Masuka's *múti* with such wonderful exactness. And the King was greatly pleased at that saying, and the white man made a friend of the old Mosutu, who saw at once—as what did he not see?—that here was no rival claiming to be greater than himself and to steal away the favour of the King from him. In truth, also, *Nkose*, the words of the stranger were well said, for since Masuka had been made the father of the King's magic, few indeed of our people had been smelt out, and then only when they had been guilty of evil-doing, as in the case of the conspirators of Ncwelo's pool, whereas, formerly, our own *izanusi* were ever clamouring for "witch-findings," ever hungry as vultures for the flesh of men; wherefore, our nation loved the old Mosutu, and we who heard were glad because there was not to be another set up in his place.

"I see that the heart of the King is good towards me, and I

rejoice," said the white man before he withdrew. "For I would fain sow the seed of the Word of Life among this people before I travel South. Then there are those who shall return, and water and tend it, before a long time has gone by."

We saw a look steal over Umzilikazi's face at these words, and it was a look we knew.

"So it is thy purpose to travel to the South, my father?" said the King, speaking softly and low.

"Such is my purpose, Black Elephant," was the answer.

"Ha! the journey to the southward is long, and not over-safe," went on the King. "There are bad peoples and tribes who will do thee hurt, my father."

"That I must brave, Great Great One; for the soldiers of Him whom I serve often meet with hurt, and even death, in His service."

"Something was said but now about sowing the seed of the Word of Life among this people, my father," went on the King, still speaking softly, and with a strange look upon his face, as he gazed fixedly at the other. "Now, why should it not be sown among this people as well as among the peoples of the South?"

The face of the white *isanusi* lighted up for joy at these words. He replied:

"Great is the Mighty One who dwells above; who has put such into the mind of the King! Here, then will I dwell for a while, and the people of the Amandebeli shall drink by degrees of the Fountain of Life."

But while he thus praised, we, who listened, laughed secretly within ourselves, for we knew what thoughts were within the real mind of the King. And these were, that the day when the white *isanusi* was to start upon his travels for the dwellings of the peoples to the South should arrive never—no, never!

CHAPTER XV.

"LOST!"

Now, as time went by, this white *isanusi* still continued to dwell in our midst in great contentment, for the King ordered that his treatment should be of the best; and, indeed, it was so. From time to time he and the Gaza would offer sacrifice together, as we had first beheld it. Howbeit, he did not importune us with this new teaching, but busied himself in going in and out among the people, talking to them, and acting as a friend to all—even among the very lowest of the Amaholi and enslaved captives. To these he taught that there would come a time when they should be free—but the way to such freedom lay through the gates of death; and this caused the slaves to shake their heads and jeer. Their lives were hard, and they wanted to be free; but if the land of freedom was only to be reached through the gates of death, why, then they preferred to remain in the land of the Amandebeli. Yet among all was this white *isanusi* loved, because his words were ever soft and kind; and soon the name by which he became known among the people was that of "Father." There was one thing, too, which he never failed to bring into his teaching—and this was that, although the King was equally subject to the Great Great One who dwelt above the skies, yet the people were none the less bound to obey the "word" of the King and the orders of his *indunas* and captains. And, this being so, he retained the favour of Umzilikazi, who had set spies to watch him secretly, and report what his teachings really were.

It happened that a few days after his arrival among us the white stranger was with the King, for often would the Great Great One invite him to an *indaba*, that he might listen to wonderful tales of far countries beyond the sea. Yet when the *isanusi* would tell once more that marvellous tale which he had first told, and begin to set forth its teachings, Umzilikazi would laugh softly to himself, and bring round the talk to other matters. It happened, *Nkose*, that on the day I named, an idea seemed to strike the King.

"See, now, father of the strange *múti*," he said. "Do all the white people believe that great tale?"

We who were watching the stranger's face saw a troubled look come over it, as he answered that nearly all did.

"Do the Amabuna believe it?" went on the King.

"They believe it, Great Great One—but not the whole of it."

"Ha! Not the whole of it! They are a lying and treacherous race, deadly as a swarm of locusts! Say, my father, if they believed the whole of it, they would lie, and steal land, and make slaves no more?"

"That is so, Black Elephant."

The King smiled grimly to himself as he took snuff. We, too, smiled. Here were teachings which would never do for us—for although we of the Zulu race did not lie, yet we took land and slaves, even as the Amabuna did, and made war. Now these were customs we could not by any possibility give up. Then the Great Great One leaned over, and whispered a word to me.

Now the little white child we had taken from among the Amabuna was fast becoming one of ourselves. Yet not; for those with whom she played she would somehow cause to *konza* to her, even in their games, as though she were born to rule. If they played at building kraals, she it was whose hut was always the largest. If the boys were playing soldiers, it was always before her they came, singing the mimic war-song, and forcing the defeated side to *konza*. She reigned among them as a little queen. Even my two younger wives, who had the care of her, she seemed to rule. They would not, however, allow her to run wild with our children, but, as her clothing wore out, they made her garments of the softest of dressed fawnskins, ornamented largely with the most valued of beads. And now, as in obedience to the word of the King, I led the little one forth into his presence, and the stranger looked for the first time upon the fair skin and flower-like little face—the heaven-blue eyes, and hair like a stream of sunlight falling down the beaded robe of the child—he made as though he would have leaped from his seat.

"See now, my father," said the King, as the little one put up her hand and cried the *Bayéte*, "here is one of thine own colour, though but a tiny child. See now if thy story of the God of Peace is known in any way to her."

Now the white *isanusi* hardly waited for the word of the King, and the change which came upon him was strange indeed. He sprang to his feet, and advanced to the little one, who stared at him with her great blue eyes, yet did not shrink from him as in fear of a stranger. Then he put his hand over her head, and, looking upward and then down at her, his lips moved.

"*Au!* he is placing a spell upon her," growled one who sat near me.

"It is not a spell that will harm," murmured another in reply. But no more was said, for now the stranger was talking quick and fast in his own language, and the little one might have been his own child, long, long lost; for tears stood in his eyes as he talked, and soon rolled down upon his great beard. *Hau!* It was a strange sight. He wept, this white man who knew not fear: yes, here, in the presence of the King, and of we *izinduna* and war-captains, he wept, and that at the sight of a little blue-eyed child!

But here was another strange thing. The little one's face wore a blank look. Clearly she did not understand a word of what he was saying. Truly a strange thing! These two white people—the old man and the tiny girl—meeting thus by chance in the midst of our nation, understood not each other's tongue!

"Speak to her with the tongue of the Amabuna, my father," said the King.

But of this language the white *isanusi* had but scant knowledge, and in the end the only tongue with which these two whites could converse was that of the Amazulu. No, *Nkose*, not as yours was the tongue in which that *isanusi* spake. It was quicker—far quicker—and accompanied with more movements, like that of ourselves.[1]

"There, my father," said Umzilikazi. "The little one is of thine own colour. Now begin with her, and teach her about this strange God, which seems to me to be teaching more fitted for her than for us black ones."

The white man's face lighted up with joy at this permission, and he poured forth many words of praise for the goodness of the King. And we, too, we echoed the words of *bonga* with a loud voice. And the little one, she too seemed glad because of those words; and not

[1] That this travelling priest was of French nationality was somewhat confirmed, for on hearing that language spoken, although unable to recognise any specific word, Untúswa declared that it seemed to bring back to his mind something of the stranger's speech.—Mitford's note.

long after, in the presence of the King, and all who were then at
Kwa'zingwenya, the white *isanusi* performed strange ceremonies
over her, of which the principal seemed the sprinkling of water, and
declared she was now especially a child of that great God of whom
he had spoken. This Umzilikazi was very willing to sanction, for
was not the child white—and a girl? But when it came to teaching
warriors a belief that peace was better than war—*Au!* that was a very
different matter.

Now I had been kept so busy all this while, attending to the affairs
of the King and the nation, that no time had I to visit the mountain
of death and her who dwelt in the secret chamber thereof. Yet my
mind was ever in flight thither as I beheld its flat top standing out
through the haze afar off. Wherefore I resolved, for good or for ill,
to journey thither, as though to hunt.

Once well beyond the last outpost of our people I began to run,
travelling with a speed worthy the days when I was the King's chief
runner. At length I stood beneath the mountain and began to ascend
its slopes, and I sang softly to myself a song of gladness and of love
as I thought how soon I should be drinking in the strange sweet
sorcery of Lalusini's words and looks.

I had nearly gained the summit when a loud and savage growl
brought me up motionless in my own footprints, and, taking the
great Assegai in my right hand and advancing my small shield
forward a little in the left, I peered eagerly in search of the enemy.

Not a moment had I to look. The flaming eyes, the long, yellow
shape, the shaggy mane, almost blurred up as they were by the
brown of the mountain-side, represented nothing less than a lion—
an enormous one, crouching for a spring. There was no turning
aside. Face to face we had come, in this narrow gully. Neither could
give way. One must advance over the body of the other.

Whau, Nkose! This was no light matter; for to kill a full-grown
lion, single-handed, with spears only, is a business we never willingly undertake. But this one gave me no choice, for, with a savage
snarl, he launched himself into the air.

I know not how I avoided that onslaught; but I was quick in
those days, *Nkose*, quick as any wild beast. What I did was to run
in upon him, flinging myself *right under* his spring. Then, as he flew
over me, I flashed upright, and, poised on tip-toe, quick as lightning

I hurled one of my casting spears. It sang, quivering on its way, striking the mighty beast slantwise in the ribs and sinking deep. With terrible roars and snarls he rolled over and over, snapping at the spear-haft, and biting his own skin in the agony of his pain, and, the more he struggled, the deeper sank the spear. Now I saw what I would do. It would be quicker and far safer, and I did not want to brave over much danger just then. A great mass of loose rock stood poised upon a firmly embedded one immediately above the body of the lion, which, with hideous roars, was writhing and struggling beneath. Running to this, I mustered all my strength for a push. It swayed and tottered. Another mighty effort, the huge stone swung over and went crashing down the slope. The aim was good. With a frightful yell the great beast yielded up his life, and lay with ribs and spine shattered, while the rock tore down the mountain-side in leaps and bounds, splitting into fragments as it rolled.

"*Bayéte!*" I cried, in my exultation; for I had done something really great. "Hail, king of the plain and the mountain! A short burial shall first be thine."

Collecting stones, I piled them upon the sinewy frame of the mighty beast to protect it from the vultures; for I desired not to tarry then, so eager was I once more to behold Lalusini. Then, having gained the flat summit of the mountain, I took my way cautiously to the secret entrance of the sorceress's retreat.

And now, as I threaded the dark passage through the earth, I began softly to sing a song of love, which should let Lalusini know that I was coming. But there came back no answering song. *Whau, Nkose!* Warrior as I was, I felt weak then, and my pulses began to beat. I sprang down into the great rock hollow. It was empty.

Then I felt like a man who would willingly die, so strong was the witchery of the spell which this sorceress of Zulu blood had woven around me. I called her by name, first softly, then louder, for I thought she might be doing this to try me, and, even then, might be watching me from somewhere, and laughing to herself at my discomfiture. Still, no answer.

Then a hideous thought took possession of my mind. That great lion I had slain! Had not Lalusini herself made mention of having heard its voice rolling upon the mountain at night? Had she not expressed some fear lest the beast might find its way in through the tunnel? As a man who has gone mad, I sprang to the hole and examined the ground for traces. But there were none—none such as would have been left by a lion forcing his way in, and returning, dragging a heavy body. So the possession of my senses returned, and I fell to making an investigation of the place. Ha! The mystery was a mystery no longer. Lalusini had, indeed, gone, but she had departed of her own free will, for most of the articles necessary to her comfort, such as clothing, cooking utensils, and so forth, had disappeared.

Yes, *Nkose*; my heart was sore within me. Whither had she gone? Was it to return once more to that great, yet distant, people, among whom she had promised to make me great? Wearied with the length of time I had been forced to leave her unvisited—in the light of my hesitation to agree to throw in my lot with hers under such mad circumstances of peril and hazard—had she decided to leave me altogether? It seemed like it. Yet, I would track her—would find her. And then I laughed at myself for a fool, for how knew I, after all this time, which way to turn to seek her? She might be far away by that time.

Sore at heart, I went up into the outer day again, and there upon the summit of the mountain I sought long and hard for footprints. But I sought in vain. There were none. Lalusini might have vanished like a bird into the air. All that day I searched. There might be other hiding-places upon the mountain, even more secret than the one which was known only to me and to her. But if this was so I know not. I only know that, search as I would, no trace could I find of such.

Then I went down again into the rock hollow to pass the night, thinking she might chance to return. But when I lay down to sleep, sleep would not come, or if it did, only so lightly as to be more wakefulness than sleep; and it seemed that the face of the beautiful sorceress hung over me in my dreams, but when I would start to clasp her, calling her by name, there was nothing, no sound but the howling of beasts, ravening upon the mountain slopes throughout the night. And when the sun rose at last, then mounted higher into the sky, and still Lalusini did not return, I knew then that I had lost her forever, that never would I behold her more.

So, with heart heavy and sore, I dragged myself away from the place, and returning to where I had left the dead lion, cut off the head and forepaws and the tail-tuft of the mighty beast, and, thus laden, took my way back to Kwa'zingwenya, sorrowing exceedingly for the loss of her who had thus bewitched me.

CHAPTER XVI.

A LIFE FOR TEN LIVES.

I RETURNED to Kwa'zingwenya with the head and paws of the great lion I had slain, and those who beheld it envied, crying, "What a hunter is Untúswa! In the chase, as in war, his is the weapon beneath which falls the mightiest!" The King, too, was pleased when he beheld those trophies. But Nangeza, seeing them, said:—

"Ah, ah, Untúswa. Thy skill is in truth wonderful, who went forth to find a young heifer and found an old lion."

This she said jeering, and with her eyes upon my face. But I, while affecting not to notice, found food for much thought in the words. Had Nangeza indeed discovered my secret? Was she concerned in the disappearance of Lalusini? Ha! I resolved to watch her narrowly, and were my suspicions verified, why then, indeed, there would be room in my house for a new *inkosikazi*.

Now at this time, things being quiet and our nation settling down in its new land, I gained the King's leave to build myself a kraal some little distance from Kwa'zingwenya, and thither I removed with all my possessions—my cattle and my wives—and my brother Mgwali also came with me with his wives, and two other sons of my father, and soon I was the head of a large kraal of a score and a half of huts. But as time went on, and my duties in the way of seeing to the strength and efficiency of my own half of the army became greater, so far from beginning to think less of Lalusini I thought of her more. In the sunshine, darting in gold through the forest trees, it seemed that I could see her eyes, in the soft whispers of the wind at evening I could hear her voice. In my dreams I beheld her, was with her. *Au!* I was bewitched indeed. But although I made more than one journey again to the mountain of death, never did I discover any sign which should show she had revisited her hiding-place. All there had fallen more and more into decay, as though she had gone never to return.

"Of a truth, Untúswa, thou shouldst be an *izanusi* thyself," said the King one day when we were sitting alone together in debate.

"Thou hast a gift for finding *izanusi* and bringing them hither—first Masuka, now this white stranger; concerning which last my mind is in darkness, for I know not what to do with him."

"Is he not content, Black Elephant? Does he not fare well among us, teaching those who care to listen—ah, ah! those who care to listen?" I added with meaning.

"For a time yes," said Umzilikazi. "But the day will come when he will desire to travel again."

"Let him travel back by the way he came, Calf of a Black Cow," I answered, still with meaning. "For him the way of the South is not safe. There indeed are peoples that would do him harm."

The Great Great One shook his head in discontent.

"Verily, Untúswa, I know not how this will end," he said.

"Let be for the present, my father," I answered. "The stranger is happy now, teaching the slaves. It may be that things will right themselves in this matter."

I spoke darkly, *Nkose*, not seeing light. But both I and the Great Great One little guessed in what manner things would right themselves, and that at no great distance of time—ah, no! little could we foresee that.

Now this was the meaning which underlay my words relating to the white *isanusi* and his teaching of the slaves. The last thing the King desired was that this white man should journey South, to bear, mayhap, the word to the Amabuna or to Dingane: "Yonder, to the North, in a fair and well-watered land, dwells Umzilikazi, and his warriors number so many, of whom a large proportion are of no account—being dogs and slaves." The white stranger and the Gaza, Ngubazana, were but two men: what easier than to kill them secretly and thus end all trouble? There were not wanting some among the *izinduna* who spoke darkly to this end. But to such counsels Umzilikazi's ears were shut. The white stranger was his friend. He was not of the race of the greedy, lying Amabuna; moreover, for himself it was easy to see he desired nothing, neither lands nor possessions; and though his teachings were not such as to be accepted by a warrior nation, there was no harm in them, no subversion of the greatness of the King. Not upon any considerations should he be harmed—neither the Gaza, his follower.

But he must be kept among us; and in furtherance of this end the

King gave secret orders that a few of the lowest of the slaves should listen to his teaching, and slowly and by degrees bring themselves to accept it, or pretend to. Then a few more were added to these; but ever with caution, lest the white *isanusi* should suspect. But he did not suspect; on the contrary, his heart was filled with joy at the readiness wherewith these received his teaching, and at length—for this took time—he put them under the same rites as those which he had performed over the little white girl. So he was content to dwell with us; and while we laughed among ourselves over the trick we had played upon him, yet we were glad that this other road lay open to him besides that to the South, which would have caused us trouble, and that into the Dark Unknown, which might have caused it to him.

I had left Kwa'zingwenya after this *indaba* with the King, and was returning to my own kraal along the river bank, sad at heart, and pondering ever upon the disappearance of the Bakoni sorceress, when I came upon an old man, stumbling along, bent double, nosing and peering on the ground. It was old Masuka.

"Greeting, my father!" I cried. "Are you seeking *múti* herbs?"

"Perhaps I am seeking for that which shall give sleep, son of Ntelani," he replied, laughing at me out of his eyes. "Ha! my dreams were strange last night—strange, and they were about thee, Untúswa, about thee!"

"About me, my father?" I cried.

"E—*hé!* But, first give me *gwai*, thou holder of the King's Assegai, for I have none left."

I took out the long horn snuff-box which was stuck through the lobe of my ear, and, squatting down, we both took snuff in silence. Then the old man burst into a chuckle.

"My dreams took me to the summit of the mountain of death, son of Ntelani. The ghost of Tauane was there—searching for something."

"For what was it searching, my father?"

"For a strange thing. For an outward chamber in the cliff, like unto the place of an eagle's nest."

"Ha!" I cried, staring at him wildly, my snuff-spoon in mid-air.

How his old eyes laughed; for my confusion was great. And well it might be, for these were the very words wherewith I had taunted the chief of the Blue Cattle on his flaming bed of death. Yet old Masuka had been nowhere near at that time, nor had any who understood that tongue.

"And why could not the ghost of Tauane find that place, my father?" I said. "Being a ghost, he could fly through the air until he found the chamber in the cliff like an eagle's nest."

"Not thus would he find it, destroyer of the Bakoni," was the answer. "'Through the darkness of the earth'—such were his words."

"Ha! Was it for good or for ill he spoke thus? Were those all the words of Tauane's ghost, my father?"

"Not so, Untúswa. Soon the ghost went winging through the air, crying and wailing that the place like an eagle's nest was there, but that the she-eagle had flown away. Why art thou sad of late, son of Ntelani?"

"Thy *múti* is wonderful, father," I replied. "Will the she-eagle return? Tell me. Will it return?"

"It will return. Ha! yonder alligators are hungry. They shall be fed. Oh, yes, they shall be fed. The she-eagle will return."

I liked not his tones, *Nkose*, and my blood ran chill. For his speech, though dark, could have but one meaning. Lalusini I should behold again; but one or both of us should find death in the alligators' pool. Well, what matter? One could but die once; and so great was the spell cast over me by the Bakoni sorceress that it seemed, once more to behold her, once more to have speech with her, I would gladly pay the price of death.

"I have a black cow, well in milk, which is one too many in my herd, father," I said. "It shall be driven forth to-morrow to the place where thy cattle graze."

But he paid scant heed, which was strange, for he loved cattle, and always welcomed such gifts. With his head on one side, as though listening intently, he repeated softly to himself:

"Yonder alligators are hungry. They shall be fed; oh, yes, they shall be fed!"

You will remember, *Nkose*, a certain pool in the river, which the King and I had lighted upon one evening soon after arriving at our new resting-place, and into which he had caused some calves to be driven that the alligators might seize them. Now this pool had been turned into a place of execution. No longer were those adjudged to doom led forth to die beneath the knobsticks of the slayers, as formerly, but were forced to leap, or were thrown into the pool, and from it none emerged alive. As I sat and talked with Masuka, I remembered that the Pool of the Alligators lay at no great distance from us, and between ourselves and the great kraal. Upon it the old Mosutu seemed to be concentrating his attention; and, as I listened, sounds were wafted thence.

"Evil-doers are about to meet death!" he said, at last. "Come, we will witness it."

We rose and took our way along the river-bank. As we crested the rise, which brought us near the brow of the cliff from which the victims were thrown, we saw a multitude streaming down from the great kraal, and in the forefront of the crowd were men armed with sticks, and driving before them two other men, who were bound.

These were already half-dead with fear, and could scarcely walk, but the blows of the slayers urged them onward until they stood right upon the spot whence they should leap into the jaws of the hungry alligators. We could see at a glance that they were slaves, and sadly, indeed, they looked. From the people we learned that these two, being in charge of a flock of the King's goats, had suffered wild dogs to break into the fold at night, whereby upwards of a score were slain. So Umzilikazi, declaring that if his goats were only fit to feed wild dogs with, assuredly two base Bakoni were only fit to feed alligators with; and they had been led forth.

Now, this scene did not move us in any way, *Nkose*, for the death of a slave more or less was nothing. But we just lingered to see these leap in.

Yet they would not. When driven to the edge they hung back, then cast themselves on the ground weeping and groaning for mercy. Already the surface of the pool below was alive with slimy, stealthy life. Widening lines upon the water told that the alligators well understood the cause of the tumult overhead. They moved silently to and fro, awaiting the plunge which should bring them the prey they had learned to love best—the flesh of men.

Now the slayers had grasped the screaming wretches, and were about to fling them out, when between the cliff brow and the victims a figure suddenly sprang forth, arising, as it were, by magic. All gave a shout of wonder, and the executioners paused in their work. The black robe, the long, flowing beard, the countenance stamped with a great horror and pain, were known to all. It was the white *isanusi*.

"Hold! my children!" he cried. "Hold! I beg of you!"

The slayers hesitated, and growled to each other. With arms outstretched, there the white man stood on the cliff brow between the hideous, hungry reptiles and their weeping, shivering victims. To fling these in was impossible without flinging him in too.

"It is the King's will, father," growled the chief of the slayers. "Know you not that did we hesitate we should be even as these? Stand aside."

"Not yet, not yet," he pleaded; and there was weeping in his voice. "Not yet. Wait—only until I hasten to the King! He will hear me, for he has given me the lives of such as these!"

"It may not be, father," was the answer, made now with more alarm. "*Whau!* it is on us the *izingwenya* will feed, if not on these. Stand now aside."

"Ah! have pity! Untúswa will take my side," he cried in a glad voice, catching sight of my face. "Stay their hands, Untúswa, if only for a while, till I bring back the King's pardon."

"It may not be, father," I, too, replied. "The King's sentence has been given. It is even as the men say. Their lives are as the lives of these if they hesitate. Would you doom to death many men where two will suffice? Let them do their work."

Now, I know not, *Nkose*, how this thing would have ended; for the white *isanusi* still continued to stand and plead, and none dare remove him by force, remembering in what high honour he was held by the Great Great One. But just then loud shouting made itself heard upon the outskirts of the crowd, which bent low suddenly, like a forest struck by a gale. And there advancing, with his head thrown back and a light in his eyes such as none of us cared to behold, came the Great Great One himself.

He stalked straight up to where stood the white *isanusi*, to where lay the doomed ones and the executioners, who, having hesitated to perform their work, counted themselves already dead. He was attended by the old *induna* Mcumbete, to whom he now turned.

"See," he said, in a voice which made many tremble, "I am no King. I am only the lowest of the Amaholi. For the word of a King is obeyed; yet my word, though long since uttered, is not obeyed. *Hau!* What sort of a King am I?"

And the terrible frown of anger upon his face took in the white man, even as it did ourselves.

"Mercy! Great Great One! Mercy for these!" cried the stranger, pointing to the doomed slaves.

We who watched trembled for the life of the speaker; those of us who did not tremble for our own—and of these there could be but few—for this was a terrible thing which had happened, such a thing as had never before been known, that any man, white or black, should dare to interfere between the king's decrees and their execution. But still the white priest stood upon the brink of that grisly pool of death pleading forgiveness, not for himself, but for those two miserable slaves. Ha! That was a sight indeed.

"You do not know us yet, O stranger!" went on Umzilikazi, now in bitter and sneering tones; "else had you not thought to save the lives of these two by any such means. For now have you doomed many to death, even all those whose errand it was to carry out my sentence and have allowed themselves to hesitate in doing so. For they, too, are dead men."

A gasp of horror, which was almost a sob, ran through the multitude. The *izimbonga* bellowed aloud in praise of the King's justice; but even their voices were not without a quaver. But the white priest stood facing the angry countenance of the King; and upon his own was stamped a great and deep sadness, but never a trace of fear.

"Be merciful, thou ruler of a great nation!" he pleaded more earnestly. "Mercy is the quality by which a King may show himself truly great. We have been friends. Oh, slay not these men, when the fault is entirely mine."

"Not entirely. The fault of the man who hesitates to obey my word is entirely his own, and the penalty thereof he knows," said Umzilikazi, pitilessly. "We have been friends, white stranger; but of what sort is the friendship which teaches those who are my dogs to laugh at me? Friend as thou art, I know not how thine own life shall be left thee after such an act as this."

Something in the words seemed to strike the white *isanusi*. His face lightened up.

"See now, O King!" he replied. "The fault is mine. If I am a traitor in your eyes, who were my friend, take my life instead of the lives of these. Take my life, but spare theirs."

"Ha!"

The gasp of amazement which softly left the lips of the King was echoed by a shiver from the crouching multitude.

"Think carefully, O stranger," he said. "Look below. See the upturned glare of the alligators' eyes. Mark their number—their great size—their hideous shapes. This is no pleasant or easy death."

"Nor is it for these, Great Great One," was the reply, with a sweep of the hand over the doomed men, who, victims and executioners alike, crouched motionless in the silence of despair. "And for them such a death may be more terrible than for myself, who humbly trust that it may be the opening of the gate of a new life whose glories are beyond words."

"I think words enough have been spoken upon this matter," said Umzilikazi, coldly. "Take thy choice, white *isanusi*. Thyself to the alligators—or these."

"My choice is made, Black Elephant."

"Leap, then!" said the King, with a wave of the hand towards the brink.

"I may not do that," was the reply, "for it would be to take my own life, which my teaching forbids. The slayers of the King must throw me in—that they themselves may live. But, first, I desire a few moments wherein to pray that the Great Great One above may receive my spirit."

To this Umzilikazi gave assent, and the white priest knelt down, and, drawing out the cross, with the Figure of a Man upon it, he kissed this. And then, for the first time, some of us noticed that the sign he made upon himself with his hand more than once was in form even as that cross.

Whau, Nkose! that was a strange sight—stranger, I think, I never beheld. The sun was near his rest now, and his fading beams fell upon the surface of the hideous pool beneath, painting it and the numerous snouts of the hungry monsters lurking there as it were blood-red. And above the crouching, awe-stricken multitude—the only movement among which was the rolling of distended eyeballs, the grovelling figures of the doomed ones, grey with fear, and not knowing yet if their lives would indeed be spared—the stern, upright figure of Umzilikazi, terrible in the offended majesty of his disobeyed commands, and the subdued, shrinking countenance of the old *induna*. And, in the midst of all, the kneeling priest, in his black, flowing robe, the tones of whose voice, rising and falling quickly in prayer, being the only sounds breaking in upon this dead and awesome silence. And to us who gazed it seemed as though a strange light rested upon the face of the white *isanusi*, imparting to it a look which had nothing in common with the set, motionless expression to be seen upon the face of a brave man doomed to die; but this might have been caused by the long rays of the setting sun darting upon it. At length he arose.

The King made a sign to the slayers. Not this time was any hesitation to be found among them. Leaping eagerly to their feet, they sprang forward and laid hands upon the white priest.

"A moment!" said this one, signing them back. "Bid me now farewell, son of Matyobane! for I wish thee no harm on account of my death, and for it I forgive thee freely. Nay, more, I thank thee for it! since, through it, thou sparest the lives of these, who number more than half a score."

He stretched forth his open hand. Umzilikazi grasped it, yet let it not go; and thus for a moment they stood, gazing into each other's faces. And that of the white man expressed the truth of his words; for in it was no evil look, no sign of fear, or of a desire for revenge. Still they stood thus, uttering no sound. The strain was becoming terrible. In crushed, breathless silence the multitude hung upon what was to follow. Was the King bewitched? Could he not relax his grasp? A dull splash was heard beneath, as one of the alligators turned on the water. And now the sun rested on the western heights, like a wheel of red flame. Then Umzilikazi spoke:

"The alligators may go hungry this night, for thou art a brave man, my father; too brave a man that thy life should pay for the miserable lives of such as these. Yet for thy sake I will spare them too, though I know not whether after doing so I am a King or as one of their dogs!—*Hau!*"

"A greater King than ever, son of Matyobane," was the reply, uttered solemnly. "The Great One above will bless thee, my friend."

Now the shouts of *bonga* which rent the air were deafening, and from one end to the other of that vast multitude rolled the praises of the mercy of the King. And, indeed, it was wonderful, for this was the only occasion upon which I ever knew Umzilikazi spare any man when his "word" had once gone forth that that man should die. And this time he had spared upwards of half a score, owing to the strange madness of a white priest who had offered to give his own life for theirs.

But some there were who murmured darkly that the King was bewitched, and among these were our own *izanusi*. Yet they dared not so whisper otherwise than darkly—ah, yes, very darkly indeed.

CHAPTER XVII.

THE RETURN OF THE "SHE-EAGLE."

Now, *Nkose*, I am about to tell of the strange and momentous events that next befell; for upon reaching my home that night, which you will remember was at some little distance from the great kraal, I found my family and followers in a state of wild consternation and grief. The little white girl was lost!

She had not been wandering, not even playing outside with the other children. When last seen she was creeping through the door of the hut wherein she usually dwelt—that of Fumana, the youngest of my wives—and this hut she had never been seen to leave. When last seen it was shortly before the setting of the sun.

This was a matter to be turned inside-out, and that speedily, to which end I called up all those concerned, and questioned them one by one; the children who had last been with her, my wives, and the Bakoni slave-girls. But while my two younger wives were half-mad with grief—for they loved the little one—Nangeza only laughed evilly, saying that it could be but a small thing to a mighty chief like myself the loss of a wretched little whelp of the Amabuna: for thus she would often speak to anger me, knowing that I always held Kwelanga to be not of the Amabuna at all, but of a far greater race.

"So, woman!" I replied, pointing my stick at her menacingly, "it may be a small matter to myself, but it will be a weighty one for all here concerned, for did not the King give Kwelanga into our care? Ha! the alligators have been robbed of their food to-night—it may be that to-morrow they will be full."

I could see fear upon the faces of those who heard my words; but again Nangeza laughed evilly. I was resolved now that the end of such doings had come. The morrow would show.

"Now to the search!" I cried. "The little one may have wandered abroad and have sunk down to sleep in the forest. She may not be far."

"Perhaps yonder moves her bed," said Nangeza, with her black laugh, as the wild howling of a hyæna sounded very near. "While

such are moving about it is little enough will be found of any child
who has sunk down to sleep in the forest, and it has long been
night."

A murmur of approval greeted these words, for few among us
liked to move about at night. And the voices of the hyænas and other
beasts wailing dismally through the forest sounded as the ravenings
of ghost animals scenting the blood of those who still lived as men.
But for such considerations I cared little then. I gave my orders, and
no man there but preferred to face the ghost animals to facing me
having disobeyed them. So we set out, by twos and threes, on our
search.

There was a half-moon low down in the heavens, and by its
light we searched—ah, yes, how we searched! We hunted hither
and thither like wild dogs questing a scent, beneath the dark shades
of the forest trees, where the beasts would howl dismally across
our path, and the rustle of huge serpents fleeing away in the brake
would make our hearts leap—not knowing what evil beings of the
night were abroad. We searched over the openness of the plain, and
among the rugged rocks where we had found the white *isanusi*. We
searched indeed far out beyond any distance such a little child could
travel. But we searched in vain.

Not only through the night did we search, but well on into the
next day. Sometimes our hearts would chill as we saw something
white, like a skull or bones, lying away from us, but on drawing
near it would prove to be a stone, or perchance the skull of a kid or
a buck, devoured by wild animals. I sent runners to all the outlying
kraals around us but these returned bearing no news, and at last so
thoroughly had we searched that I was constrained to believe that
it was as Nangeza had so evilly suggested—the little one had wandered away from the kraal, and, having lost herself, had been carried
off or devoured by wild animals.

Now my own heart was sad and sore, for, *Nkose*, I loved this
little creature, with the eyes of heaven and hair like the sun, whom
I had saved from the spears of our young men, and who had come
to look upon me as her father; and, indeed, she would sometimes
place her tiny white hand upon my great dark one and laugh, and
ask whether hers would grow black, too, when she became old. And
now I should see her no more; hear her rippling, joyous laughter

never again—ah, *Nkose*, my heart was very sore. But my younger wives, Nxope and Fumana, they made terrible moan, far more so than they would have made over child of their own blood.

It came about, however, that some there might have even greater reason to make moan, and that on behalf of themselves; for at day-dawn on the third morning after the disappearance of Kwelanga an armed force stood at the gate of my kraal, and in a loud voice summoned those within the huts to come forth in the King's name.

Now, many of these, looking upon the armed men, felt themselves already dead, deeming that Umzilikazi had sent to "eat up" my kraal, by reason of the manner in which its trust had been fulfilled; nor was I myself for the moment at ease.

"Greeting, Ngubu!" I said. "What is the will of the Great Great One?"

"This, son of Ntelani," answered the leader of the armed band, that same Ngubu who had headed the party in pursuit of me that time I had fled with Nangeza, and who was present when I slew Njalo-njalo; "this—that thou betakest thyself at all speed to the Black Elephant, who would confer with thee. That for thee. For these, they must go with us, every one, to the last man, woman, and child."

"Whither, Ngubu?" I asked, troubled. "Into the Dark Unknown?"

"Not so, Untúswa. Into the presence of the King."

They looked relieved at this I thought, though it might be but the lengthening out of their agony, for the assegais of the "eaters-up" are swifter than the teeth of the alligators. And so they started, hemmed in by the spears of the warriors, while I alone strode on in advance, by no means easy in my mind because of what was to befall, for some, assuredly, would look into darkness long before that night.

A little way outside the great kraal Kwa'zingwenya was a grassy mound, crested by two large and spreading trees, and from this the plain sloped away, smooth and open, to the brink of the cliff over-hanging the Pool of the Alligators. Beneath the shade of these trees Umzilikazi was wont to sit sometimes throughout the whole day, hearing and settling disputes, talking over the affairs of the nation, or it might be reviewing one or two of the young regiments practis-ing drill upon the open plain before him. Here now I found him.

"Well, Untúswa? And so there have been *tagati* doings at your kraal?" he said, when I had saluted. "Where is Kwelanga?"

"Now are all our hearts sore, Black Elephant," I answered, "for search has been diligently made, but in vain."

"Yet I gave her into your keeping, son of Ntelani. There has been *tagati* herein, and some shall die."

"The will of the Great Great One is the delight of his children," I replied. "Lo—now here are they who must answer for this business."

Now there came in sight across the plain the whole company of my people, surrounded by the spears of the warriors who custodied them. All, as they drew near, bent low before the King, shouting aloud the *Bayéte*, and on every face was stamped varying stages of fear and dread.

"Here has been *tagati* at work," said the King, after eyeing them in silence for a few moments. "I think, Untúswa, the women it was who had the care of Kwelanga?"

"That is so, Black Elephant," I answered.

"There are thy three wives and two Bakoni slave-girls—five in all," went on the King. "Five women, and they are not able to custody one little child! Ha! If a woman is unable to do this, of what use is she? Not to give us the aid of her counsels in war," with a frown at Nangeza. "Clearly these are of no use at all. Away with them! The alligators are hungry!"

But before the slayers could spring forward, my two younger wives flung themselves on the ground at the King's feet.

"Spare us, father!" they wailed.

"She who is gone was more to me than my own children," howled Fumana.

"Our own children will die of grief for loss of her," groaned Nxope.

"Spare us, Great Great One, that we may never rest until she is found," cried Fumana.

"No *tagati* is there among us two, Father—among us two," screamed Nxope.

"What mean you—witch? Ha, Nangeza, *inkosikazi* of Untúswa! Hast thou nothing to say, no tears for Kwelanga—for thine own life?"

While the others had thus been bemoaning and praying for mercy, Nangeza was watching them with contempt in her eyes, which latter would flash into the most intense hate and menace as she met my glance. Now she answered:

"I have much to say, if the King will hear it—ah, much to say"; and her glittering eyes sought my face in the triumph of their hate.

"I think we have heard enough of this babble," said Umzilikazi, with a bitter sneer; for he loved not women, deeming them, though in some ways necessary, yet of no account whatever, and only producing mischief if allowed to raise their voices at all. But even the Great Great One had reckoned without the length of Nangeza's tongue. Hardily she went on:

"There has been *tagati* indeed; but not among us wives of Untúswa must such be sought. Ho, Untúswa! Where is the witch thou didst save alive from the slaughter of the Bakoni? Ha, ha, Untúswa, where is she?"

Now, *Nkose*, my heart turned to water within me; for such a suspicion, once implanted in the King's mind, would surely bear fruit sooner or later. And the offence was among the most deadly I could commit. But at the words, I laughed; threw back my head and laughed softly, while murmurs of amazement went up from those who heard.

"Hear you the words of this woman, Untúswa?" said the King.

"I hear them, Black Elephant."

"They are strange words, son of Ntelani. Hast thou no answer to make to them?"

"Now, my Father, who am I that I should weary the ears of the Great Great One by crossing answers with a woman in his presence?" I cried.

"That is well said," muttered Umzilikazi. Then aloud, "So, woman, where doth she dwell, this witch whom Untúswa saved alive from the slaughter of the Bakoni?"

"Upon the Mountain of Death, the mountain whereon her people were slain," said Nangeza.

"And how is she named?"

"That I know not, O Elephant; but if Untúswa ever whispers her name in his sleep, it is Fumana or Nxope you should ask, O Calf of a Black Bull," she said, in a tone full of meaning and of malice.

Now I thought and thought how Nangeza could have obtained even that amount of knowledge of my secret. Could she have followed me, stealthily, the last journey I made to the Mountain of Death? It almost seemed so. Or had she set others on to watch me? Anyhow, I felt not over-certain of seeing many more suns set.

"And is that all thou hast to say, wife of Untúswa?" said the King, softly, and putting his head on one side, as his manner was.

"This, too, Father. For many nights past I have heard, as it were, a woman's voice singing around our kraal. I doubt not it was the voice of this witch, and that she hath lured the little one into the forest, to devour her, as the way is with such evil-doers. But it is Untúswa who has brought her about our ears to blight us with a curse."

"In truth, thou art an excellent wife—a very milch-cow of price," said the King, mocking her. "In truth, it is worth a man's while to throw away his life for such as thee. Thou art, indeed, worthy to be the chief wife of one of my best fighting-captains. Thou who wouldst seek to throw on to his shoulders the consequences of thine own neglect, and fill up our ears with such childish tales of witches singing around the gates! And thou, Untúswa, thou art happy, indeed, in the possession of such! Well, woman, such babble is of no avail. The alligators are hungry."

The *izimbonga* raised a chorus of praise, and the frightened company of my people, seeing that only five of their number were to suffer, joined in. And now, bending low before the King, I craved a boon.

"The wisdom of the King is great, and his justice is terrible," I said. "But these, it is for these I would speak," pointing to my younger wives.

"Say on, Untúswa," said the King.

"Not for me is it to question the will of the Great Great One. But I would ask, Father, that these might be spared, at any rate, for a few days longer. It may yet be that Kwelanga is found, and then, my Father, what will she do, finding that those who took care of her are no more?"

"Strange care have they taken of her, Untúswa," replied Umzilikazi. "Hold! Whom have we here?"

For over the plain a great multitude was advancing. As it drew nearer, we could make out that at some paces in front of it walked a woman. That she was tall and straight, and beautiful of build, we could see even from there. Nearer—nearer, she drew; advancing direct to where was seated the Great Great One. In silence the people parted to make way for her, and, not hesitating a moment, she paced up to the King, her head thrown slightly back, proud, stately of bearing, as though she were a queen. Then, halting, she bent down, yet not very low, and cried, "*Bayéte!*" And we who looked thought we had never beheld so fair and gracious a type of womanhood; while I, for my part——*Whau Nkose!* it seemed as though the end of all things was at hand, for she upon whom I now gazed—upon whom we all gazed—standing there before the King, was none other than Lalusini, the beautiful sorceress who had bewitched me with her love.

CHAPTER XVIII.

IN DARK WARNING.

THERE she stood—she on whom my thoughts had dwelt day and night—she for whom I had sought so carefully and yet so fruitlessly—she whom I had never expected to behold again. There she stood, and as quick murmurs of amazement, of admiration, went up from all who beheld, her eyes swept around our circle and rested upon my face—yet hardly rested—for in them there was no brightening, no recognition. She looked at me as she looked at the others—as though she had never seen me before.

Now I remembered Masuka's strange, dark, prophecy—how that the "she-eagle" should return, but that then the alligators should be fed. The King would remember the name as spoken by Tauane—and that, coupled with Nangeza's accusation, ah—good night! Well, I cared not. I, like others, leaned eagerly forward as I crouched, straining my eyes to gaze upon the beauty of the sorceress. Yet even then, while her glance was not directly meeting mine, I seemed to read in her eyes an unspoken, yet none the less vividly-flashed, message—even as I had read the glance of old Masuka that dreadful day upon which I stood between the King's assegai and doom. And the language I read in this glance was—"Caution!"

She was attired in the short, apron-like girdle of the Bakoni, ornamented with rich bead-work, and a light mantle of dressed fawn-skin similarly adorned hung from one shoulder. As when I saw her first, she wore upon her arms and neck bands of solid gold, after the manner of the richer of the Bakoni, and her hair was gathered up from the scalp into a high cone as the Zulu women wear it.

"Who art thou, my sister?" said the King, not choosing to show the astonishment which even he felt.

"I am of the Bakoni, Great Great One. I am called Lalusini," she answered in purest Zulu.

"Of the Bakoni? Lalusini? *Hau!* That is no name ever brought forth of the twisted tongues of those chattering dogs. It is a full ripe Zulu name, born of the race of the Heavens," returned the King.

"Say now, Lalusini. What wert thou among the Bakoni dogs whom we have stamped flat? A prisoner?"

"Yea and nay, Black Black One. I was the Queen of their *múti*."

"Ha! Yet another magician! It seems that all the magicians in the world find their way, or are brought here: first old Masuka, then the white man—now this one," said Umzilikazi. "Ha, Untúswa—thou magician-finder! How is it thou didst not find this one—thou who didst find the rest?"

I only made murmur, for I guessed that the King was mocking me. And the moment was in truth a trial as he went on—

"Say now, Queen of the Bakoni *múti*. How didst thou escape death or capture when my children stamped flat thy people?"

"By the name thou spakest just now, Black Elephant—Queen of the Bakoni *múti*. Now of what use is *múti* if it fails in the day of necessity?"

"Thy story I will yet hear," answered the King. "Now say, Lalusini, knowest thou Untúswa?"

"Untúswa? I seem to have heard that name. Surely it was that of the King's messenger, who with only one young man, and he unringed, did hold the Bakoni in defiance like a lion at bay."

"And thou hast not beheld him since that day?"

"I think not, Great Great One—and that day only from afar did I behold him. Nay I saw him once at the council, and then nearer. He was a tall man, who carried a very large spear."

"Look around, my sister, and tell me if he is here to-day," said the King.

Lalusini looked first among such groups of warriors as were mustered around. Then she stepped over to the assemblage of *izinduna* among whom I sat, and looked long and earnestly. Umzilikazi, meanwhile, was watching her narrowly.

"I think that is the King's messenger," she said, gazing into my face. "He has the look of such a warrior as that one was."

But before anything more could be said Nangeza sprang forward, and her eyes were glittering with hate, and in her voice was a snarl as that of a wild beast.

"She is the witch whom Untúswa saved from the slaughter, reserving her for himself. Look, O King! Now they pretend not to know each other," shrieked Nangeza, darting her hand furiously forth as though it contained a weapon.

Now, *Nkose*, it was a dreadful moment for me, for at first there was dead silence. All were too amazed even to exclaim. I merely uttered a disdainful click, shaking my head. But Lalusini—she turned towards Nangeza, glanced her up and down, and laughed—laughed softly, musically. Then, waving her hands into the air, she began to sing, and the words were in the tongue of the Bakoni, which none there present understood. Yet her voice was musical and sweet, and in it there thrilled a mystery. All watched in silence as she moved her hands and feet to the measure of her chant. Since I understood this tongue, *Nkose*, I listened as though a great serpent were tightening its coils more and more around me, for her words were dark and full of a strange and terrifying mystery. Her song ceased.

"What dost thou seek here now, my sister?" softly said the King, for even he could not refuse to acknowledge the influence of her charm. "Is it to make *múti* among thine own people, having had enough of the Bakoni dogs whom we have eaten up?"

"I think there are enough who make such *múti* here, Black Elephant," she answered. "Not for this have I come. I am here to save the Father of a new nation."

"*Hau!*" we gasped, stricken well-nigh dumb, for the words were spoken slow and sad, and with weighty warning. None doubted but that they applied to a near attack on the part of our most to be dreaded enemies, and at once all men's minds flew to the *impis* of Dingane advancing upon us in force—or, perhaps, the Amabuna, or even both in concert. Dismay was on every face, for we liked not to be thus taken by surprise. But upon that of Umzilikazi was a frown of terrible import, which meant badly for those from whose quarter the foe should first appear, they having failed to report it.

"Thy words are dark indeed," he said. "Explain, sorceress, for time does not wait."

But Lalusini, for reply, only returned a swift, silent glance. Then once more she burst into song, again in the Bakoni tongue. Her head was thrown back, and she seemed to be gazing at some momentous object invisible to us. She seemed to lose herself, to utterly forget our presence, as her voice rose wild and sweet and clear. Yes, indeed, there was a mystery in her song, and it seemed to me that the words had a very certain meaning; also that, all the while standing facing me as she was, her glance betimes met mine quickly, as in a flash, and with a purpose. It was, I felt, in her mind that I should mark her words and weigh them well. Thus they ran:—

> "The Lion sinks
>   To the serpent's fang;
> The eagle drops
>   To the bowstring's twang.

> "Great is small;
>   Little is great;
> Great ones fall
>   When the mean deal fate.

> "The serpent's coil
>   Hides the fangs of death;
> *A coil of blue*
>   Veils the serpent's breath.

> "See the White Bull's pride
>   O'er the Black Bull wave;
> *Now, the White Bull's hide*
>   *May the Black Bull save.*"

Whau, Nkose! Then was amazement my master—I its slave! The "coil of blue!" Such a blue-beaded girdle was that of Nangeza's skirt, beside which she wore little else when summoned before the King. Upon this my eyes fixed themselves, only, however, to follow once more the meaning glance of Lalusini. And the King sat wondering, yet not understanding the *múti* song. And above his head, waving softly to and fro in the hand of its bearer, rose aloft the royal white shield. It was as the buzzing of bees within my ears that I heard the voice of the Great Great One.

"I have a mind to end this *indaba*," he was saying. "Thou, Nangeza, hast a pestilent tongue and an evil heart; wherefore my servant Untúswa must seek a new wife, for *thy place among us shall be empty.* Take her hence. The alligators are hungry."

"So, too, is Death, thou fool who art King!" yelled Nangeza. I saw her hand swift at her girdle. Something flashed through the air. It struck—struck hard and quivering—into the great white shield, which, quick as the movement, as the flash itself, I had snatched from the shield-bearer, and whirled down so as to cover the person of the King. It was one of those short, javelin-shaped arrows, such as were used by the mountain tribes, and sometimes among the Bakoni. And the point thereof was green and sticky with the most deadly of poisons.

That was a scene—the wild, quavering gasp of horror that went up from all who beheld! Nangeza, yelling, and biting like a wild beast, in the grasp of those who had seized her; myself, immovable as a stone, still holding the shield with the poisoned dart sticking through it—exactly as I flung it between the Great Great One and certain death. And the only two who were completely unconcerned were Lalusini and the King himself.

"*Whau!*" cried Umzilikazi, having taken a pinch of snuff. "I think that would have made me sneeze, Untúswa. See, the point was coming straight for my face, and it was flung hard—flung hard! Yet thou hast saved me from such a scratch, Untúswa—and it was well! Strange, too, that thou shouldst have been the one to do it, seeing that she was thine *inkosikazi!*"

There was suspicion in the tone—deadly suspicion—as the King sat looking at me with half-closed eyes, speaking softly withal.

"It is not strange, Father, seeing that I was the one who alone understood the Bakoni witch-song," I replied.

"Ha! And what said that?"

"'A coil of blue veils the serpent's breath.' Also, 'Now the White Bull's hide may the Black Bull save.' And, indeed, was it not so, Black Bull, whose horns gore not merely, but kill?" I said.

"This, then, was the warning thou wouldst have conveyed, thou strange sorceress," said the King, pausing a moment, while shouts of amazement and of *konza* went up from all. "Verily, thy *múti* is great. But of this witch first. The alligators are hungry; but their teeth are not sharp enough for such royal prey as this. The stake of impalement is a still sharper tooth. Away with her! Yet for the alligators we will find some meat. It seems that Untúswa's wives are of a bad disposition—at any rate, after dwelling side by side with yonder witch, they will have drunk in some of her evil mind. Let them, therefore, be taken to the alligators."

Now, *Nkose*, my heart was sad, for I loved my two younger wives, who were ever laughing and pleasant, and needed not to be told twice to do a thing. But these, as the slayers sprang forward to drag them forth to the terrible pool of death, flung themselves on the ground weeping.

"Spare us, Father!" howled Fumana. "She who has done evil is nothing to us."

"We only live by the light of the King's presence," groaned Nxope.

"Spare us, Great Great One!" wept Fumana.

"We are only weak women, and fear the dreadful death, O Elephant who art strong!" screamed Nxope.

"Peace, witches!" said the King. "Well, Untúswa! And thou! What hast thou to say? Do not these deserve to die?"

That was something of a question, *Nkose;* and one which it might cost a man his life to hesitate in answering. For did I not at once agree, after what had happened, the people would howl for my death, as being privy to the bold attempt upon the King's life, just made by my chief wife; and I suspected the question was put to try me. Yet I was fond of these two women, who had always done well by me; nor did I ever err on the side of timidity in those days. So I made answer—

"I think these two are innocent of the other's evil-doing, Great Great One. The wisdom of the King is great, and his justice is terrible. Yet I would crave the boon of their lives; for I have never known them do or think harm. So, too, shall I be left without wives at all, if these are taken from me."

"New wives shall be found for thee, Untúswa—and better than the old ones," answered Umzilikazi, half in mockery. "Ha! I think thou keepest thy wives too long. *Whau!* A bowl of *tywala,* when fresh, is needful and pleasant; but if kept too long, it grows sour and unwholesome, even harmful, and is only fit to be thrown away. So it is with a woman. But thou, sister, whose *múti* is great enough to discover serpent's fangs beneath a witch's girdle—what sayest thou? Is it well that these two should live?"

I looked at Lalusini and saw that her eyes were full of pity for these two horribly frightened women crouching there before the King, and then I knew that her heart was not dark and fierce as that of Nangeza, else had they certainly been dead.

"I think it well they should live, Great Great One, for they are innocent of the other's ill-doing," she answered.

"Ha! sayest thou so? Well, I give ye your lives, ye two. Begone! For the other, it seems that the stake is long in making ready."

This dreadful form of death, remember, being seldom used amongst us, some time must elapse while its instrument was preparing. Meanwhile, all crying aloud in praise of the King's mercy and justice, Nangeza seized the opportunity of wrenching herself from the grasp of those who held her, and before any could stay her—so lithe and active was she—she was darting across the plain in leaps and bounds, fleeing with the speed of a buck.

"To the alligators!" she cried, laughing wildly. "The alligators are hungry. They must be fed! They must be fed!"

The ground was open, the way but short. Before any could come up with her she had gained the brink of the cliff overhanging the pool. She turned and stood facing us, and there, in sight of all, shrieked out a last curse upon the King, upon me, and upon the whole nation; then, just as the foremost of the pursuers sprang to seize her, she flung herself backward from the brink. There was a loud splash, but no cry, and they who hurried to look declared that the water was lashed into a red-and-white foam, as the ravenous monsters rushed upon their prey, rending it limb from limb in a moment; and, indeed, though this is a hideous death enough, it is but a mere passing pang when compared with the black, lingering agony of the stake of impalement.

Thus died Nangeza, my *inkosikazi*, she whom I had stolen from the *isigodhlo* in times past, and in doing so had thrust my head deep within the red jaws of death. Now she died thus, brave, fierce, defiant to the last; and, *Nkose*——I think it was about time she did.

CHAPTER XIX.

THE WHITE SHIELD.

"PRAISE on now, ye *izimbonga*, shout aloud, my children," said the King, "for we are rid of a most pestilent witch, even though Untúswa has lost his *inkosikazi*. Well, what matter? We can find him a new one. Look, Untúswa. This stranger is fair. Will she not make a noble substitute for the evil-doer who sleeps yonder beneath the water?"

Now, *Nkose*, my heart leaped within me at the words; yet I did not like the tone, for I could see that the King was mocking me, and I suspected a trap; for Umzilikazi's ways were dark at times, and of late his suspicions, in one direction or the other, were seldom at rest. Still, I answered, as was my wont, boldly—

"She would indeed, Father. Is this, then, the 'word' of the Lion to the lion-cub?"

All gazed silently and in wonder at my boldness, for none doubted but that this beautiful stranger should reign queen in the *isigodhlo*.

"Ah, ah, Untúswa," mocked the King. "Know you not that she is a sorceress, and such can wed with none? Yet, it is a pity—a pity," he added, gazing longingly at the beauty of Lalusini, who stood with a half smile on her lips, looking down at us as though we were a couple of children discussing our games. Indeed, there were not wanting some who thought, that, noble and stately as the King's presence was, the aspect of this strange woman was the more royal of the two.

Now, Umzilikazi took up the great white shield, and began examining the little hole, or rather slit, made by the poisoned dart, murmuring softly to himself the while. Then, carefully, he picked up the little weapon itself, which I had immediately plucked from the royal shield, and flung down in disgust. An idea seemed to strike him.

"See, Untúswa, here is a great *múti* shield," he said. "It will make a fitting mate to the dark-handled *umkonto*. And as it has once stood between my life and treason, so may it always. Take it, Untúswa, my shield-bearer. It will be seen afar in the line of battle, when the meat stands ready to the teeth of the lion-cubs. Take it, Untúswa. It is thine."

Speaking thick and fast the words of *bonga*, I bent down and received this great gift from the hand of the King. It was a splendid bull-hide shield, of pure white, and not bound with black facings, as was the way with those borne by the royal guard. It was a royal shield, and of the royal colour, and was tufted with the tail-tuft of a bull, also pure white. And now I held two royal gifts: the King's Assegai, and the great white shield of the King. And since I had held the first naught but success had been mine. What would not follow upon the possession of the last?

The arrow which Nangeza had thrown we examined also. It was larger somewhat than those usually shot by the mountain tribes, and looked as though it had been made for this purpose. The point, too, was thick and green with an ugly poison, which was not all snake-poison, but a mixture of such with something of the nature of distilled herbs. Now, from whom had she obtained that secret? Then the King and I put our heads together, and whispered, and some of the royal guard bounded forth, to return immediately, dragging two men whom we knew to be of our own *izanusi;* yet not altogether, for they were of a lower class, who assisted our witch-doctors without being altogether of them. They were not our own people, both being of the Bapedi, and as they were brought before the presence, their knees knocked together, and their eyes protruded with fear.

"Take that arrow, ye dogs who are no *izanusi*, but cheats," said the King. "Now touch each other with the point thereof."

"We are but dust beneath the feet of the King," whined one, yet not obeying.

"To do this is death, Great Great One," moaned the other.

"Ha! And do ye hesitate? Who hesitates to face death at the word of the King? And if it is death for most men, ye jackals, is not your *múti* strong enough to render this of no avail? I speak not twice."

So these two grasped the arrow—first one, then the other—and obeyed the King's word. And we, bending forward, watched them keenly and with joy for we hated these crawling snakes of *izanusi*, who would have made of themselves, King, army, nation, all rolled into one. And we took care that there was no trickery in what they now did. So it happened that not long after they had pricked each other with the arrow they grew heavy and sleepy, and soon rolled over dead, and frothing at the mouth. For Umzilikazi judged that these two had supplied Nangeza with the poison, and there was nothing he loved so much as making the evil which one had prepared for another the manner whereby that one himself should fall.

"Now talk we of Kwelanga," he said, when the bodies had been removed. "Thou, Lalusini, will the little one ever return to us?"

"They who wander abroad by night without weapons of defence run great danger, O Elephant," she replied. "When such are but little children, what chance have they?"

"Yet the witch who is gone accused thee of a hand in her disappearance?"

"Then did she lie, Great Great One," answered Lalusini softly. "No part did I bear in this. Yet one thing my serpent tells me. Not for ill was this child of the sunshine saved from reddening the Amandebeli spears what time the other children of the Amabuna perished thereby. Wherefore, when her voice again shall be heard, neglect it not, lest a nation be a nation no more. Lo, it groweth dark and all things are night! I hear the sound of a trampling of feet, of the quiver of spears as the forest boughs in a gale, the clash and roar of hosts in battle, the song of victory!"

"And to whom the victory, my sister?" said the King.

Lalusini turned wonderingly at the voice and passed her hand once or twice over her brow. Her eyes came back to earth again, and she seemed as one who has but awakened from a long, deep sleep. And we who beheld it were stricken with awe, for we knew that the sorceress had parted with her spirit for a time; and this, soaring away through the fields of space and of the future, had beheld that to which her lips had given utterance, and, indeed, a great deal more to which they had not. And now, her vision ended, it was not within her power to reply to the King's question.

"Get thee gone now, and rest, my sister, for I perceive that thy powers are great," said Umzilikazi with a wave of the hand. And at the signal, some of the women who hung upon the outskirts of the crowd, came forward to lead the stranger to a large new hut which had been prepared for her reception.

When the assembly of the people had dispersed, the King and I still lingered talking over these matters.

"Is it for good or for ill she has come among us, Untúswa?" he said.

"For good, Great Great One."

"Ha! So thou ever sayest. Yet her prophecy as regarded the little one was strange."

"Strange it was, Black Elephant, but it was not lightly spoken."

"She is a greater magician than this white man, for no such saying, light or dark, did he ever utter concerning us."

"That is true, Father. Yet he is a good man."

"And the sayings of that witch who was thy chief wife, Untúswa. They, too, were strange."

"*Whau!* They were the ravings of a jealous and evil-tongued woman, Calf of a Black Bull. But now I am without a chief wife, give me, I pray thee, this sorceress, Father, for there is that about her which I love, O Stabber of the Sun."

"So, so!" said Umzilikazi, laughing softly, and there was a look on his face which brought back the days when I, being a boy, desired leave to *tunga*. "So, so, Untúswa? She would make a noble substitute for thy dead witch? Ha! Yet be content, thou holder of the royal spear and the royal shield."

There was that in the words—in the look—as the King dismissed me which left an uncomfortable load upon my mind; and, indeed, I felt as though I had acted like a fool.

Now, as I returned to the huts I occupied when at Kwa'zingwenya upon the King's business, my two younger wives came about me with words of love and thankfulness, because my voice had been raised on their behalf when they were adjudged to die the death which had overtaken Nangeza. Yet for these I had no ears and but little patience, for my mind was filled with the Bakoni sorceress. Moreover, I now foresaw strife between these two; for, Nangeza being gone, these would not rest until one or other of them had taken her place, nor would they suffer me to rest—for so it is with women: each must always be the greater. So I answered them but shortly, bidding them gather up their possessions and start back at once to my kraal—happy that they could go back well and strong in the flesh, and not as weeping ghosts whose bodies were dead moaning over the ashes of their former home. But for my part I chose to remain at Kwa'zingwenya for a space, for I feared lest Lalusini should escape me again. Yet was I as powerless with regard to her as the lowest of our Amaholi; for was not her life the property of the King, even as the lives of all of us? Truly within the nation I was great. Yet did my will cross that of the King and—*Au!* where is the smoke of yesterday's fire?

Thinking such thoughts, I was wandering at eventide between the great kraal and the river when I came upon old Masuka gathering herbs.

"Greeting, thou holder of the royal spear and the royal shield," said the old man, looking at me sideways, like a bird, out of his bright eyes. Again I felt uneasy, for his words were exactly those which the King had uttered—his tone mocking and ill-omened.

"Greeting, my father," I answered, trying to seem unconcerned. "Now we have yet another magician among us—this time a female one."

"That is so, Untúswa. Ah, ah! what was my 'word' to thee? 'The she-eagle will return—and the alligators shall be fed.' Did I lie in that?"

"Not so, my father. Truth was there in the word, for it has been shown this day."

"Your black cow has given good milk, my son. *Whau*, Untúswa! You should be an *isanusi* yourself, who did so readily read the way of the Bakoni witch-song. But now great things are to come upon us—upon you: yes—strange things."

"What is the strangest thing which is to come upon me, my father?" I said, again seeking to pry into the future.

"Ha! The place of the Three Rifts," he answered, darkly.

"But I know not such a place, my father."

"Thou wilt know it, Untúswa; thou wilt know it—one day."

No more would the old man tell, and so I left him, pondering greatly over these things as I went. And it seemed to me that the air was dark with sorcery and magic, and that snares lay spread all around, lurking for the steps of him who should tread unwarily; and, indeed, this was so, for the old Mosutu's foresight was no mere empty frothing, but of portentous weight, as, indeed, were all his utterances.

While these things were in progress, *Nkose*, the white priest was

absent from Kwa'zingwenya; for since the day of his interference at
the Pool of the Alligators, the King chose, when possible, to find some
pretext for removing him to a distance what time evil-doers were to
die the death. For if the stranger were again to interfere, he, too, must
die, for it would be impossible to overlook such rebellion a second
time, even from a white man. Now, Umzilikazi did not desire his
death, wherefore he would direct that some should lure the stranger
to a distant kraal, on the pretence that certain people there were eager
to listen to his teaching, all in accordance with the crafty scheme which
had kept him from pursuing his journey to the south, and rendered
him content to remain among us. And, no matter what the weather,
no matter how great his own fatigue, upon receiving such a call, the
white priest would start immediately, through heat or cold or storm,
though the rivers were in flood or sickness lurked in the low-lying
swamps. So it had been in this instance; and not until several days had
gone by since the death of Nangeza did he return, weary with travel,
and sad that his teachings should be of so small avail.

But very much more sad was he on learning of the disappearance
of Kwelanga, and he wept, that white *isanusi;* for he loved the little
one, who, after all, was of his own colour, the only one of such among
us. And he, like ourselves, doubted not but that she had been slain and
devoured by wild beasts. Yet, loudly did he give thanks to the King
who had permitted him to perform the water-rite over her; since by
this, he said, though her body were dead, her spirit should live in happiness forever. And we, hearing these words, glanced at one another
with meaning. Did they not accord with Lalusini's saying, that again
should Kwelanga's voice be heard, though with a warning, forasmuch
that not for ill had we saved her alive when all others were slain?

Now, although this white priest had declared in a friendly manner
towards old Masuka, and, indeed, showed no enmity towards our
own *izanusi*, his mind seemed evil towards Lalusini. Her he could
never be brought to regard with over-great friendliness, but yet was
guarded in his utterances; and, while he looked upon her coldly, said
naught against her. But she, for her part, in nowise seemed to return
his manner, for she ever spake softly and kindly to him—even as she
did to all—but in a way as though she herself were too great to feel
enmity or ill-will to such small things as those around her. And this,
indeed, was partly true.

CHAPTER XX.

DREAMS—NEW AND GREAT.

Now, time went by, and of Lalusini I saw nothing, nor could I find opportunity of speaking with her alone. I was greatly troubled in mind, too; for I thought the King desired her—he who cared not usually about women—and my days were heavy and my dreams dark.

We were seated alone, the King and I. We had been talking over many things, as our way was; for Umzilikazi seemed to trust me more and more, till it was whispered that I had become the most powerful man in the nation, young as I was—more powerful than Mcumbete, the chief *induna*, or even than Kalipe, the commander of the army. As we sat thus, the King said—

"It seems to me, son of Ntelani, that we have sorcerers enough and to spare. Now this one which came last among us is one too many. Wherefore, as she is young and well-favoured, I will take her to wife, so shall she practise sorcery no more."

Here was a dark curtain for my eyes—I, who loved Lalusini. But I only answered that it was good—that the small wishes of the King were the great ones of his children.

"That is well said, Untúswa! Go now, and bring hither this sorceress, that she may learn to what great end she was born."

I saluted, and, going forth, proceeded straight to Lalusini's hut, sending in women to tell her the Great Great One desired speech with her. Then I returned to the King, fearing to be alone with Lalusini, lest I should by word or look betray myself—betray us both. And as I went I remembered her words, spoken first in the hiding-place up yonder, on the mountain of death: "There is that by which even Umzilikazi dare not wed me." What was behind this saying? For a matter which should come between the King and his will must indeed be weighty—nothing less than one of life or death.

Lalusini stood before the King, royal in the stately splendour of her beauty; her large eyes smiling down upon him as she uttered the *Bayéte* in a voice like the murmuring of trees, yet not bending over much.

"*Whau!* It shall be so!" I heard him mutter, after gazing at her for a short space in silence and admiration.

"Hearken, my sister!" he said aloud. "Among this people there are sorcerers and diviners enough already. And now thou art another of them—yet thy *múti* is great."

"Would the King sit here to-day, but for that *múti?*" she answered. "Here or on a darker seat? Yet it matters not that I should wander again if I am to find no resting-place among this people. Still, there are others."

"That is not my mind, thou who art from nowhere," said Umzilikazi. "Thou art indeed fair and goodly enough for a queen—and a queen thou shalt be. Thou shalt be at the head of the *isigodhlo*, and the delight of a King."

Now my eyes were fixed upon the face of Lalusini; but over it came no change.

"That cannot be, Great Great One!" she answered.

"Cannot be? Ha!" cried Umzilikazi, gazing at her in displeasure and amazement. "Are, then, the wishes of a King to be uttered twice?"

"Thou art all-powerful, O Black Elephant," she said. "The elephant may rend down forest-trees and loosen rocks with his might. Yet even he cannot walk against a broad river in flood. There is a law which is greater than even the wishes of the mightiest of kings."

"What meanest thou, my sister?" said Umzilikazi, in a low but terrible voice.

"Thou doest well to call me thus, son of Matyobane; for within me runs the blood of Matyobane."

"Ha!"

So great was his astonishment that for a space, save that one amazed gasp, no word could the King utter. Now stood revealed the meaning of that saying of hers; for, *Nkose*, so strict is this custom among us Amazulu, that no man may take to wife any girl within whose veins runs a drop of his own blood, or, indeed, as to whom exists the barest suspicion that such may be the case. Wherefore, in declaring herself to be of the blood of Umzilikazi's father, Lalusini knew that even the King himself dare not take her to wife; nor, indeed, would he desire to, once convinced of the truth of her words.

"Is this indeed so?" he said at last, frowning suspiciously, for a king likes not to be balked in the desire of his heart, be the reason never so good. "Say, then, who was thy father?"

"First look at me, Great Great One. Are we not of a royal tree, we in whom runs the same blood?"

Now the King started slightly, and I, too, marking that royal stamp which rested upon Lalusini, saw for the first time a certain degree of likeness between them.

"Of my father I cannot speak," she went on. "My mother was Laliwa, sister of Matyobane."

"Au!" "A wonder!" broke from myself and the King at once. For she had named one of the inferior wives of Tshaka the Terrible. Well might we cry out in amazement. This strange beautiful woman, this sorceress of the Bakoni, whose witcheries had inspired both of us with love for her, was of the royal house of Senzangakona, was the daughter of that mighty king, the terror of whose name spread as far as it was known—and even among ourselves—the great Tshaka, from whom we had revolted and fled. Truly indeed had she spoken when saying that she came of a stock greater than that of Umzilikazi.

"Wonderful things have we heard to-day," said the King. Then jestingly: "Say, daughter of the Lion whose roar is now silent! Here is a valiant fighter, my war-captain and councillor, Untúswa. Wouldst thou not wed with such, the gates of the *isigodhlo* being now closed?"

Lalusini turned her eyes full upon me for the first time, and the glance expressed amusement, yet beneath it I could discern something more.

"Did I mate with any, it would indeed be with such a warrior," she said. "But this is not the day for thoughts of such things, O son of Matyobane, for great events are maturing."

"And these events—are they for good or for ill?" said Umzilikazi.

"For good or for ill? Ha! There is a darkness over the earth, yet not the darkness of night. Lo, I see the world beneath the glow of the full moon, and it is bright as noonday, though softer. And now it is dark, and the face of the moon is wrapped in blackness until it shines forth once more. Then beware, King and founder of a new nation; for the scream of the vultures is borne upon the winds from afar, crying that a banquet awaits—yes, a banquet awaits!"

Now, Lalusini had sunk back into the state of one who dreams, and when she awakened, returning as it were to earth once more, she seemed not to know what words she had uttered, or, indeed, if she had uttered any. But the King and I forgot them not, and often afterwards did we talk them over together.

Now Lalusini began to sing in a strange, far-distant tone, and low, but the words were in the Bakoni tongue, and were mysterious enough even to me. And the song was of a shield, and seemed to tell of battle and of blood.

"See, Great Great One," she cried, ceasing, and pointing to the white shield which the King had given me. "He who bears yonder shield must not part from it, even for a space, until after the blackness of the moon. Then it may be that he will part with it forever—yet not."

Her words were dark now, yet, in the fulness of time, were they to be made plain enough. But the King, dissatisfied, pressed for an explanation.

"Seek not to look into the mysteries of my magic, son of Matyobane," she replied, utterly fearless, "for to do so is to render them evil."

"And I fear not such. No dread do I stand in of the sorcery of any. Ask now, my sister—where is Isilwane, once head of the *isanusi?* Where Notalwa—and others?" said Umzilikazi, frowning.

"Yet, let well be. Say, Calf of a Black Bull—was my *múti* for good or for ill, that guided the shield now borne by Untúswa? The magic of the Bakoni is as superior to that of the Amazulu as the might in battle of these last is to that of the peoples they have made an end of."

"What now is thy story, my sister?" said the King, leaving that question. And some of her story Lalusini gave us then and there—how that she alone of all his children would Tshaka the Mighty recognise, even if there were any others who were not slain, for that King desired not children, lest, growing up, they should plot against him and depose him. Lalusini, however, he destined to some great though hidden end, and caused the land far and wide to be searched for those who could teach her the deeper and most hidden myster-

ies of their magic. Then it befell that the two brothers of Tshaka—
Dingane and Mhlangana—rose up against the Great One and slew
him, and Lalusini with her mother, Laliwa, and some others, fled
afar to escape the death of the spear, and after many wanderings and
perils reached the land of the Bakoni, which they deemed remote
enough from Dingane. Here Tauane, the chief of that people, would
have wedded her, but she would have none of him or his plans.

"*Au!* that dog who is burnt!" cried Umzilikazi. "I would he were
here again, that I might make him once more taste fire. *Au!* A dog, to
think to blend the branches of the royal stem of Senzangakona with
the rank weeds of his jackal tribe."

"Not to no purpose had I learned the magic of the wise," went on
Lalusini. "I divined your coming, Great Great One; yes, long before
Untúswa's first embassy appeared in the land, and I welcomed it.
Nothing of it did I say in warning to Tauane and the People of the
Blue Colored Cattle, save darkly, and, as it were, in jest. And they
mocked."

"If you welcomed our coming, my sister, why didst thou disappear into air for a space thereafter?" said Umzilikazi cunningly.

"Ha! no evil lay behind that, son of Matyobane. Can two bulls of
equal size dwell in one kraal? Yet Zululand is now just such a kraal,
having two kings, Dingane and Mhlangana. Yet it should have but
one."

"*Hau!*" cried the King. "Should that one be Dingane?"

"Not Dingane should it be, Elephant of the Amandebeli," she
replied.

"Mhlangana, then?"

"Not Mhlangana, Great Great One in whom flows the blood of
my mother."

"Ha! Who, then, Queen of the Bakoni *múti?*"

"Umzilikazi, the son of Matyobane."

"Ha!" broke from us both at the surpassing boldness of this
declaration; and for some moments we sat staring in silence at this
wonderful woman. Then the King took snuff, and, as he did so, I
well knew what was passing in his mind. For, had but another regiment or two cleaved to us, what time the Amandebeli and we of the
Umtetwa tribe, and others, fled from Zululand, no flight need we
have made at all. We would have marched to Dukuza, and eaten up

the whole usurping House of Senzangakona. Ofttimes had the King thus talked to me since; sorrowing even now, when it was too late, that the opportunity should have been allowed to pass. And now this woman—this sorceress of a strange tribe, yet claiming mighty descent—came thus to hold before Umzilikazi's gaze a vision of such power as, even in the fulness of his might, the great Tshaka had never wielded. To combine the warrior strength of our nation with that of the parent stock of Zululand! *Whau!* there was a destiny!

We should rule the world itself with such a power behind us. No wonder a strange light gleamed in the eyes of the King as they beheld such a vision.

"And how shall this be brought about, Lalusini?" he said; more to say something than because uncertain as to what her reply would be.

"What nation can *konza* to two kings?" she answered. "Sooner or later its choice must be made. One or both must fall. Then is the time for him who was born to be great."

"And if but one fall?"

"Then let the other follow, and speedily. Ha! who would be great and run no risks! There are many in Zululand yet—many who are still young, as well as others—who remember how the son of Matyobane led them in battle. Many who, sitting in their huts at night, whisper, with their hands to their mouths, the name of Umzilikazi. For the foot of those of the House of Senzangakona treads heavily."

"And how know you all this, my sister?" said the King, looking sharply at her.

"Wherefore did I disappear into air for a space?" was her reply, with just a shade of meaning, quoting Umzilikazi's words.

"Ha! And when the House of Senzangakona is overthrown, what wilt thou, Lalusini, thou who art of that house thyself?"

"Revenge!"

"Revenge? For the death of the Black One who begat thee?" said Umzilikazi.

"Revenge!—and one other thing, and this the King will not refuse?"

"And that is——?"

"The time to declare it is not yet, Great Great One."

CHAPTER XXI.

"THE PLACE OF THE THREE RIFTS."

Now, in the days which followed upon the revelation of Lalusini's birth and parentage, and the prospects and possibilities at which she more than hinted, the mind of the King seemed to contain but one thought, and that was the greatness which might be his by boldly risking all to seize it, by judgment in choosing the right time. To this end he would converse with her for a whole day at a time, and, in some wise at least, every day. Indeed, the predictions and influence of the beautiful sorceress seemed to thrust those of old Masuka quite into the background, and seldom now were his divinations required. Yet, *Nkose*, that astonishing old bag of bones seemed in no wise to resent this waning of the royal favour. His bright, keen eyes would flash forth a laugh when he met or passed Lalusini, but in his greetings of her there was no tone of envy or of ill-will. Even the white priest the King seldom conversed with in those days; nor was this strange, for with such an immense undertaking before our eyes, involving war and bloodshed, such as, perhaps, the Zulu nation— and certainly our own—had never seen, Umzilikazi had little desire for the conversation of one whose preaching was all of peace. *Whau!* What had we to do with peace, we who sought the overthrow of mighty Kings? But the white man cared little for this neglect. As long as he was allowed to go about the country striving to win men to his teaching, he was happy.

Now, in these conversations I also took part, I alone being in the secret, for Umzilikazi ordered that no word as to Lalusini's birth or his own schemes should leak out. Moreover, now I found opportunities of talking alone with her, such as I had dared not before seek.

"Well, Untúswa?" she said, mockingly, one day, when we two talked alone. "So, when the eagle's nest was empty and the she-eagle had gone, your first thought was that the lion you had then slain had robbed the nest?"

"Who says I slew a lion that day, Lalusini, for I searched the whole mountain, yet upon it was none, save only myself?"

"Ah, ah! son of Ntelani," she laughed. "Thou who, with one other, didst fight against the whole Bakoni nation, art a child before the Bakoni *múti*. Be patient. Great things will happen soon."

"Patient—*Hau!* It seems to me that we draw no nearer one to another, Lalusini. And I like it not."

"Yet I have managed to keep outside the *isigodhlo*, Untúswa," and again she laughed. "Did I speak truly in that matter?"

"Truly, indeed," I answered.

"That is well said, valiant fighter, whose greatness is gained by means of women."

"By means of women?" I repeated, thinking she was again mocking me. "Now, how can that be, Lalusini, seeing that I lead the King's army, and am ever in the front of the battle?"

"And how camest thou to win the King's Assegai, and with it the place of a commander in the King's armies? Was it not through a woman? Tell me that, Untúswa."

"It was, indeed," I answered, remembering Nangeza, and how my foolishness in stealing her from the *isigodhlo* had won me life and great honour, instead of the death which I had expected and deserved.

"And how camest thou to win the white shield—the *múti* shield? See thou part not from it, Untúswa. Was it not through two women: she who would have dealt the death which it turned away, and she whose wisdom entered thy brain at the right moment? Tell me that, son of Ntelani."

"That, too, is the truth, daughter of Kings," I answered. "But I would ask this: If Umzilikazi sits in the seat of Dingane, in whose seat am I to sit?"

She laughed softly, musically.

"Ah! ah! Untúswa. Remember my offer to you in the cave of the eagle's nest. Was it not to rule over a great nation?"

"*Hau!*" I cried in amazement, seeing the whole truth. Yet could it be real? I, Untúswa, who, though now an *induna* of weight, was but yesterday a boy. I, Untúswa, had been chosen by this daughter of a royal house—a powerful sorceress, and withal beautiful beyond any woman I had ever seen—to aid her in recovering the throne of Tshaka the Mighty, and to rule over the great Zulu nation as King. And this greatness I had thrust away from me!

"Thou art young yet, Untúswa, though thy deeds have been many and thy name is feared," she answered, smiling up at me in a kind of pity, and yet I thought with much love in her eyes. "Yet what thou hast done is only a beginning, and what the white shield has done is only a beginning. See thou part not from it."

"Never will I part from it," I declared. "And so, Lalusini, this greatness which was held out to me in the cave like the eagle's nest is now held out to Umzilikazi?"

"Young still—impatient ever—yet an *induna*," she said, looking at me as she had done in the old days, when I kept her hidden away, and my visits were stealthy, and made at the risk of my life. "This greatness is for him who may seize it—thou who wouldst love the daughter of a race of kings."

"That will I do, and seize upon the greatness also," I said. "Give me but the chance, Lalusini."

"The chance shall come, but by a way of fear and blood, *induna* of the King, who hast but begun to live. It may be that we shall be great together—or—shall sit down in darkness for ever[1]—yet not even that, for the vultures and jackals will grow fat."

Now, towards the full of the moon I was sent by the King upon military business—which was to levy drafts of young men upon certain outlying kraals to the southward. This occupied many days, for the distances to be traversed were great, yet so eager were all to bear arms in those days that even the very children would beg to be enrolled, and parties of them, flourishing sticks and singing war-songs, would march for some distance beside the new warriors on their journey to the military kraals whither these were consigned. Upon this service I was accompanied by my brother, Mgwali, and four men of my own kraal. Our journeyings brought us to a high jagged mountain range, called Inkume, beyond which lay a wild waste country, where none of us dwelt, for it was swampy at the time of the rains and not over-healthy, though some of us would now and again visit it to hunt, for game abounded there.

---

[1] This is an allusion—first, to the Zulu method of burying the dead in a sitting posture; second, to the custom of leaving the bodies of those executed for a criminal offence exposed to the carrion beasts and birds, a practice somewhat analogous to the not so very old English one of gibbeting highwaymen and other malefactors in chains.—Mitford's note.

Now, *Nkose*, I know not how it was unless that, having so much to do with magic and sorcery, I was becoming half *isanusi* myself, but something moved me to penetrate beyond this range. I told myself it was to hunt; yet it was not to hunt. I told myself the lions on that side must be strong and large, and I would kill one or two and make for myself some famous war adornments with the mane and tail; yet I knew that I cared little if I found lions or not. Something within myself seemed to urge me onward. Each jagged and fantastic point of overhanging rock seemed to beckon me forward. In the voices of the male baboons crying hoarsely from the crags, in the scream of the black tufted eagle wheeling lazily in the blue heights, I seemed to hear words—tones—calling me ever onward. It was fearsome, it was as a thing of *tagati* as I plunged deeper and deeper into the great pass which wound through the heart of the mountain range. The lofty cliff walls overhanging my way seemed to stoop, as though to overwhelm me in the mournful blackness which now brooded from the gloomy mountain-shadows; for the sun was already beginning to sink.

I had sent back Mgwali and the others, for something moved me to undertake this expedition alone. I was armed with the great and splendid spear—the King's Assegai—two or three light casting ones, and a heavy short-handled knobstick; also I carried the great white shield which had saved the King's life, for, although, when not on a war expedition, it is our custom only to carry small ornamental shields, yet, remembering Lalusini's oft-repeated warning, I never parted with this one, even when I slept.

The land here was rolling and grassy, dotted with little clusters of trees and bush, and over the plain herds of game were frisking. Far off, waving above the tree-tops, I could make out the snake-like necks of tall giraffes, browsing on the tender shoots; and yet the desire to kill game seemed to have left me, as I walked on and on, thinking of Lalusini and the strange things she had presaged as about to befall our nation—also the great destiny which she had darkly hinted might await myself.

When I turned to retrace my steps, lo! the sun had set below the rim of the world. But upon the tall, smooth-faced cliffs, which sheered upward to the sharp ridge of Inkume, lay an afterglow of surpassing brilliancy—a strange, weird, boding light, as though they had been plunged in a sea of blood. Blood-red, too, were the spurs of the great range. *Hau!* It was wonderful, it was terrifying, it was *tagati!* Never did I behold anything like it before.

And now, as I gazed in marvel and awe, the redness grew deeper, then faded; and the great rocks took on a colour as of the livid blue-blackness of a mighty thunder-cloud. And as the shadows were thrown out thus clearly, and every line stood forth, while every hollow receded into gloom, I noticed that the mountains here swept round into almost a half-circle. In front opened the mouth of the pass through which I had come, while on the one hand and on the other a deep, gloomy rift—bushgrown, overhung—ran up far into the heart of the range. *Hau!* It was as if a cold thing were creeping up my back; for now, as plainly as though they were shouted in my ears, came old Masuka's words, "The Place of the Three Rifts!"

So I stood and gazed, my hand to my mouth, in amazement, in awe. This, then, was "The Place of the Three Rifts." Here it was that strange things were to come upon me—so had predicted the old Mosutu.

Now day had faded into night, and already the shadows of forest and plain were blended together. Already the voices of the darkness were raised—the howl of ravening hyænas; the shrill cry of jackals; the wild, yelling bay of wild dogs, ordering the plan of their hunt! and, withal, the croaking of innumerable frogs in the adjoining reed-bed, the screech of the tree-crickets, and the whirr of the night-hawk. And beneath the misty loom of the tall cliffs it seemed to me that the voices of dark ghosts were calling one to another. "The Place of the Three Rifts!" *Whau!* I would rather engage the waggon-fort of the Amabuna again single-handed than face what might be before me ere morning should break upon that fearsome wizard glen.

While I stood thus, with a strange *tagati* spell upon me, as firmly rooted as one of the trees growing around, a glow burned in the sky afar, and the land grew light again, as a broad, full moon rose beyond the rim of the world, soaring slowly aloft, a great golden ball. And now the fear began to leave me, for I could see again. Moreover, it is only in the darkness that evil ghosts love to move; or, at any rate, are at their worst. Yet ever, in the tones of the wild creatures of the plain—in the cavernous echo of the sentinel baboon's resounding bark, high up among the crags—it seemed that wizard voices were calling—grim, threatening, unceasing.

Now I moved forward, as though to root up the dread that was upon me. Moreover, I feared to face that dreadful pass—full of *tagati* and all evil things—in the darkness. And even then there broke from its portals such a wild, wailing, ghost-like howl, which rose in innumerable clamours, surging in a hundred voices around the caves and corners of the rocks—now roaring, now in strange and whistling scream. *Hau!* All the terrors of this spell of wizardry returned. Right in the moon-path, between each jutting elbow of the cliff portals, was a huge beast—ghost-like unto a hyæna, yet four times larger, and more evil-looking than the largest of those foul and loathsome creatures in mortal life. Squatted on its haunches, its horrible head thrown back, and fangs, now glistening white, now concealed, it bayed hideously to the moon; and I, who feared not death in blood, in any shape or form, felt this ghost-voice go through me, turning my blood to water. This was no real animal, but a terrible ghost. Not to sit in the seat of Dingane would I again thread that pass until the fair and beauteous sun-rays should once more make glad the face of the world, dispersing such to their own abodes of horror and of gloom.

Silently I drew back among the shadows, for I feared to be seen by this ghost-like animal. Then spying a place where the rocks above me seemed to offer a secure hiding-place, which could only be approached from one side, I seized a branch of a tree which was rooted in a cleft, and swung myself up as noiselessly as possible.

I was right in the selection of my hiding-place so far. There was but one way up to it—that by which I had come. Yet behind anything, anybody, might drop down upon me from above. And now that I was here the spell of dread which had been upon me seemed to fade. I thought I could hear the wild, sweet singing of Lalusini, soothing me to sleep. The next thing—*au!* I was asleep. At first, strange visions chased each other across my dreams. Then I dreamed no more, but slept heavily, for I was weary.

Au, Nkose! How shall I say what next befell? For I saw before me Kwelanga, the little white child whom I had saved from the red spear-blades of our warriors in the waggon-fort of the Amabuna. There she stood, the golden sunlight of her hair dispelling the night; her great blue eyes wide open, and fixed upon mine in terrible fear and anxiety. Then my sleep became dreamless once more.

"Untúswa, my father! Wake, Untúswa, for thy life's sake!"

Clear—clear through the night—sounded her voice, the voice of the little one whom we had lost. It sounded in warning.

"Waken, waken, Untúswa, my father! Waken for thy life's sake; lest a nation be a nation no more!"

Now I leaped up; noiselessly, cautiously, as is our habit when alarmed. So strangely clear, so distinct the voice, that I gazed eagerly around, expecting to behold the little one standing before me in the moonlight. And her last words! "Lest a nation be a nation no more." *Whau!* Even such had been the words of Lalusini, in her divining vision, when she declared that again should that voice be heard in warning, and charging that its utterances should not be neglected. But the apparition of my dream had faded. I was alone in the silence of the night.

Then, *Nkose*, I could have wept, for I had loved the little one; and now, deceived by my dream, had hoped to have, by some wonderful means, discovered her, alive and well. For the moment, I forgot all wizardry and presages, as I peered around, calling her softly by name. And then came a sound which put all other thoughts to flight, and stirred my blood until it tingled again—the sound which is as no other—the quivering rattle of assegai-hafts held bunched together in the hands of warriors.

Who were these, moving thus abroad at midnight? Surely, none of our people would find themselves away here in this wizard spot at such an hour. Ha! Could it be some of our own people who had come in search of me, seeing I did not return? Yet, somehow, this did not seem the explanation of it.

While I listened, the sounds were drawing nearer, and they were above me; and now, with the rattle of the supple wood, came the deep smothered tone of a voice or two. Then, before I could move to carry out the plan of concealment which my instinct prompted, there dropped down into the little hollow wherein I stood ten or a dozen men.

CHAPTER XXII.

OF THE BLACKENING OF THE MOON.

THEY were fully armed, these men. Each carried the large war-shield and broad assegai. Further, they were plumed and otherwise adorned as warriors upon a hostile expedition. In the light of the moon I could see that they were all *amakehla*, or head-ringed men, of middle age, straight and tall, and, indeed, the very pick and flower of such an *impi* as any *induna* might be proud to command. But who were they? Not one of their faces was known to me. Clearly they were not of our own people; and, if not, who were they?

They halted on seeing me, uttering a quick murmur of surprise, yet not of a surprise that was over great. Then they lowered their weapons, and, tossing aloft their right hands, they exclaimed—

"*Bayéte!*"

Yes; to me they cried the *Bayéte*, these warriors—*Bayéte*, the salute of a King—to me, Untúswa! In truth, the old Mosutu *isanusi* spoke not falsely when he declared that the strangest thing would happen to me in the Place of the Three Rifts, for here was I being hailed by armed warriors as a King. For a moment the thought crossed my mind that the Great Great One was no more, and that the people had elected me to sit in his seat, and had sent to find me, but only for a moment. For the light of the moon was strong, and of the faces of these not one did I know.

"*Yeh-bo!*" I answered, in a deep, muttering tone, some instinct moving me to hide my real voice as much as might be. And I stood straight and erect, waiting for them to continue.

"We have explored this mountain range far on either hand, O Greater of the Twin Stars of the Heavens," said the foremost, "yet there is no way by which our *impis* may cross save by yon gloomy pass. And in the mouth thereof sits some strange wizard beast and dismally howls."

"It is even as Silwane has said, more valiant of two Kings," declared another.

"Greater of the Twin Stars of the Heavens!" "Way by which our *impis* may cross!" Who was the man addressing? To what *impis* did he make reference? *Hau!* was this part of the wizardry of the place? And then, *Nkose*, as the real truth flashed upon me, I knew not whether I were living or dead. These warriors were the advance guard of an *impi* coming from Zululand. *"Bayéte"*—the royal salute; "Greater of the Twin Stars," must have been intended for one of the two Kings, brothers, then reigning over Zululand, Dingane or Mhlangana. And for one of them these men were mistaking me.

I would ask you, *Nkose*, was ever any man in such a position? The invading *impi* must be of immense size if commanded in person by a King, and it was sent to crush us. That was as clear as noonday. Now, indeed, I had a part to play. Were the mistake discovered, I could hardly escape with my life, and, in that case, our whole nation, taken completely by surprise, would be assailed without warning, and, it might be, utterly exterminated. Fortunately, my back was to the moon, whereas they were facing it.

"What is thy will, Father?" went on the man who had been named Silwane. "Shall we send back to hurry on the companies, and force this pass tomorrow night? Yet, it will be better to leave it until the night after."

"Till the night after?" I said, questioningly, desiring to speak in as few words as possible, lest my voice should betray me, and yet thirsting for more information.

"It will be better so, Greater of two Kings," went on Silwane. "Unless we fall upon these Amandebeli by surprise, *au!* the good fortune which was theirs on the Kwahlamba may still be with them; for, unless they have *impis* out elsewhere, the force they can bring against us can hardly be less than our own."

This was news which caused my heart to leap with joy, only to droop again immediately, for I recollected that a large *impi* had gone forth under Kalipe to eat up two chiefs who dwelt to the northward, and who had failed to pay their tribute, thinking themselves strong enough. True, its return was daily expected, but up till now there had been no sign thereof. Of course, in my character of supposed King, I was in favour of the delay, and, indeed, would have ordered yet further, but dared not. The more uncertain were my orders the better, for he whom I was now personating might really have decided views of his own of a contrary policy. *Whau, Nkose!* in truth was I walking between spears, even as when I put my own words into the mouth of the Bakoni chief in the sight of Umzilikazi and the whole nation. Fortunately, boy as I was before we left Zululand, I had often seen the princes of the House of Senzangakona, and remembered their voices, which I now strove to imitate. And I wanted to find out which of the two Kings I was supposed to be.

"Thy plan is good, Silwane," I said, and then, carelessly, "*Whau!* I know not. I who am but a child. I would that the other of the Twin Stars of the Heavens were by me now, for his judgment in such matters is greater than mine. What think you, Silwane?"

"*Au!*" he cried. "He who sits at Umkunkundhlovu has the wisdom of nations. But it is thou who art skilled in war, O Mhlangana, Twin Star of the Amazulu."

Ha! It was Mhlangana then whom I was representing, not Dingane. But where was that prince himself? He might appear at any moment, and then——!

"Umzilikazi knows well how to use mountain passes," I said, laughing to myself as I thought of the way we beat back Tshaka's *impi*. "Wherefore, move not the soldiers until moonrise to-morrow night, and enter the pass when darkness shall fall on the night after. Meanwhile let none draw near this mountain chain, lest they be sighted by those whom we are come to stamp flat—none, no, not one."

"And those who are already posted upon the height, father?"

"Let them remain," I said, "but let them keep well concealed. Stay, where are they posted?"

"Yonder, where the two patches of scrub crown the projecting spur, Great Great One," said the *induna*, pointing to a place which I could see, luckily without turning my head, for had the moonbeams fallen on my face that moment I were lost.

"Ha! But one picket? It seems I ordered two to be posted," I said carelessly.

"One was indeed thy order, Serpent of Wisdom," replied Silwane. "Yet there are five men in it. Shall I send up and bid two of them take up other position elsewhere?"

"Let be, it matters not," I answered, still carelessly. "Ten eyes should surely, from such a point, command half the world."

You will observe, *Nkose*, that I had found out four things: that a huge Zulu *impi* was advancing to surprise and utterly destroy us; that in strength it scarcely exceeded that of our whole nation; that it was led in person by Mhlangana, one of the brother Kings of Zululand; and that it would cross the mountains at a certain time. It only remained for me now to do one thing more to complete the trap into which I intended that the might of Zululand should advance—and fall.

"That look-out is sufficient," I continued, after a moment's pause. "Yet I think that it is not needful to wait until dark to enter the pass. It may be done at mid-day, if those upon the watch-place signal that none are about. Then that night shall the flames of Kwa'zingwenya light the triumph dance of the might of the People of the Heavens. Let it be known, then, that a white blanket be waved thrice if the way is open."

"We hear you, Father," answered the warriors. "The plan will not fail. By the King's white shield, but the rebel Umzilikazi may soon sit down in darkness forever."

"*The King's white shield!*" Now I saw yet further light. For, accompanying these words, the glances of the warriors had fallen meaningly upon the white shield which I carried—the pure white shield without spot of any other colour—the shield which had saved the life of a king, and was now the means of saving the life of a king once more, and also the life of a nation. This was how the mistake occurred; this was how they had taken me for Mhlangana, seeing the great white royal shield in the moonlight. But where was Mhlangana?

I said just now, *Nkose*, that there only remained for me one thing more to do, yet, having done it, I found there remained another; and this was, to effect a speedy and safe retreat from a position to which any moment might bring an end—resulting in my own death and the destruction of our nation. How was this to be effected? I dared not move or turn ever so slightly lest the light, falling upon my face, should betray me. To send these men away, and myself remain behind, might arouse their suspicion, and, over and above these considerations, the real Mhlangana might appear at any moment. Truly, *Nkose*, it required all the *múti* that old Masuka, and the white *isanusi*, and Lalusini, and all the greatest magicians the world ever saw, could devise to find me a way out of that trap.

But while these thoughts were racing through my mind a confused murmur rose among the group of warriors. A murmur of astonishment, even of a little alarm. Their faces were turned skyward, seeming to look beyond me as I stood; and, lo! the light had grown so dim that scarcely could I distinguish their features, up till now so plainly visible.

"*Au!*" they cried. "The moon! The moon! It grows black!"

Now I turned also, deeming it safe to do so, yet with caution, and covering half my face as though bringing my hand up in astonishment. And what I beheld was indeed portentous.

Over the face of the moon a black curtain was spreading slowly, slowly—veiling it not as a cloud veils it, but completely. While we had been talking, we had not noticed the fading light. Now, as we looked, lo! the half of the great golden ball was black. Higher, higher—farther, farther, crept this curtain, till none was left but the outside rim. All the rest of it was black. The world was in darkness.

Now, I had seen something of this kind before; but never before or since have I seen the moon grow so utterly, so completely, black. It seemed darker than the darkest night; yet, in reality, it was not so; but there was a cold and wizard-like breathing in the night air, and even the voices of the creatures of the waste were hushed. And heavy upon my mind lay Lalusini's warning, and the words of her waking vision, uttered before the King, and relating to the blackening of the moon and of the feast which awaited the vultures. It was all plain enough now; ah, yes! the vultures would soon have a gigantic feast, indeed; but——of whom would it consist—of ourselves, or of the invading might of the two brothers, the Zulu Kings?

Now I saw in the darkness a wide door open for my escape from my perilous position.

"We will return now, my children, having found out all we desire to know," I said.

"*Yeh-bo, Nkulu 'nkulu!* assented the warriors, bending down and uttering words of *bonga*. Then they opened for me to pass, but I signed them to precede me; and so we all climbed up the rocks till we soon found ourselves on the slope of one of those great rifts which ran down into the half-circular hollow or basin which I had marked out for the death-trap of Mhlangana's *impi*.

"*Whau!*" muttered Silwane, who walked just in front of me. "The moon is dark for the mourning of a nation, for the death of a king."

"I think that is even so, Silwane," I said grimly, my meaning not being his.

The steep slope along which we were proceeding was thickly sprinkled with growths of bush, and here and there great formations of boulders and stones, which rendered the way difficult and toilsome. And now a bit of the moon began to reappear. At all risks I must slip away, even if it aroused suspicion.

I had already drawn back somewhat, falling farther and farther into the rear. Already I judged the distance between myself and the warriors great enough, and the spot favourable, for it was rugged and rock-strewn, and overgrown with bush. Already I had turned the darker side of my shield towards them, and in a moment more would have dropped into concealment, and glided away with the silence and rapidity of a serpent, when, *Nkose*, the strangest of strange things happened.

Between myself and the warriors in front there was a shape. It seemed to appear out of empty air, for assuredly I had seen it spring out of nowhere. It was the shape of a man, tall and broad. Unlike the warriors in front, he was not adorned as for war, but like myself, though wearing only the *mútya* as usual, he was fully armed. His back was towards me, and, as I stared wildly at him in the now fast lightening darkness, a movement he made brought full into my view the large war-shield which he carried. *Hau!* The shield was pure white, like my own—a royal shield. This, then, must be the real Mhlangana.

The time had come, *Nkose*—had fully come—to take leave of that party, for assuredly had Mhlangana looked back he would have taken me for his ghost, stalking behind him, and who would wish to frighten any so great as one of the brother Kings of Zululand? *Whau!* So I dropped quietly behind a bush to wait until the party were out of hearing. But before it was so I could hear Mhlangana talking to the warriors; but his words were few, and their tones were even and showed no suspicion that they had been receiving their orders and plan of battle from Umzilikazi's second fighting *induna*. And, indeed, as I thought of it, I laughed so to myself that I was forced to sit down upon the ground and take snuff. For these skilled warriors and captains had cried the *Bayéte* and bent low and uttered *bonga* to me, Untúswa, who was but yesterday, it seemed, a boy in Zululand; and from me had they taken their orders, which would be for their own destruction. *Whau! Nkose!* The world may have contained more ridiculous positions, but somehow I hardly think it possible.

"*Hamba gahle*, Mhlangana! *Hambani gahle*, warriors of Dingane!" I murmured in scornful farewell.

It did not take me long to reach the entrance of the pass. The wizard beast was no longer there, but even had a hundred such been waiting to bar my way, they would have delayed me no longer than the time it would take to fight my way through them. No fears had I now of ghosts, or shapes of *tagati*, or any such thing. All such fears had disappeared in the face of this real peril which threatened us as a nation. I laughed at such fears as I sped through that grim pass, its gloomy depths rendered still blacker by the bright moon rays—for the moon was light again now—striking upon the tall cliffs high overhead. And I could hear stones falling among the rocks as though ghosts were at play, and weird wailing voices with shrill, sharp screams of fear, or savage snarls, and indeed, many sounds issuing from the shadows; but of such I took no heed—but, indeed, nothing—neither ghosts nor animals—could, I think, have a wilder, fiercer appearance than mine, as, with head bent forward, and gripping my shield and weapons, I sped through that grim, black defile which was at one moment in shadow, then in moonlight, bearing with me that which was of all things the most portentous—the fate of a nation.

CHAPTER XXIII.

THE MUSTER.

NEVER before, *Nkose*—not even in the days when I was young, and for my swiftness and endurance was chosen by Umzilikazi as his chief runner—did I cover the ground as I did that night, wherefore the night was not very far spent when I reached the kraal where I had left Mgwali and my four followers. At me came a troop of dogs, opened-mouthed and baying, but I hammered them soundly with my knobstick, and, recognizing me as no enemy, they slunk away yelping and ashamed. But the people turned out, in some alarm, wondering at the suddenness of this midnight disturbance—wondering still more on beholding me; for it was easy to see that I had been running fast and far.

I went into the hut of the headman, and while I was refreshing myself with a bowl of *amasi*,[1] I issued my orders.

"Listen, Mgwali. Remember you the two shrubs just below the highest point of Inkume, beneath which we speared the she-leopard when last we hunted here?"

"Perfectly, son of my father."

"Good. At that point lie five Amazulu——warriors of Dingane. These are the eyes of a mighty *impi* which is advancing against us from the south. But the eyes of Umzilikazi must take the place of the eyes of Dingane."

"*Ou!* I am ready, *induna* of the King!" cried my brother, springing to his feet, and gripping his shield and weapons.

"*Gahle!*" I said putting out a restraining hand. "Take the four who accompanied us hither, and, for security's sake, take other four or five, so shall you be two to one."

Then, Malula, the headman of the kraal, called up two of his sons and three other young men, and ordered them to proceed with Mgwali.

"Now," I said, "the way is long, but the night is still young, and

---

[1] Unpasteurized fermented cow's milk drunk either straight or poured over corn meal (also known as *Inkomazi*; *mazi* means "female animal," cow, ewe).

so are ye. Hearken, son of my father, and all of you. Before break of day must this be done. Not one of those warriors of Dingane *must leave his post*. If but one escapes, why, then shall ye all writhe upon a seat of pain for many days. When you have taken their places, and they sleep forever, send down one of your number to pass along the word to me and to the Great Great One; then shall ye have further orders when to signal, and how. Mgwali is chief of this party. Now go."

They started, those youths, and I knew that if a single one of Mhlangana's outlook escaped, it would only be because Mgwali and his nine followers were all dead.

Now, I started too, being refreshed, and as I went straight as a line for Kwa'zingwenya, I posted runners at different points of the way, for such, *Nkose*, is our system when we desire to pass the word quickly; and, indeed, I think the wonderful speaking wires of you white people can hardly convey tidings with greater swiftness. Further, I despatched messengers to every kraal on that side of the country, that every man should proceed swiftly, but secretly, to Shushuya, the military kraal of the "Scorpions" regiment, but for the rest none were to flee, and the women and cattle were to go about as usual, and that, did any fail to do this, or seek to flee in panic, assuredly that kraal should be eaten up and its people given over to the assegai. This, in case Mhlangana had other pickets out overlooking our country, for, did the royal general learn that we were not unprepared, it might bring about an entire alteration in his plans, and, of course, in mine. All these orders I gave without halting, they who received them running by my side as I ran. Nor did I fear failure to obey them; for the women, however they might dread the chance of the spears of Mhlangana, would still more fear the certainty of those of Umzilikazi. And the word of a war-captain of my standing at such a time was as the word of the King himself.

Now, as I ran, my mind was busy with the plan I had formed, which was simple. The *impi* from Zululand should be signalled to advance by Mgwali and our people, who had slain and taken the place of its own outpost. Once in the hollow formed by the spurs of the mountain closing down upon the Place of the Three Rifts; it should be fallen upon by our entire force—save a portion placed in reserve at the narrowest point in the pass; and, being thus taken completely by surprise, I had little doubt but that a panic would ensue which should place it entirely at our mercy. *Whau!* In that event not many warriors would return to Dingane to tell how deadly was the goring of the horns of the Black Bull whose kraal lay in the north. Nor had I much fear lest the invader's plan should be altered; for the counsels of Silwane and the others would weigh with Mhlangana; and the bent of those counsels I had fully gathered what time I was receiving royal homage when the moon grew black.

Never had I known till then, *Nkose*, how great was the secret dread which our King had entertained for the might of Dingane. For when I reached Kwa'zingwenya, and unfolded to him my discovery—the peril that threatened us, and the steps I had taken to meet it—his whole mien grew dark as the moon had done over the Place of the Three Rifts, as troubled as the stirring of shrill winds among the scud of the storm wrack.

"Know you, Untúswa, that we have little more than half our strength to fall back upon?" he said. "Kalipe's force is away, and of its return there is no sign."

"Let swift runners be sent to meet it, Great Great One. It may yet arrive in time. Failing that, the pass of the Inkume shall be to the *impi* of Dingane and Mhlangana what the pass of Kwahlamba was to that of Tshaka."

"Great talk!" growled the King. "But I think, Untúswa, thou art not much greater than a fool; for instead of yet further delaying our enemies, while speaking with the mouth of Mhlangana, and thus allowing time for Kalipe's return, thou didst even hurry on the hour of the battle."

"Had I done otherwise suspicion would have been aroused, and the *impi* would have been thrown forward at once. Then what time should we have had to muster our forces, O Black Elephant? Now, instead of the hunting dogs of Dingane and Mhlangana surprising us, it is we who shall surprise them, father of a new nation."

"Ha! that sounds not so ill," muttered Umzilikazi.

"There is yet more, Serpent of Might," I said. "Had suspicion been aroused, that moment I were assuredly dead. Who then would have carried warning of the approach of those who come against us?"

"That is true, son of Ntelani. And so they cried the '*Bayéte*'? And for once thou wert a king."

Now I liked not Umzilikazi's tone, for it was bitter and jeering—suspicious, too. But his next words scattered all apprehensions on my own account.

"This sorceress—she shall be slain." He was muttering more to himself than to me. "She it is who has brought her own people upon us."

"The will of the Great Great One stands," I said. "Yet let the King pause; for weighty has been the service she has rendered us."

Umzilikazi looked at me, and his face was clouded with suspicion.

"So, Untúswa? I begin to see," he said. "The men of Mhlangana are coming to set up a new King here—and a new Queen! Ah, ah, Untúswa, she is fair—the strange sorceress!" he jeered.

"Now have the dreams of the King been bad—even as at the time of Ncwelo's conspiracy," I replied, bold as ever. "If you doubt your servant, Father, slay him now, or after we have rolled back the men of Mhlangana."

The King looked gloomily at me, then he said—

"The sorceress—let her be sent for."

I gave the order to those without, and soon the door of the hut was darkened and Lalusini entered.

"See, thou witch," said the King, pointing at her with his spear, "I am minded to slay thee, for now I know whose wizardry has brought the enemy to our gates what time the half of our fighting force is away. Thus, then, was thy flight turned to account after the Bakoni were eaten up."

But there was no trace of fear in Lalusini's eyes as she gazed upon the terrible threatening countenance which to any of us would have seemed to bring death very near—only a slight look of wonder.

"Is it for this I have saved the life of a King—the life of a nation?" she said, her clear sweet tones firm and without a tremor: "I would ask the Great Great One—what started Untúswa from his sleep? A voice of warning? Would the warriors of Dingane have spared him, think you, had they come upon him slumbering? How did they mistake him for Mhlangana, and thus fill his ears with their plans? Was it not because of the shield—the royal shield—the white shield? And how did he escape from them to carry hither the word of warning? The blackness of the moon, was it not? And the shield?

Who warned him not to part from it day or night *until after the blackness of the moon? Au!* In a word, who predicted all these things, in warning? and have they not come to pass? Now, son of Matyobane, say. Am I to die?"

She stood, drawn proudly up, and her tone had been that of rebuke. And such is a terrible one to adopt towards him whose word summons the slayers.

"Hearken, my sister," said Umzilikazi, now speaking softly. "Thy words are not without truth and reason, yet I trust thee not overmuch, being of the blood of those who come against us. Thou art great at making *múti*. Now, in the battle before us, the odds against us are heavy. If thy *múti* wins us this battle, then thou shalt dwell in great honour and obtain any wish thou shalt express. If we lose it, thou shalt die, and die hard, as the worst sort of witches die."

"And is this the word of the King?" said Lalusini, a smile gleaming in her great lustrous eyes.

"Such is my word, sister, and my word never fails; else had Untúswa not been seated here this day."

"I hear the King, and am glad," she answered. "My word, too, never fails—I, a daughter of the House of Senzangakona. You shall win in this battle, son of Matyobane, shall win it through my *múti*. Is it permitted that I go now and prepare the same?"

"Go, and may it be well for thee and for us," said Umzilikazi.

When she had gone forth the King sent for old Masuka.

"The might of Dingane is at our gates, my father," he said. "Shall the victory be ours?"

"*Ou!* Who may say for certain, and time has not been given me to look into the future, lord? Yet the white shield—the white shield. Twice already hath its efficacy been great. It has guarded the life of a King, also that of a nation."

"The white shield!" repeated Umzilikazi, in vexation. "Are ye all in league, vultures of *izanusi?* When I ask for an omen, for a glance into the future, ye all croak about a white shield. Go now, old man, and make thy *múti*, for the army must be doctored before set of sun."[1]

---

[1] Doctoring involved hallucinogenic potions designed to make the warriors feel stronger and invincible: a mixture of herbs including an extraordinary cannabis (THC levels extremely high, without the CBD sedative); also, a tea made of

Masuka saluted and crept out. Then being restless, the King rose and followed. In the gate of the *isigodhlo* stood the white priest, desiring speech with the King.

"Ha! Yet another magic-maker," growled Umzilikazi. "Say now, talker with the spirits of the air, will thy sacrifices aid us against the might of Dingane, for they who come against us number more fighters than ourselves, Kalipe being still absent?"

"I had heard that, O King," said the white man. "To no magic do I pretend, yet it may be that the Great One whom I serve will remember in its hour of need the nation which has received with kindness the humblest of His servants."

"Ha! I think they who come against us would not so have received thee, my father," replied Umzilikazi, somewhat impatiently. "Yet practice, I pray thee, thy mystic rites on our behalf, for with this foe at our gates we need all the aids we can get—whether of sorcery or not."

"That I will gladly do, O King," replied the white priest. And as he saluted and turned away, I noticed that he looked ill and tired— perhaps through over-much journeying. But soon we saw certain of the slaves entering the dwelling which he kept for his sacred rites, and heard the tinkle of the little bell, and now and again the soft murmur of the white sorcerer's voice.

"Now, Untúswa, I think we have enough *múti* of one kind or another," said the King. "Go, therefore, and muster the fighters who wait without."

It must not be supposed all this time, *Nkose*, that nothing was being done. I had sent forth, ordering every regiment to repair immediately to headquarters, and every man who had been enrolled, or who was capable of bearing arms, to assemble without a moment's waste of time. Further, I had ordered the establishment of chains of scouts and runners to watch and swiftly report any movement on

---

a wild bulb called *isibuko* (from *buka*; hence an *instrument* for seeing—the "looking-glass or window" bulb), containing alkaloids with powerful stimulant and pain-killing properties; and a hallucinogenic "red mushroom" of the *Amanita* genus containing the psychoactive alkaloid muscimol that increased both coordination and ferocity—and produced during battle a terrifying, glazed stare. These bulbs and mushrooms were extremely toxic at high levels; at the desired "doctored" dosage an added benefit was that in the preliminary war-dances the soldiers "saw the gods."

the part of the foe, whom as yet none had seen excepting myself. From all sides now, people were pouring—men mostly—armed men in groups and bands streaming over the plain, all converging on the great kraal, and among these, a compact cloud, huge and dark, marched the splendid regiment of The Scorpions, nearly two thousand strong, young men mostly, and strangers to fear, of which I was the chief commander. On they came, singing the war-song of Umzilikazi, and, filing into Kwa'zingwenya, took up a position in a huge half-circle within the great central space. These, occupying as they did a military kraal of their own, were already fully armed, but others from without were not, and as the latter swarmed in a rush was made upon the places where the shields were kept. But a strong guard had been placed over this, and soon the distribution was finished, and the shield-houses were nearly emptied. Then all were doctored for war and proceeded to the great plain outside to dance the war-dance.

The while, *Nkose*, I had my hands very full, for in the absence of Kalipe I was the general in command, and, indeed, so great was my pride in that position that I would rather risk disaster and defeat than be once more put down to second again. But almost every moment my runners were coming and going, yet not noisily and with fuss, but as though seen by hardly any among us. So far everything had gone well. Mgwali and his scouts had surprised and slain Mhlangana's outposts, so that none had escaped, and had dragged the bodies far down the mountain on our side, lest the vultures gathering in clouds should be visible to the enemy and convey a warning. Of our men two had been killed and several wounded, nor did this astonish me. No further move had been made by the foe, who still lurked behind the forest belts of the flat country beyond Inkume, little dreaming of the reception we were preparing for him.

Now, as I looked round upon the muster, I felt pride and joy in the host I was to lead forth. The war spirit gleamed in every eye, and in the restless twitching of the limbs of the warriors was a fiery impatience to behold the enemy. None was a stranger to it. Even Ngubazana the Gaza, coming out from helping the white *isanusi* to perform his rites, looked wistfully at the mustered legions, and upon his face came a warrior light there was no mistaking.

"How now, son of a kindred race?" I said, for I was passing him at the time. "I think this is not the first day thou hast seen warriors mustered for battle."

"That is so, *induna* of the regiment of Scorpions," he answered, with a longing glance at my own especial fighting rank.

"I think, on such a day, thy place is among these, rather than acting as *induna* to a king of peace, Ngubazana," I said, somewhat mockingly.

"*Whau!* You are my father, Untúswa!" cried the Gaza, in a quick, eager, suppressed voice, as though fearful of being overheard by some one. "Give me a shield—give me a broad spear, that I may join them."

A great shout of laughter, of delight, broke from the warriors; and, at a sign from me, some ran to the shield-house, so that in a moment Ngubazana was fully armed.

"Thy follower is going to help us against Dingane, father," I cried aloud to the white *isanusi*, who had just appeared. "*Whau!* This is no time for thoughts of peace, but for deeds of war!"

"*Yeh-bo! Yeh-bo!*" chorused the regiment.

"Well, let him go," said the white priest, quite tranquilly, noting his follower's hesitation. "Go, now, Ngubazana, and fight like a brave soldier for the King who has sheltered and favoured us. Yet, shed no more blood than is necessary, and slay none when already defence-less. Show mercy, and spare. So, take my blessing with thee."

Now the first words filled all with great delight, but for the last, *au!* We, who when we "see red" spare nothing that has life, how should such words commend themselves to us? But we remem-bered that this was a man whose business was peace.

So Ngubazana bent before the white *isanusi*, who blessed him with one of his strange signs. Then he leaped with joy into the ranks of The Scorpions, clutching his weapons, and humming to himself the war-song.

CHAPTER XXIV.

THE SONG OF THE SHIELD.

THE regiments, organised and armed, and decorated for war, filed through the great entrance of the kraal Kwa'zingwenya, and formed up in a vast half-circle upon the plain outside, whither the King had already proceeded, and the *Bayéte* was roared forth in tremendous volume as the Great Great One stalked majestically into the open formation thus left. His words were few:

"Warriors," he said, "yonder is a nation's death or a nation's life." Then he gave the signal for the war-dance to begin.

This was short, for we had no time to spare for ornamental ceremonies. When the dance and the song were at their height, they ceased suddenly, and there was dead silence.

Umzilikazi was standing in the midst, clad in his full war costume of white flowing hair and leopard-skin and beadwork, his head crowned with nodding ostrich plumes of black and white. In his left hand he held his lion-skin shield, tufted with the tail of the beast, and a light casting spear.

Now, as we waited, breathless, he took the little assegai in his right hand, and, poising it for a moment with a quivering motion, he hurled it from him—hurled it fast and far—in the direction of the Pass of the Inkume, in the direction of Dingane's *impi*, and, as it fell to earth, he pronounced in a loud voice—

"Go, children of Matyobane!"[1]

A great and mighty shout rent the air, and, falling into marching rank, my own company of The Scorpions leading, our *impi* set forth. In strength we numbered about seven thousand, of whom between two or three thousand were those who had been enrolled from among conquered peoples, and, of course, not equal to those of pure Zulu blood. The strength of Mhlangana's *impi* I could only guess, but estimated it to be about ten thousand strong. Wherefore, you see, *Nkose*, our chances were not great, and depended almost

---

[1] Mitford's scene echoes the blood-stained spear or "dart" that, according to Dion Cassius' *Roman History*, the Caesars hurled towards the enemy from the pillar of war in the Campus Martius.

entirely upon our being able to strike the enemy unexpectedly, and roll up his battle rank in the panic of surprise.

While these preparations were going forward, the white *isanusi*, sad and troubled at heart, in the course of his wanderings ran against Lalusini, who gave him greeting.

"Will your *múti* avail to bring victory to yon host, my father?" she said, with her sweet smile.

"I know not. If it is the will of the Great Great One who sent me, I have no fear," he answered.

"Is your power, then, so doubtful, O maker of strange ceremonies?" she went on.

"I pretend to no magic; on the contrary, I reprobate such," said the white priest, shaking his head, for he distrusted and disliked the beautiful sorceress. "It is not given to us to pry into the future, which is in the sight of One alone."

"Why, then is my *múti* greater than yours, white stranger," she replied. "For I *can* look into the future, and I foresee that this nation shall win the battle. Yea, I know this."

"I hope it may be so, Lalusini," said the white man, still sadly. But the other women who stood by, hearing this presage, cried aloud in astonishment and delight, repeating Lalusini's words again and again, till they had turned them into something of a song.

As we marched forth thus to war the sky was by degrees blackening up for rain, and a deep, distant roll of thunder was heard from time to time creeping over the ridge of the world. The old women, whose furrowed faces and ragged top-knots stuck over the kraal palisades as they watched us deploy into rank, were dumb and shaking with apathy and fear, for in them still lived an ingrained terror of the might of Tshaka, whereas we young people had almost forgotten it, and with us it was a mere tradition. Of young women and girls there seemed to be none in the kraal, or if there were they were keeping in hiding. And though my thoughts now were all of war, I could not refrain from looking backward to try and obtain a glimpse of Lalusini. But in vain.

Not backward should I have looked, however, but forward; for now, as we turned the corner of a hill, a sound as of singing was heard in front. *Whau!* There on a little rise stood Lalusini herself. She was arrayed in her beautiful beaded dress, and wore her heavy

golden ornaments. Behind her came a great number of girls, all carrying green boughs in their hands and singing songs of war and of
victory, as was their wont to hearten us when we set out upon any
expedition of weight and importance.

As we came near, Lalusini drew a little apart from the rest, and
standing thus upon the summit of the rise, in full view of the whole
army, her proudly-reared head and splendid form thrown out by the
livid thundercloud behind the hill, she lifted up her voice and sang,
this time not in the dark tongue of the Bakoni, but in pure Zulu.
And the wild sweetness of her voice was of the sort which renders
warriors mad.

"A song of the Shield,
     In the battle's ring!
A droop of the Shield
     Guards the life of a King.

"Proud tuft, proud hide,
     Which the White Bull gave!
Now the White Bull's pride
     Shall a nation save.

"Burnt kraal, stamped field—
     Thick the vultures soar,
And laugh o'er the Shield
     In the van of war.

"Rolls the battle song
     On the war-wave's crest,
Bringing might to the strong,
     To the weak ones—rest.

"Great is small,
     Little is great.
Who may fall
     In the coming Fate?

"Who may fear
     On the death-soaked field?
None who hear
     The Song of The Shield!"

Now the last words were taken up by her band of attendant girls, but the voices of these were soon lost in the great rolling volume of the warriors' chorus, which was caught up and tossed along the ranks as the roaring of a mighty ocean—

> "Who may fear
> On the death-soaked field?
> None who hear
> The Song of The Shield."

As they marched past, a quick, keen flash darted down from heaven immediately upon the singer, whom all men thought was stricken— yet not; for in the sudden silence that followed, and the muttering rumble of the thunder-tone, she still stood—that splendid daughter of a race of kings—her eyes still turned skyward, her form outlined in its beautiful curves against the livid blue of the storm-cloud.

After this we marched in silence, no more singing or noise of any kind being allowed. But as we held on swiftly through the night, this great array of armed men, like a destroying flight of locusts in its straight, fell course, the echo of that wonderful song was still in every ear, its burden in every heart; and it seemed to each warrior that he had the strength of ten; for the Song of the Shield was surely the song of victory.

To us came from time to time runners, bearing tidings from Mgwali. No move forward had been made by the *impi* from Zululand, yet now and again, far below upon the plain, our outpost, which had taken the place of that of Mhlangana, could discern a point of white, which was the swift signal of those who had been posted at intervals to watch, and pass along word to Dingane's leaders.

"*Whau!* We will give them a brave good-morning, Untúswa," said the King, as, having gained our position along the ridges of Inkume, shortly after midnight, the Great Great One and I had crept carefully up to Mgwali's outlook. "See, now, I desire not to hurry the battle, yet the sun will not be very high before we shall whisper them to come on. Thy strategy has been good, Untúswa, yet per-chance they will remember the pass in the Kwahlamba and fear to enter this. Ah! would that we could roll down the mountain itself upon them here as there. It would save us many men."

This we could not do, for the straight cliffs shooting up from the defile were smooth and firm. No loose rocks were here, hardly a few small stones, so firm were the iron crests of the mountain.

Now I had endeavored to dissuade the King from accompanying us, pointing out that in the event of our destruction he could, on receiving tidings thereof, safely fall back upon Kalipe's *impi* and thus retreat, building up the nation afresh. But my words were laughed at.

"What, Untúswa? Shall I show my back to an enemy because he is strong?" had said Umzilikazi. "Have the horns of the Bull been cut off that he can no longer gore? *Whau!* thou art brave, son of Ntelani— braver there is none—but young. The generalship that rolled back the *impi* of Tshaka shall roll back that of Dingane, or——*Whau!* I would rather die with a great nation than live to reign over a small one."

Thus spake Umzilikazi, and I think, *Nkose*, he knew that the life of our nation was an uncertain thing that day, for he took in all the lay of the ground, every stone, every rock, every place or point that could offer us the smallest advantage, with the eye of the great leader he was. Yet with my generalship he interfered not one jot, thoroughly approving it.

Beneath us lay the entrance to the pass, where I had beheld the huge ghost-animal squatted howling, and this widened out into a broad hollow, opening on the outer side, as it were, through great gates between slanting ridges or spurs, rocky and steep; and on the nearer side of these ridges ran up the two great rifts: one on the right hand, the other on the left.

Our force was divided into three. Under cover of the darkness, as the moon sank low, we disposed companies of warriors in each of these side rifts, while, some little way back, within the pass, and where the rocks narrowed, so that but a few men could hold it against an army, were posted picked fighters, including a section of my regiment, The Scorpions. These were to hold the passage against the invaders, while we, swooping down upon them from either side, would have them in a trap.

The party within the pass was under one Gasibona, a brother of that Gungana who had held the command which was now mine, and a brave and skilful fighter. The bulk of The Scorpions were under the second chief, Xulawayo, for the King had ordered me to remain with him during the earlier part of the battle.

"The white shield will be needed later, son of Ntelani," he said. And I understood.

The sun rose in a ball of flame, and the world grew light. Far away over the plain beneath us we could see the dewdrops sparkling on the grass and in the bush sprays; but there was no game in sight, not even a small buck. It had fled from the disturbing presence of the Zulu host. Fair and bright now seemed this place, which seen by night was awesome and ghostly. Time went by. Our warriors, rank upon rank, squatted behind their shields eager for the moment, for here, indeed, was an enemy worthy of our strength. No miserable Bapedi or skulking Barutsi these, but men of our own blood, the disciplined troops of mighty Zululand.

Now the word was given to show the signal. Three times it waved—the white blanket—and, immediately after, we beheld a white spot showing far away on the plain beneath; then another beyond this. The word was being passed along the line of sentinels that the *impi* might now advance in safety.

The King, with Mcumbete and two of three more of the *izind-una*, lay hidden among the crags at the highest point overlooking the pass, hence he might direct our operations by signal, which we then and there arranged. My plan was simple—namely, to draw the host of Mhlangana into the hollow formed by the Place of the Three Rifts, and, at the moment they were about to enter the pass, to fall upon them flank and rear. By this means I hoped to strike terror and confusion among them, so completely would they be taken by surprise. I reckoned that we should slay a great number in the first moments of panic, and, by reducing the odds against us, could, without difficulty, defeat them with enormous slaughter. *Au!* but I reckoned without the generalship of Silwane.

"They come, Great Great One," I whispered.

Now we could see the sheen of spears, as the *impi*, looking like an immense mass of black ants, appeared in the far distance. We watched it draw near, and it seemed that our victory was assured. It was advancing in loose order, having no fear or thought of surprise, as indeed why should it have, seeing that its own outpost had signalled the road clear? Ah, they little knew, those warriors of Dingane, that ours was the outpost—ours the signal—luring them to destruction and defeat.

"By the head-ring of my father, but yonder are splendid soldiers!" said the King as we watched the *impi* draw near. "Yet had we but

Kalipe's force not one of them should be left alive to return and tell
Dingane of the strength or weakness of the Amandebeli. Say now,
Untúswa. Which is Mhlangana?"

"I see him not, Black Elephant. Perhaps he lingers in rear of the
march, fearing no attack."

"Ha! It may be so. Go now, son of Ntelani, for the hunting dogs
of Dingane draw very near. They shall soon feel the horns of the
Bull."

As I started off to join my division, which was halted in the great
rift beneath, which ran up from the hollow on the left of the King
as he faced it, I could see that the *impi* was still quite unsuspicious.
I saw, too, that in numbers it was slightly inferior to ourselves; but
then, against that, our force comprised about two regiments of
enrolled slaves, who could not altogether be depended upon, even
to save themselves from the assegai. Excepting the few warriors left
to guard the pass, our entire force was massed in these two rifts,
half in each, and we lay facing each other, awaiting the signal of the
King.

But the strategy of Silwane baffled us. Instead of approaching in
the same loose and open order to thread the defile, he sent forward
an advance guard of about four hundred men.

They passed our hiding-place, for we lay securely concealed. But
when they came opposite the mouth of the other rift, they somehow
discovered the presence of warriors—armed and lurking. Then
Xulawayo, who was in command on that side, ordered a charge,
hoping to fall on these men and slay them before they could convey
the alarm to the rest. It was a vain thought, however, for these soldiers of Dingane, so far from giving way, raised their war-cry, and
stood awaiting the attack.

Further concealment was useless. The whole *impi* came pouring
into the hollow, fearless, but widely alert.

Kept well in hand by their sub-chiefs, they fought splendidly at
first. Directly they came in touch with our lines they charged, and
charged straight. *Whau!* We had not reckoned upon this, and soon
our regiments of slaves gave way and began to flee, throwing us
back in confusion.

Ha! Then followed a wild din. The hollow was a mass of broad
shields and fighting forms, surging wildly hither and thither, and the

rocks rang with the clash of wood and hard hide; the thunder of the war-shout, the wild death-yell, and the choking groans of the wounded, smitten unto death. Ha! we "saw red"; our one thought was—blood—blood—ah! and it flowed—yes, it flowed! *Hau!* that fight was short and sharp. Nearly half our strength lay slain or sorely wounded, and the men of Dingane had lost nearly as many. Yet we had been stamped flat that day but for a rumour that spread among our enemies that a large force was advancing to cut them off on their rear. That saved us. They began to retreat, yet not hurriedly and in rout, but facing us and fighting their way. We, for our part, made no pursuit—*au!* we were glad to let them go—and after making a show of pursuit we retreated, battered, wearied, and utterly disheartened, to the heights above the rift, where we had lain concealed at first. Some there were among us who declared we ought to rejoice, for that, great as had been our losses, still we had beaten back the might of Dingane, who in future would leave us in peace. But I knew better than that, wherefore I would not withdraw the remnant of our forces from that position, but watched and waited.

Now when the retreat began, Ngubazana the Gaza, deeming it a rout, had called a number of young warriors of The Scorpions to follow him, and this band of hotheads had plunged into the thickest of the Zulu ranks. But these turned. *Whau!* That was no rout, and in a moment there was not one of those young fools left standing. But Ngubazana, who was much older and should have known better, was the last to fall, and he fell fighting, for quite a ring of Silwane's people went down before his spear. At last they threw a heavy knob-stick at him, which felled him, so that he dropped upon the slain which he had heaped up there, and they made an end of him.

Thus he died the death of a warrior, fighting bravely to the last; and it was a strange death for one who had left his country to become the follower and servant of a teacher of peace.

CHAPTER XXV.

THE BATTLE OF THE THREE RIFTS.

WITH gloom around our hearts, and mightily discouraged, we lay and rested, and soon there came down to us a runner from Mgwali's outpost to tell that an immense *impi* was advancing from the direction in which the defeated and retreating Zulu force was last seen, and then we knew, if we had not known before, that, as we rested there with our shattered and broken remnant, it was but for a breathing space before renewing a most desperate conflict which could have but one ending. Beneath, the hollow was heaped up with corpses—the hillsides, too. There they lay, the fiercest, bravest of our warriors, and of those of Dingane, likewise of ours the poorest; for our regiments of incorporated slaves could not stand before the stern might of Zulu, but were swept away like sheep, lying as they had fallen, in a fleeing attitude. Disheartened, dispirited now, we waited for the end. Even Kalipe's *impi*, did it arrive, could hardly avail to turn the fortune of war now; yet we were resolved, determined as ever, that if a new nation were to die that day it should die hard.

While we lay thus thinking there came about a strange thing. Over the heavens a lurid cloud had been spreading, and it might have been this which had brought the matter back to men's recollection. For in the air there thrilled the notes of that sweet, strange song—the Song of the Shield. Did it spring out of the very heavens? None could tell. All gazed eagerly up, for all heard it. Those who were weary and resting sprang to their feet, filled with fresh life. Those who were binding up wounds let that be, and, staring around, uttered ejaculations of awe and surprise. It seemed to spring from beneath the brow of the great iron-faced cliff, and to soar out thence in wreaths of sound. Could the singer be there hidden? No; that was impossible. But we—we listened, and it seemed that life lay outspread anew before our eyes.

Now there befell that which made our ears deaf once more to the Song of the Shield. Afar on the plain beneath came into sight that which we had been expecting—the remnant of the Zulu host, and the *impi* which had reinforced it, spread out in half-moon formation, covering an immense distance. It swept on, black and terrible, and we could see the glittering roll of its spear-points like the breaking crest of a huge wave in the sunlight, could hear the sweep and clash of its shields like winds shaking a forest. *Whau!* It looked terrible, that great *impi*. Fresh and strong, it would eat us up easily, for it was almost double our own numbers, and we were already crushed, dispirited, and weary.

And now the foremost of this new host came beneath, marching in dense serried ranks, victory already gleaming in the eyes of the plumed warriors almost visible to us where we lay; the countless array of broad shields, and the splendid discipline of their march— all this we marked as we lay. Sweeping rapidly onward they came, company after company. Their numbers seemed to have no end. And then the war-song of Dingane came rolling up the slope:

> *"Us' eziteni!*
> *Asiyikuza sababona!"*[1]

In fierce, long-drawn, throaty barks, the words were jerked forth, like the baying of an army of large and ferocious dogs. And we were their game. Then, as the song was hushed for a moment, there quivered forth upon the air—this time loud and clear, and strong—the melody which turned our hearts to iron once more—the Song of the Shield.

Its words were caught up by our warriors, and thundered forth in a frenzy of delight. Now we believed we should defeat that huge host. *Au!* and we were to them but a handful!

The song of Dingane had ceased now, and in silence the great *impi* was climbing the spur of the hill, which it had already shut in with the dense half-circle of its formation. Behind us was the hard, smooth cliff—the face of the mountain—before us, Mhlangana's spears. *Whau!* it recalled to my mind the day we stormed the fortified hill of the Bakoni. Only to-day these should find lions—not miserable jackals—lions who knew how to die biting.

---

[1] "Thou art in among the enemy! We shall never get to see them!" meaning: "There will be none left by the time we come up!"—Mitford's note.

Now, looking up to the high point where the King sat and watched the battle, and at times directed it, I beheld a signal—a strange signal, whereat I marvelled greatly, for it directed me to leave the high position we were on and charge down upon the densest ranks of the Zulu "horn." But discipline among the King's troops was absolute, wherefore I hesitated not a moment, but crying to my "Scorpions" to follow me, I went—we all went—I waving the white shield aloft. Below we could see the astonished looks of those whose spears were upraised to receive us.

The place we were now in, *Nkose*, was a hollow, half way up the slope, and shut in by steep walls and terraces of rock like the stairs in a white man's house. And now I beheld another signal—the signal to turn and stand.

Down the stair-like place a crowd of men were pouring after us. Yet their look was not that of warriors in triumphant pursuit, such as it ought to be, for these men were the men of Mhlangana and they were sure of us, had us securely trapped, we being shut in between lines of spears. They wore rather the look of men who flee, and, indeed, such it appeared was the case, for above I could see the other half of my regiment of "Scorpions" showering down assegais upon them, pressing them hard down this steep and stony path which they knew not, but which we knew.

Now as we rushed forward to make an end of them before those below could climb up, I beheld upon one of the rock stairs a man—a tall, broad man, whose back was turned to me as he gave some order to those he led. *Whau!* I knew that back, for I had seen it before; had seen it rise out of nowhere, the night that the moon grew black. I was about to launch a casting assegai, which could not have missed, when, hard as our case was, I remembered that it was not fitting that one of the brother Kings of Zululand should be slain from behind, pierced through the back.

"Turn, Great Great One, brother of Dingane!" I cried.

Mhlangana turned; and, as he did so, zip! went my casting spear. Then he laughed. It was quivering in his shield—the great white shield which was like my own.

"Take back thy spear, thou whom I know not!" he cried; and I, it was all I could do to catch the assegai as he had done, or, rather, to turn it off.

"Ha! bearer of the other white shield!" I cried. "It may be that my day is done, but so is thine." And I hurled at him another assegai. This struck him in the side, wounding him, for I saw the blood flow.

"*Bayéte*, brother King!" he called out mockingly. And then I knew that he mistook me for Umzilikazi.

We got within striking distance, but he was a little above me, and, covered by his shield, I could hardly reach him. I sprang upward, driving at him with a long-handled spear, and our shields clashed, as we met in full shock. *Whau!* they crashed together, the two white shields, but I felt I had wounded him again, and he began to totter. A moment more, and Dingane would have reigned sole King, when, I know not how it came about, but the whole crowd of Mhlangana's picked men swept furiously down upon us, rolling us back, themselves pressed down by the other half of my regiment of Scorpions driving them from above. Then I could no longer see Mhlangana, for the gully was filled with men, fighting, struggling, stabbing, and the air was resonant with groans and hissing, and the slapping of the hide shields together, as warriors met in mortal shock, each fighting now to his own hand.

But the pursuers had by this time become the pursued; for, in turn, a great body of the Zulu force had surged up the ridge, and was driving The Scorpions before it. We were hemmed in completely now. We were cut off from the pass, through which the bulk of us might have escaped—others covering the retreat—for below, the other horn of Mhlangana's force had closed in, and was merely waiting—waiting grimly until we should be driven down upon its spears. Then the Amandebeli would be no longer a nation.

In despair, still keeping our ranks close, we retreated slowly, fighting our way step by step, up the outermost of the three rifts. We could not escape, for now were we hemmed in on either side by rocks. Our tongues were swollen by thirst, and we panted like dogs. Many of us were gashed with wounds, and streaming with blood; but those who fell were immediately speared and ripped by the men of Mhlangana. Our shields were hacked and bent and our weapons dripping. Still the Zulu host seemed to hesitate, and now a voice cried from its ranks—

"Ho! leopards who are securely trapped! Come forth! Yield now to the mercy of the Great Great One! Come forth, thou Umzilikazi,

who callest thyself King, and place thy neck beneath the paw of the
Lion of Zulu!"

I can recall the thrill of delight which ran through me, even in
that moment of death, *Nkose*, on being again hailed as King; for it
was clear that Mhlangana, seeing me in the forefront of the battle,
waving the pure white shield, had mistaken me for Umzilikazi,
though the Great Great One himself was far above us on the mountain crest, waiting and watching. But I answered fiercely defiant—

"Come, now, and place it there thyself, Mhlangana. But few of
thy *impi* shall return to Dingane by the time that is done."

A roar of fierce laughter went up from the bravest and staunch-
est of my followers. But most were silent, gloomily silent, and the
silence was ominous. I even heard murmurs among some as to the
uselessness of further resistance, since we and our enemies were of
the same blood, and we might as well live to fight in the army of
Dingane, who would spare us, as die in that of Umzilikazi, who was
already a dead king.

Leaping up, I sprang upon the nearest of these, and with one
blow of my broad spear—the King's Assegai—laid him dead at my
feet. Then, rolling my eyes over my dispirited remnant, I cried—

"Who is of the base blood of slaves to talk of yielding? Have The
Scorpions no sting left? We will die as we have lived—stinging."

Our enemies, thinking we were deliberating surrender, remained
halted below in silence. As I finished speaking, there rang out once
more, soft and clear upon the air, from the heights above, that wild,
sweet voice—

> "Great is small,
>   Little is great.
> Great shall fall
>   In the coming Fate.
>
> "Who may fear?
>   Who to-day will yield?
> None who hear
>   The Song of the Shield!"

"*Ou!*" cried the warriors, their hands to their mouths. "The
shield! The Song of the Shield again!"

"Hear ye what the words say?" I cried. "'None who hear.' Now, those hear not the sound, wherefore it is we who need not fear. Behold it, the white shield!" I cried again, in ringing tones, holding it aloft. "We will die beneath it. But we yield not!"

"The white shield! We will die beneath it!" they chorused, springing up, freshly heartened. But I restrained them, for I wished to parley with Mhlangana and his leaders, only, however, to gain time in order that, being rested, we might recommence that unequal fight with renewed vigour. And then, to my unbounded surprise, I, looking up, beheld from where the King sat on the heights above the signal to move downward—the signal to charge.

Au! I hardly knew whether I were dreaming or already dead. To charge? It was madness! Why, that host whose spears awaited us was four times as great as our own, fresh and untired, and thirsting for battle. It would eat us up in a moment. Umzilikazi's brain must have turned at the impending fall of his power. Such an order was that of a general gone mad. Or had the enemy, unknown to us, surprised and captured the King, substituting others, even as we had done in the matter of Mhlangana's outpost, who were signalling us to our sure and easy destruction. All these thoughts flashed through my mind like scorching fire: yet, even while this was so, I was already issuing my directions, for with ourselves in those days, *Nkose*, an order was given to be obeyed, not to be questioned.

And as we marched down—quietly at first—to fling ourselves in full charge upon the Zulu host, we could hardly believe our ears. The sound of a war-song rose upon the air, nearer and nearer, as though sung by men coming up the great pass—

> "Yaingahlabi!
> Leyo 'Nkunzi!
> Yai ukúfa!"

Ha! It was our own song—the war-song of the King. Our enemies heard it, too, though the Song of the Shield had not floated to their ears, being audible to ourselves alone, for the dense ranks, which had been squatting on the ground as though to rest, sprang into life, and heads were eagerly turned in the direction of this new force. We, however, hoped but little from this, for those who had been left to guard the defile under Gasibona would be but a mere mouthful in the open field of battle. But, as I saw the shields of the foremost emerging from between the cliffs, I glanced upward once more. The signal was to charge—to charge swiftly, and at once.

"Follow me now, my children!" I cried. "Follow the white shield!"

We hurled ourselves forward, and for a moment nothing was heard but the hissing of war-whistles and the rush of feet. Then—*au!* a crash as of a wave upon a hard rock. So hard had we struck them, so fierce had been the shock, that we rolled them back—at first. Hundreds lay dead and writhing, and still the burning hiss of the spear as it did its work!

At first—only at first. They came at us again. They were closing round us. I saw panic in my ranks.

"The shield! the white shield!" I roared. "Come beneath it, ye who fear."

The shrinking, their spirits renewed, answered with a wild yell. Then we "saw red" as we stabbed and struggled. Ha! they yield. Yes, that dense host was falling back before us—before us—a handful of men! A wild shout arose from its midst—a shout of dismay. And as we pressed them, giving them not a moment wherein to recover themselves, we beheld the reason.

Pouring around the end of the spur came a great cloud of dust, and through it shields and spears. We needed not the alarm and confusion of the Zulu host to tell us that these were our own people, as, indeed, they were. It was Kalipe's *impi*. Roaring the war-shout of Umzilikazi, they fell upon Mhlangana's force, and at the same time the warriors who had issued from the pass assailed it furiously upon that side. Dismay and panic now took hold of the great *impi*. Thus suddenly attacked on three sides, realising that they had underestimated both our strength and strategy, the warriors of Dingane turned and fled by the way which was still open, yet fast closing up, and we—we purposely refrained from closing quite their way because we could slay more of them in their flight, and with small loss to our own side, whereas, did we hem them in—these fierce and desperate Zulu lions—there was no foretelling the issue of the fray, for even yet they were equal to us in numbers. Panic alone was their destruction.

But although we thus left a way open for them to flee, we pressed them hard—*au!* we pressed them hard. We smote them as they fled, striking them down by scores, but I and Kalipe, and the other war-captains were too wary to allow this to continue, even if we had not seen the King's signal of recall. So, singing in mockery after them the war-song of Dingane, we left the pursuit and returned in triumph.

Au, Nkose! that was a sight. I have seen your countrymen lying in heaps at Isandhlwana,[1] and I have been in many a hard-fought battle since that of which I am telling. But never have I seen so vast a number of slain as that evening at the Place of the Three Rifts. They lay, here in heaps, there thickly strewn in twos and threes. Many of my kindred and friends fell there, and of our captains and valiant leaders not a few, while two whole regiments of our incorporated slaves had gone down before the Zulu spears. Far and wide they lay, and of the enemy the number of slain was as great as ourselves, and among them some of our older men recognised many whom they had known before our flight from Tshaka. But among the chiefs and leaders we found not the body of Mhlangana nor that of Silwane.

Thus we returned, weary with the flight and the pursuit, but with pride, and joy, and triumph in our hearts, for we had beaten back the most formidable of our foes, and of whom we had gone in dread ever since we had been a nation. And already, though the day was nearly done, vast clouds of vultures were gathering in the heavens, which beholding, many laughed exultantly, remembering the presage in the Song of the Shield. But as the sun sank below the rim of the world, again the great smooth cliffs of the mountain face glowed blood-red, even as I alone had seen them glow the evening before the last, and so wonderful was this omen that many cried out that the mountain itself was bleeding afresh for those who lay slain beneath it, and that it was a place of *tagati*. And, indeed, who shall gainsay this, remembering the strange things which it had witnessed; yet was such magic good towards us though evil to our foes, since but for the heartening result of that wild, sweet, mysterious song, and the *múti* of the white shield, even the King's strategy, perfect as it was, could hardly have availed to save the life of a nation. And this, and nothing less, is what was accomplished that day at the Place of the Three Rifts.

---

[1] The first battle of the Zulu War (1879) at which a column of well-armed but overly confident British were surprised and wiped out.

CHAPTER XXVI.

LALUSINI'S CHOICE.

"So, Untúswa! My commands were those of a general gone mad?"

"Not so, Serpent of Wisdom," I answered, "for the eyes of one who sits aloft see farther than those who watch below."

"Yet the order must have seemed passing strange. *Whau!* but these bore their part as cubs of the lion indeed," went on the King, his snuff-spoon arrested in mid-air, as he rolled his eyes in pride over the assemblage of our warriors, who, squatted in rank, were resting after their hard-won victory. "I almost looked to see you give way, for the host of Dingane was terrible in its might, and ye—ye looked but a mouthful to it."

"See yonder, Great Great One," I said, pointing upward to the cliff. "No living thing surely could find foothold there, yet thence floated forth a wondrous song, and that song saved the day, Calf of a Black Bull. For it hardened our hearts, which were already sinking, so that we fell upon our enemies each man with the strength of ten. And that song was the Song of the Shield!"

"What tale is this, Untúswa?" said the King, mockingly. "Thy song must have been piped by a bird, then, for assuredly nothing human could find foothold there."

"One man may, in truth, be mistaken, Father," I answered. "Yet——ask these, ask all who followed the white shield this day."

Now a murmur arose among those who were with me attending on the King—Xulawayo and Mgwali, and other fighting leaders.

"*Yeh-bo!*" they cried. "It is even as Untúswa has said, Father. The Song of the Shield was the same as that sung by the stranger sorceress when we went forth to war."

Umzilikazi's countenance clouded somewhat, I thought.

"The sorceress has won," he muttered. "Yet is all this passing strange."

That night we lay upon the heights of Inkume in battle formation, for we knew not whether another *impi* might come against us. Yet, weary as we were, we slept not over-much, for when the moon rose it seemed to look down blood-red upon the field of strife; and we—we thought we could see the bodies of those who were slain and gashed rise up once more and fight and slay each other again. *Whau!* And of the slain there were thousands, for in those days we met shield to shield, spear to spear, and every man slew his enemy or was slain by him. Thousands were there, and when the day dawned the rising of the sun was well-nigh darkened by soaring clouds of vultures, swooping and wheeling on their great soft pinions, awaiting our departure to settle down upon their feast.

With great triumph did we return to Kwa'zingwenya, for although we who had gone forth thence came back with little more than half our number, yet with Kalipe's force—which, joining us in time to turn the conflict into a rout, had suffered but small loss—we made a brave show; for we had won a great victory, and, I think, *Nkose,* we had a strangely swelled opinion of ourselves, and that every man thought himself the greatest warrior in the world. Yet we had some cause for our pride, for we had once more met and rolled back the mighty Zulu power, had met and defeated a larger force than our own, one composed of the picked warriors of Dingane's regiments.

As we drew near to Kwa'zingwenya we heard singing, and lo! A great company of girls, clad in their gayest dancing dresses, came out to meet us. They carried green boughs, which they waved as they sang, and at their head was Lalusini. At sight of her the warriors cried aloud her name, hailing her as their deliverer, for her *múti* it was which, when their hearts were as water, had turned them to iron once more. But she, smiling kindly at them, turned herself to the King, hailing him by all his titles. This time, however, she sang not the Song of the Shield, but the warriors did, for it was roared forth by the whole *impi,* and, indeed, it became one of the great songs of our nation, nor do I think it is forgotten yet. Also they sang this song:—

> "Are they sharp—the horns of the Bull?
> They are sharp. They are strong.
> The Lion rushed upon them—
> The Lion from the South—
> *Ou!* Where is he—that Lion?
> His head was high—loud was his roar:
> His tail, too, was high;
> But the horns of the Bull are sharp—
> Ha! Ha!
> Now the Black Bull roars alone."

We went through the rites of purifying after the shedding of human blood, and then there was great feasting and rejoicing; for our losses, which were heavy, were not to be spoken of at such a time, and songs of victory and rejoicing filled the air—not those of death and mourning—for great, indeed, had been our triumph. And we were still a mighty nation.

Death, too, had been busy at Kwa'zingwenya during our struggle for a nation's life. For it had called to the white *isanusi* to come over into the Dark Unknown. The stranger was dead. He had been seized with sickness in certain swampy lands, while travelling to outlying kraals to spread his teaching, and had come back to die. And those who were with him say that he died very quickly, and without pain or fear. Now, I thought the King was not over-sorrowful about this; for, although the white doctor was his friend, yet, sooner or later, these two strangers would want to go forth from our midst—which we did not desire. And now both were dead: one on a bed of sickness, the other on the field of blood, as a warrior, making his dying bed of the bodies of those he had slain. *Au!* It were better so; yet were we sad as we buried the white priest—burying with him, too, all his possessions and articles of clothing and sacrifice, even as he used to wear them, deeming that he would need to make *múti* where he had gone, even as he had done here. Yes, we were sorry, for he was a good man and a brave man, that white teacher, and although I have seen and heard many since, *Nkose*, never did I hear any who spoke words quite as did that one.

Meanwhile, there was a thought ever present in my mind, and this was the matter of Lalusini. The King, too, when we were alone together, would, at times, talk strangely on that subject, as though he would read my thoughts; and I, recollecting, wondered if I had rendered Tauane's last words as darkly as I had intended, or if some inkling of the Bakoni chief's real meaning had not come back to the Great Great One's mind. But when things had quieted down after our feasting and rejoicing, the King sent for Lalusini.

"Hail, Black Bull! whose horns are too sharp for the Lion!" was her salute.

"To thee, greeting, whose voice, singing from the air, brings life to the dead hearts of defeated warriors," answered Umzilikazi. "Tell me now, sister, how was that done?"

"Nay, son of Matyobane," she said, with a smile and a shake of the head. "That may not be. Sufficient is it that I have from the King's own mouth that my *múti* did raise the drooping hearts of the warriors, and thus cause them to triumph over the Lion of the South. Does the word of the King stand?"

Umzilikazi looked disappointed. Yet it was scarcely a fair thing to question a sorceress as to the secrets of her magic; and I, sitting there, hearing her claim the fulfilment of the King's promise, remembered how I, too, had once done the same, though, then, my case had been, indeed, a most desperate one.

"What, then, dost thou ask, sister?" he said.

"This, Great Great One. I am tired of wandering. I would fain rest within the kraal of the Black Bull, and dwell with this nation forever."

"That is granted, daughter of the Mighty," said the King.

"Not all my request is it, Elephant. I am tired of sorcery, I would fain abandon it and live as others do."

Now we all cried out in surprise, we *izinduna* who were in attendance upon the King. After the proof she had given of her astounding powers, to desire to leave all this and dwell among us as any ordinary woman! *Whau!* It was a marvel.

"The word of the King was that there were already magicians enough in this nation," she went on, fearlessly. "Now I would retire from among such. I would wed."

"*Hau!*" we all cried, in amaze.

"And whom wouldst thou wed, Lalusini?" said the King.

"I would wed the bravest warrior of this nation, Great Great One."

Now murmurs of astonishment filled the air, for, besides certain councillors, several of our principal fighting-captains were present— Kalipe, Gasibona, and Xulawayo, and others—besides myself.

"*Whau!*" cried the King. "Among so many who are brave who may say which is the bravest? What sayest thou, son of Ntelani?"

"I say in the words of the Great Great One. Among so many brave who can point out the bravest, my Father!" I answered, and, as I gazed upon Lalusini's beauty, a terrible fear was round my heart lest some other should be chosen, and in my anxiety I bent forward, sweeping with my gaze the ring of set, astonished faces, and I seemed to behold them afar off, and as through a mist.

"What say ye all?" said the King, turning to the others.

There was a pause, then Kalipe answered, for he was well disposed towards me, and, moreover, liked not to wed with a sorceress himself.

"The bearer of the white shield, Great Great One. He is the bravest of our warriors—none braver."

And all the others shouted aloud in assent of Kalipe's words.

"Hear ye what these say, Lalusini?" said the King.

"I hear them, Black Elephant," she replied, turning and smiling on me now for the first time.

"Let it be so, then, for my word stands," said Umzilikazi.

Thus it came about, *Nkose*, that I took for my chief wife Lalusini, the daughter of great Tshaka, but as to this the King enjoined upon us to keep her birth a secret. And we dwelt long together and loved each other much, and there was peace in our kraal; for Lalusini was tender-hearted as well as beautiful, and not as Nangeza, who was hard and desired to be chief over all upon whom she looked. But save on very great and momentous occasions, Lalusini gave up practising sorcery, and, indeed, she told me afterwards how she had been able to sing the Song of the Shield in our ears in such wise as to turn the tide of the battle, and how that the great cliff above us was so formed at one place as to throw back the voice even when the singer was a long distance off: so had the song been heard as though it sprang out of nowhere, to the saving of our nation.

And I, after that I carried the white shield and the King's broad spear into many a fray, and the might of the Amandebeli stood as it had ever done, nor was the arm of Dingane stretched out again to strike us until——Well, there came a time.

But it will soon grow dark, *Nkose*, nor is there time to begin another story. *Whau!* And a long one indeed has this been, for I think the sun had but just risen when I began, and now it is about to sink below the rim of the world again. In the lives of men, as in the lives of nations, strange things have befallen. I have lived under the shadow of five kings—all mighty and great—but of them all, saving perhaps Tshaka, none was so great as Umzilikazi, the Father and Founder of a great and mighty nation.

EPILOGUE.

Now as old Untúswa ended, the other two Zulus—who had been intently, eagerly, listening throughout—never interrupting, though uttering an emphatic murmur of assent or astonishment now and again, fell to discussing this tale they had heard—the Tale of the White Shield. They compared it with other traditions of magic feats and magic arms, wholly heroic and three parts mythical. But the old follower of Umzilikazi stood aloof with a good-humoured, yet pitying, kind of smile. He had other stories, he more than hinted; for this stirring epic which he had just narrated covered a time which was to his life as less than the blade of an assegai is to its whole length.

Then indeed, I, the stranger and the civilised, felt a growing compunction that time—and other things—forbade further dalliance amid the wild mountain haunts of these genuinely interesting barbarians, for from where we sat to Kambúla, whither the waggon had proceeded, was a far cry at that time of night; nor was the way better known to me than any other road I had never travelled before, and it was already growing dusk. Wherefore my steed, grazing hard by, was caught and saddled, and the splendid old veteran of a hundred fights, stood holding my stirrup in his courteous Zulu manner, and thus with hearty farewells we parted.

The darkness drew down, curtaining the grey cliffs above with shadowy gloom, and now lights twinkled forth from the little eyrie-like kraal, and as I slanted down the steep side of the mountain I could still see the dark forms of the three warriors, could hear the quivering rattle of assegai-hafts and the deep bass of voices, as they took their way homeward, half-hidden among the rocks and long grass.

So, too, did I take mine, reflecting on the completeness of this grand savage epic—the Tale of the White Shield; also of that other I had heard from the same narrator. What tales they were! What deeds, too, which most of these quiet-looking, pleasant-featured, courtly-mannered savages could tell of if they chose! Dramas hardly credible as fitting in with the latter quarter of this prosaic nineteenth

century. And I marvelled exceedingly—not for the first time—over
the boundless stupidity of certain Britons of the denser short, who in
official or private capacity could move among such for a greater or
lesser period of time, and yet bring away no more of an impression
than that of a lot of "blacks" who wore precious little clothing and
were not eager to learn the arts of "civilisation."

APPENDIX

Robert Moffat, *Missionary Labours and Scenes* (1842). Mzilikazi sent two *indunas* to visit the missionary Moffat at Kuruman. Because local tribes were hostile to the Matabele, Moffat agreed to conduct the emissaries to the border of their country upon their return. They then persuaded him to continue on to see the king:

In the latter end of the year 1829, two traders journeyed into the interior for the purpose of shooting elephants, and to barter. Hearing at the Bahurutsi that a tribe possessing much cattle lived at some distance eastward, they proceeded thither, and were received in a friendly manner by Moselekatse,[1] the king of that division of Zoolus called Abaka Zoolus, or more generally Matabele. . . . When these traders returned, Moselekatse sent with them two of his *lintuna*, or chief men, for the purpose of obtaining a more particular knowledge of his white neighbours; charging them particularly to make themselves acquainted with the manners and instructions of the Kuruman teachers. On their arrival they were astonished beyond measure with every thing they saw, and as they, according to the custom of their nation, were in a state of nudity, their appearance very much shocked the comparatively delicate feelings of the Bechuanas. . . . Every thing calculated to interest was exhibited to them. Our houses, the walls of our folds and gardens, the water ditch conveying a large stream out of the bed of the river, and the smith's forge, filled them with admiration and astonishment, which they expressed not in the wild gestures generally made by the mere plebeian, but by the utmost gravity and profound veneration, as well as the most respectful demeanour. "You are men, we are but children," said one; while the other observed, "Moselekatse must be taught all these things." When standing in the hall of our house looking at the strange furniture of a civilized abode, the eye of one caught a small looking-glass, on which he gazed with admiration. Mrs. M. handed him one which was considerably larger; he

---

[1] He calls himself Moselekatse, sounding the *e* as in emit, but is also called Umselekas, or Umsiligas, by the Kafir and Zoolu tribes.—Moffat's note.

looked intensely at his reflected countenance, and never having seen it before, supposed it was that of one of his attendants on the other side; he very abruptly put his hand behind it, telling him to be gone, but looking again at the same face, he cautiously turned it, and seeing nothing, he returned the glass with great gravity to Mrs. M., saying that he could not trust it. . . .

These men had intended to visit the white man's country, the Colony, but this was found inconvenient, and involved considerable difficulty as to how they were to be returned in safety. . . . We could not help almost trembling at the possible consequences of the ambassadors of such a power being butchered on the road. Having maturely considered the subject, and implored Divine direction, it was resolved that I should take charge of them as far as the Bahurutsi country, from which they could proceed without danger to their own land and people. . . . (510-514)

On a Sabbath morning I ascended a hill, at the base of which we had halted the preceding evening, to spend the day. I had scarcely reached the summit and sat down, when I found that my intelligent companion had stolen away from the party, to answer some questions I had asked the day before, and to which he could not reply, because of the presence of his superiors. Happening to turn to the right, and seeing before me a large extent of level ground covered with ruins, I inquired what had become of the inhabitants. He had just sat down, but rose, evidently with some feeling, and, stretching forth his arm in the direction of the ruins, said, "I, even I, beheld it!" and paused, as if in deep thought. "There lived the great chief of multitudes. He reigned among them like a king. He was the chief of the blue-coloured cattle. They were numerous as the dense mist on the mountain brow; his flocks covered the plain. He thought the number of his warriors would awe his enemies. His people boasted in their spears, and laughed at the cowardice of such as had fled from their towns. 'I shall slay them, and hang up their shields on my hill. . . . The vultures shall devour the slain of our enemies.' Thus they sang, and thus they danced, till they beheld on yonder heights the approaching foe. The noise of their song was hushed in night, and their hearts were filled with dismay. They saw the clouds ascend from the plains. It was the smoke of burning towns. The confusion of a whirlwind was in the heart of the great chief of the blue-coloured cattle. This shout was raised, 'They are friends;' but they shouted again, 'They are foes,' till their near approach proclaimed them naked Matabele. The men seized their arms, and rushed out, as if to chase the antelope. The onset was as the voice of lightning, and their spears as the shaking of a forest in the autumn storm. The Matabele lions raised the shout of death, and flew upon their victims. It was the shout of victory. Their hissing and hollow groans told their progress among the dead. A few moments laid hundreds on the ground. The clash of shields was the signal of triumph. Our people fled with their cattle to the top of yonder mount. The Matabele entered the town with the roar of the lion; they pillaged and fired the houses, speared the mothers, and cast their infants to the flames. The sun went down. The victors emerged from the smoking plain, and pursued their course, surrounding the base of yonder hill. They slaughtered cattle; they danced and sang till the dawn of day; they ascended and killed till their hands were weary of the spear." Stooping to the ground on which we stood, he took up a little dust in his hand; blowing it off, and holding out his naked palm, he added, "That is all that remains of the great chief of the blue-coloured cattle!" . . . (527-528)

As the wagons had to made a circuit to arrive at a ford through the river, Entsabotluku, Mr. Archbell, myself, and two of our attendants, saddled our horses to go the direct road. When we reached the river, we found people bathing, who, seeing horsemen, scampered off in the greatest terror. We proceeded directly to the town, and on riding into the centre of the large fold, which was capable of holding ten thousand head of cattle, we were rather taken by surprise to find it lined by eight hundred warriors, besides two hundred who were concealed on each side of the entrance, as if in ambush. We were beckoned to dismount, which we did, holding our horses' bridles in our hands. The warriors at the gate instantly rushed in with hideous yells, and leaping from the earth with a kind of kilt around their bodies, hanging like loose tails, and their large shields, frightened our horses. They then joined the circle, falling into rank with as much order as if they had been accustomed to European tactics. Here we stood surrounded by warriors, whose kilts were of ape skins, and their legs and arms adorned with the hair and tails of oxen, their shields reaching to their chins, and their heads adorned with feathers.

Although in the centre of a town, all was silent as the midnight hour, while the men were motionless as statues. Eyes only were seen to move, and there was a rich display of fine white teeth. After some minutes of profound silence, which was only interrupted by the breathing of our horses, the war song burst forth. There was harmony, it is true, and they beat time with their feet, producing a sound like hollow thunder; but some parts of it was music befitting the nether regions, especially when they imitated the groanings of the dying on the field of battle, and the yells and hissings of the conquerors. Another simultaneous pause ensued, and still we wondered what was intended, till out marched the monarch from behind the lines, followed by a number of men bearing baskets and bowls of food. He came up to us, and having been instructed in our mode of salutation, gave each a clumsy but hearty shake of the hand. He then politely turned to the food, which was placed at our feet, and invited us to partake. By this time the wagons were seen in the distance, and having intimated our wish to be directed to a place where we might encamp in the outskirts of the town, he accompanied us, keeping fast hold of my right arm, though not in the most graceful manner, yet with perfect familiarity. "The land is before you; you are come to your son. You must sleep where you please." When the "moving houses," as the wagons were called, drew near, he took a firmer grasp of my arm, and looked on them with unutterable surprise; and this man, the terror of thousands, drew back with fear, as one in doubt as to whether they were not living creatures. When the oxen were unyoked, he approached the wagon with the utmost caution, still holding me by one hand, and placing the other on his mouth indicating his surprise. He looked at them very intently, particularly the wheels, and when told of how many pieces of wood each wheel was composed, his wonder was increased. After examining all very closely, one mystery yet remained, how the large band of iron surrounding the felloes of the wheel came to be in one piece without either end or point. 'Umbatae, my friend and fellow-traveller, whose visit to our station had made him much wiser than his master, took hold of my right hand, and related what he had seen. "My eyes," he said, "saw that very hand," pointing to mine, "cut these bars of iron, take a piece off one end, and then join them as you now see them." A minute inspection ensued to discover the welded part. "Does

he give medicine to the iron?" was the monarch's inquiry. "No,"
said 'Umbate, "nothing is used but fire, a hammer, and a chisel."
Moselekatse then returned to the town, where the warriors were
still standing as he left them, who received him with immense bursts
of applause. (530-532)

Having resolved on returning, Moselekatse accompanied me in
my wagon a long day's journey to one of his principal towns. He
soon became accustomed to the jolting of an African wagon, and
found it convenient to lay his well lubricated body down on my bed,
to take a nap. On awaking, he invited me to lie down beside him;
but I begged to be excused, preferring to enjoy the scenery around
me. Two more days we spent together, during which I renewed
my entreaties that he would abstain from war, promising that one
day he should be favoured with missionaries, which he professed
to desire. Having obtained from me my telescope, for the purpose,
he said, of seeing on the other side of the mountains if Dingaan,
the king of the Zoolus, whom he justly dreaded, was approaching,
I bade him farewell, with scarcely a hope that the Gospel could be
successful among the Matabele, until there should be a revolution in
the government of a monarch who demanded that homage which
pertains to God alone. A few moments before I left him, I remarked
that it was the duty of a wise father to instruct his son; and as he
called me Machobane, I thought it right again to warn him, that if
he did not cease from war, and restrain his lintuna (nobles) from
perpetrating their secret and dreadful cruelties on the aborigines,
he might expect that the eternal God would frown upon him, when
the might of his power would soon be broken, and the bones of his
warriors would mingle with those they had themselves scattered
over his desolate dominions. To this solemn exhortation he only
replied, "Pray to your God to keep me from the power of Dingaan."
... (556-557)

It appears that the farmers [Boers] had hunted on what
Moselekatse considered his dominions, and had used some people
who acknowledged his authority rather roughly. This the haughty
monarch would not brook, and sent his men more than once to
attack them; and on one occasion a desperate conflict ensued, when
the farmers repulsed their assailants, who, seizing the cattle, retired
with them, leaving many of their number dead on the spot where

they had intended to massacre the farmers. . . . It was altogether a melancholy affair, like many others, which have resulted from the restrained power of the farmers who emigrated from the Colony. . . . Moselekatse was soon taught that his shields could not resist the balls of the farmers, who were not Griquas, whom his tried warriors had hitherto routed. . . . In the last conversation I had with him I warned him against a rupture with the farmers. . . . Moselekatse's power had reached its zenith; for, in addition to the attacks of the farmers, a large commando from Dingaan came upon him from the east, when many of his men were cut off, and great numbers of his cattle taken. Overwhelmed by such superior and unexpected forces, he fled to the north. (588)

David Livingstone, *Missionary Travels* (1858):

The great objection many of the Boers had, and still have, to English law, is that it makes no distinction between black men and white. They felt aggrieved by their supposed losses in the emancipation of their Hottentot slaves, and determined to erect themselves into a republic, in which they might pursue, without molestation, the "proper treatment of the blacks." It is almost needless to add that the "proper treatment" has always contained in it the essential element of slavery, namely, compulsory unpaid labor.

One section of this body, under the late Mr. Hendrick Potgeiter, penetrated the interior as far as the Cashan Mountains, whence a Zulu or Caffre chief, named Mosilikatze, had been expelled by the well-known Caffre Dingaan; and a glad welcome was given them by the Bechuana tribes, who had just escaped the hard sway of that cruel chieftain. They came with the prestige of white men and deliverers; but the Bechuanas soon found, as they expressed it, "that Mosilikatze was cruel to his enemies, and kind to those he conquered; but that the Boers destroyed their enemies, and made slaves of their friends." The tribes who still retain the semblance of independence are forced to perform all the labor of the fields, such as manuring the land, weeding, reaping, building, making dams and canals, and at the same time to support themselves. I have myself been an eye-witness of Boers coming to a village, and, according to their usual custom, demanding twenty or thirty women to weed their gardens, and have seen these women proceed to the scene of unrequited toil, carrying their own food on their heads, their children on their backs, and instruments of labor on their shoulders. Nor have the Boers any wish to conceal the meanness of thus employing unpaid labor; on the contrary, every one of them, from Mr. Potgeiter and Mr. Gert Krieger, the commandants, downward, lauded his own humanity and justice in making such an equitable regulation. "We make the people work for us, in consideration of allowing them to live in our country."

I can appeal to the Commandant Krieger if the foregoing is not a fair and impartial statement of the views of himself and his people. I am sensible of no mental bias toward or against these Boers; and during the several journeys I made to the poor enslaved tribes, I never avoided the whites, but tried to cure and did administer remedies to their sick, without money and without price. It is due to them to state that I was invariably treated with respect; but it is most unfortunate that they should have been left by their own Church for so many years to deteriorate and become as degraded as the blacks, whom the stupid prejudice against color leads them to detest.

This new species of slavery which they have adopted serves to supply the lack of field-labor only. The demand for domestic servants must be met by forays on tribes which have good supplies of cattle. The Portuguese can quote instances in which blacks become so degraded by the love of strong drink as actually to sell themselves; but never in any one case, within the memory of man, has a Bechuana chief sold any of his people, or a Bechuana man his child. Hence the necessity for a foray to seize children. And those individual Boers who would not engage in it for the sake of slaves can seldom resist the two-fold plea of a well-told story of an intended uprising of the devoted tribe, and the prospect of handsome pay in the division of the captured cattle besides.

It is difficult for a person in a civilized country to conceive that any body of men possessing the common attributes of humanity (and these Boers are by no means destitute of the better feelings of our nature) should with one accord set out, after loading their own wives and children with caresses, and proceed to shoot down in cold blood men and women, of a different color, it is true, but possessed of domestic feelings and affections equal to their own. I saw and con-

versed with children in the houses of Boers who had, by their own
and their masters' account, been captured, and in several instances I
traced the parents of these unfortunates, though the plan approved
by the long-headed among the burghers is to take children so young
that they soon forget their parents and their native language also. It
was long before I could give credit to the tales of bloodshed told by
native witnesses, and had I received no other testimony but theirs
I should probably have continued skeptical to this day as to the
truth of the accounts; but when I found the Boers themselves, some
bewailing and denouncing, others glorying in the bloody scenes
in which they had been themselves the actors, I was compelled to
admit the validity of the testimony, and try to account for the cruel
anomaly. They are all traditionally religious, tracing their descent
from some of the best men (Huguenots and Dutch) the world ever
saw. Hence they claim to themselves the title of "Christians", and all
the colored race are "black property" or "creatures". They being the
chosen people of God, the heathen are given to them for an inheri-
tance, and they are the rod of divine vengeance on the heathen, as
were the Jews of old. (35-37)

Sol Plaatje, *Mhudi* (1930). Plaatje, a journalist and politician, whose
novel was the first in English by an indigenous African, describes
from the oral traditions of his own tribe Umzilikazi's attack on
Tauane (or Tauana, "lion's whelp"). Ra-Thaga and Mhudi recount
the massacre from the viewpoint of the victims and, despite the inev-
itable discrepancies of oral history, Mitford's and Plaatje's accounts
contain nearly a dozen small or large similarities:

[**Ra-Thaga's experiences**]:
   One morning, while Notto [Ra-Thaga's father and tribal
headman] was engaged in these occupations at the cattle-post, two
men came from Kunana who walked like bearers of very important
news. After greeting him they related this startling information:
   "Two Matebele indunas, Bhoya and Bangela, had come to
Kunana to gather the annual tribute. They duly announced the
object of their visit and asked that six young men should be supplied to carry the Barolong tribute for them and lay it 'at the feet of
Mzilikazi, ruler of earth and skies.'

"Chief Tauana," the messengers went on, "received the visitors with indifference and, without informing his counsellors in any way, he commanded some young men to take the two to the ravine and 'lose them,' which is equivalent to a death sentence. The tax collectors were dragged away without notice and almost before they realised their doom they were stabbed to death. . . .

They all stood waiting for Notto's orders when a melancholy shout rent the evening air in the bush hard by. Not having reached the town, they were till then not aware that they were in the thick of the fight already; but women began to scream in the bush around and they could hear the Matebele swords at work. Notto gave the order to fall to, and they hurled themselves into the bush from which emanated the sickening wail. It was clear, from that moment, that the sun of the peace-maker had set, never to rise again, for, by the faint light of the new moon, they noticed with horror that the Matebele were not fighting men only; they were actually spearing fleeing women and children. Ra-Thaga saw one of them killing a woman, and, as she fell back, the man grasped her little baby and dashed its skull against the trunk of a tree. The sight almost took his breath away. The next moment a woman fell beside a tree, her fall hastened by a stab from behind. She carried her baby in a springbok skin, strapped to her back. The skin loosened as she fell, and a Matebele withdrawing the assegai from the mother's side, pierced her child with it, and held the baby transfixed in the air.

Maddened by these awful scenes, the Barolong hurled themselves against the enemy and fought like fiends possessed.

The bush, by this time, was howling pandemonium, and what was seen and heard made the survivors almost delirious with grief. Looking away they saw the flames shooting up from hundreds of blazing huts at Kunana, and licking the air in a reddish glow that almost turned the night into day. Then Ra-Thaga recognised his father in the turmoil, holding a number of assegais. He had evidently done much already for he was panting heavily.

"Charge and kill these beasts of prey!" the head-man cried.

Just at that moment a woman ran past him and a Matebele from behind a tree, close by, speared her also. Ra-Thaga drove his assegai into his armpit; he could not pull it out again so he left him with it, saying as he did so, "Feel what these mothers have felt, you vampire, and may the spirits scorch your soul hereafter."

"I couldn't tell," he used to relate, "how long our struggle lasted, but eventually I found myself alone amongst a number of corpses, groaning men and expiring women." (6-9)

[Mhudi's narrative]:

"The news of the death of the two Matebele Indunas had hardly got about when the alarm sounded. We were ordered to prepare to leave with the children at nightfall, and while we were tying up some provisions, a hideous cry rent the air to the north end of the town as the enemy attacked, and we had to flee before sunset. Mother had the baby, and I carried my little brother and a few articles. The bushes on the southern outskirts of the town were swarming with a moving mass of women and children; while the tramp, tramp of the march of many pairs of feet was drowned by the wild screams of thousands of people at the far end of the town, as they received the thrusts of the Matebele spears.

"A young mother and friend of mine who joined me later in the course of our flight, gave me some harrowing details of the attack. She herself had one of her breasts ripped open by one of those human vultures and the running and bleeding exhausted her soon after she joined me. She begged me to leave her and fly with the little ones. She told me that the Matebele took her baby from her and dashed its little head upon a rock till its brains bespattered those around. Other women, she told me, met their death heroically. My cousin Baile, she said, was near her when she received a stab from a Matebele who spoke our tongue fluently; and Baile said to him: 'Kill me, you coward, go back and brag that you have killed a woman in kirtles. If that be your Zulu prowess, I admire the Bechuana trait of measuring strength with bearded men, and never defiling their spears with women's blood.' She was still speaking when another stabbed her from behind; and, as she dropped, this Matebele speared his comrade for allowing the dog of a Chuana woman time to curse his King's armies; many similar incidents she told me, before she entreated me to leave her and flee.

"We had not gone far out of Kunana when we found that the place was completely surrounded, and there was little hope of escape. Some women were already turning back, but we, who came last, had seen enough to satisfy us that it was better to meet our death endeavouring to get away. I shall never forget the happenings of that night. The screams of women and children as the Matebele hordes met us reminded me of the shambles of which my mother used to tell us; for, up till then, the women were unaware how carefully they were waylaid. There were five or six Matebele behind every little bush greeting a woman with a stab as she tried to pass a tree. And if one woman managed to pass while these gallant soldiers were engaged in slaying another woman and her children, there would be another soldier behind the next tree ready to prod her, and so things went on until my turn came. As I passed a shrub, behind which it was impossible to suspect that a man could be hiding, a big naked soldier waved his assegai in the air, and brought it down upon my little brother who was still strapped to my back. The point of the assegai just grazed the skin of my nape. The force felled me and the Matebele withdrew his spear and left me and the child on the ground. It was then, while in this position that I saw more butchery than I had ever heard of. Here a defenceless woman, there an innocent child would be ambushed and stabbed to death; the ferocious brutes were evidently pleased with the evening's work.

"My little brother on my back only moaned a little and died shortly after. I noticed that the blood around me was the poor child's and not my own, and that I had escaped with a slight scratch. Placing the child beneath the tree, near other victims, I fled from the hideous place. With my relatives wiped out, I wondered why I still cared to live, but I ran from the field of carnage to where I do not know. I had lost my bearings and knew not which was east, west or home; but I knew that so long as I kept my back towards the lurid sky, reddened by the flames of the burning city, I was running away from danger." (20-22)

www.ingramcontent.com/pod-product-compliance
Lightning Source LLC
Chambersburg PA
CBHW011353010726
47494CB00008B/2302